DONALD HAMILTON

A **_MATT_**
HELM
NOVEL

THE
INTIMIDATORS

TITAN BOOKS

The Intimidators
Print edition ISBN: 9781783293001
E-book edition ISBN: 9781783293018

Published by Titan Books
A division of Titan Publishing Group Ltd
144 Southwark Street, London SE1 0UP

First edition: April 2015
1 2 3 4 5 6 7 8 9 10

A CIP catalogue record for this title is available from the British Library.

Printed and bound in the United States.

*THE **INTIMIDATORS***

1

It was a good day, until we got back to the dock and found the messenger waiting. I didn't know he was a messenger when I saw him, of course. We seldom do, until they identify themselves. He was just an ordinary-looking man, for the Bahamas, black, rather shabbily dressed, chatting with one of the marina employees as he watched our captain back the fifty-foot twin-screw sportfisherman into its narrow slip, making the complex maneuver look as if it were so easy that even I could do it if I wanted to try, which I didn't.

I was standing aft in the open cockpit beside the fighting chair, wondering if I was supposed to be performing some useful operation with the stern rope—excuse me, line— since the mate was busy forward. As you'll gather, I'm not the world's greatest nautical expert. Then the marina gent on shore stepped up and gestured toward the line in question. I handed it to him. As he dropped the loop over one of the big dock cleats, his companion caught my eye and made a small signal, never mind what.

That was all. The next moment, the unknown man was strolling away casually along the pier, stopping to talk with another black man near the marina office, and I was trying to secure the dockline I was holding, a duty from which I was relieved by the young mate.

As I said, it had been a pretty good day up to that point. We'd raised two sailfish and connected with a blue marlin in the three-hundred-pound class. Probably because of my total inexperience, we'd missed both sails, and the big boy had managed to wrap the wire leader around his bill, snap it, and get away. Nevertheless, I'd had him on for about fifteen minutes, all three hundred pounds of him, and for an ex-freshwater-angler, brought up on little ten-inch trout, the whole experience had been fairly memorable. You might say I was the one who was hooked.

I'd discovered that, for a man in my line of work, deep-sea fishing has considerable advantages as an off-duty sport. Trolling or casting on the average inland lake, you're often within easy rifle shot of shore; wading a brushy stream, fishing rod in hand, you're almost always a beautiful target for anyone lurking in the bushes. On the ocean, on the other hand, you're reasonably safe from hostile attention. Once you've checked out the boat, and sized up the crew, and your fishing companions if any, you can relax and forget about watching your back. Unless somebody considers you important enough to send a submarine after you—and I don't flatter myself I've made anybody quite that mad—nothing's going to sneak up on you unexpectedly on a small vessel ten miles at sea.

Besides, I'd just learned, fighting a truly big fish is a hell of a lot of fun; and the rest of the time you can lean back lazily in the fighting chair watching the baits skipping astern, soaking up the sunshine, and carefully forgetting about various things including a nice lady named Laura, a colleague who'd been called back to work some weeks ago after we'd spent a pleasant Florida interlude together. Well, I guess she wasn't a nice lady by ordinary standards— there are no nice people in our business—but I'd found her an attractive and enjoyable companion despite certain strong-minded Women's Lib tendencies.

Now it was my turn to receive the summons to action. I reviewed the situation hastily. Loafing around the Florida Keys alone after Laura had left, doing a little desultory angling, I'd run into a fairly prominent Texas businessman and sportsman, a gent reputed to have a finger in various political pies, who seemed to think I'd done him a favor. I'd barely been aware of his existence when he approached me, and he must have had very good Washington sources of information—perhaps a little too good—to know about me and the assignment I'd recently completed, a job with political overtones. It had been a cooperative venture, anyway, with a lot of agents involved. Nevertheless, the success of our mission had apparently saved Big Bill Haseltine's bacon in some way and he'd been aching to show his gratitude to somebody and I'd been elected. He'd insisted on arranging for me to spend a week learning about *real* ocean fishing at a private club where, he'd said, the billfish were so thick you hardly dared go swimming for fear of being accidentally perforated by a passing marlin or casually skewered by a sail.

Walker's Cay—pronounced key just like in Florida—is the northernmost inhabited point in the Bahama Islands which, in case you didn't know, were part of a foreign country or possession called the British West Indies, or B.W.I., lying at its nearest some forty-odd miles east of Miami. I hadn't known, and it came as a big surprise to me. Somehow, never having been there, I'd had the vague impression that the Bahamas were located way down south of Cuba in the Caribbean somewhere, or maybe far out east in the Atlantic in the neighborhood of Bermuda.

Actually, Walker's Cay, although off to the north a bit, turned out to be barely an hour's plane ride from the airport at Fort Lauderdale, just up the Florida coast from Miami. The plane was a clumsy-looking and not very speedy flying boat, a private craft belonging to my hosts-to-be. Rather to my disappointment, it didn't sit down on the water upon arrival but put down its wheels again and landed on the paved strip that took up a large part of the little island. The rest of the limited real estate was mostly devoted to the clubhouse with its grounds, swimming pool, cottages, and service buildings; and by the marina and its facilities. To let us know we were really landing on foreign soil, there was a black Bahamian customs gent to greet us; but we'd already filled out the simple entry form on the plane, and the pilot took care of the rest of the formalities…

All that seemed longer ago than yesterday morning. After a day and a half on the water, I'd got into the swing of this angling existence, and all I'd had on my mind until a moment ago was fish. Now I had to figure out how to get out of here quickly without causing comment, and locate a moderately safe phone, and call Washington. What I'd just received was the "make contact at once" signal, which implies reasonable dispatch but also reasonable concern for security. There's also the simple "make contact" signal, which says take your time and be absolutely certain you don't attract attention and aren't being watched; and then there's the "make contact with utmost haste" signal, which means drop everything and grab the nearest phone regardless.

I went through the motions of thanking the captain and mate for a fine day, but my thoughts were elsewhere. I hoped they didn't notice; they'd been very considerate to a clumsy beginner at the sport. Stepping ashore, I couldn't help feeling a slight resentment. This was unreasonable. Certainly there had been times when I'd been snatched back to work unceremoniously after being promised a lengthy leave, but this wasn't one of them. I'd had most of the summer free; I was in no position to complain. Nevertheless, I couldn't help wishing that I'd either managed to land that big marlin this afternoon, or that Mac had held off a day or two and let me hook into another one.

I walked along the pier and up the hill past the swimming pool to the main building, and went into the office to do a little research on the problem of communications. The telephone company does not, of course, run its wires to islands a hundred miles out in the Atlantic. I knew the club had radio facilities—you could see the mast far out at sea—and kept some kind of schedule. I knew they could probably, therefore, get me any number in the U.S. by way of the nearest marine operator on the mainland. However, since any radio-equipped boat between here and there could presumably listen in, it seemed like a hell of a public way of chatting with Washington on subjects that would probably prove to be very private indeed.

I was selling Mac short. He'd taken care of everything. The girl at the desk, a slight, friendly looking redhead with freckles, looked up quickly.

"Oh, Mr. Helm," she said. "Any luck today?"

"We hooked a good-sized blue but I couldn't bring him in," I said.

"Oh, that's too bad," she said. "I mean, it's really too bad, because I have a message for you from Mr. Starkweather, Jonas Starkweather, editor of *Outdoors Magazine*. It just came in. He's going to be in Fort Lauderdale tomorrow night and he would like you to have dinner with him. He says it's important, something about some pictures he needs very badly."

At an earlier period in my life I'd made my living with a camera, with an occasional assist from a typewriter. It was a cover we still used upon occasion; but it was unlikely that any magazine editor remembered my name at all, let alone favorably enough to buy me a dinner.

Nevertheless, I might have considered the possibility if the man at the dock hadn't prepared me for some devious, secret-agent-type shenanigans.

"Damn!" I said. "There goes my fishing trip! Did he say where and when?"

"The rooftop restaurant of the Yankee Clipper Hotel at seven o'clock tomorrow night. He's staying there and he's reserved a room for you. I've put you down for the plane tomorrow, if that's all right, Mr. Helm. You should be down here with your luggage a little before ten…"

Flying over the island the following morning, I could see the big white sportfisherman lying idle in its slip in the marina; and I knew a twinge of regret, which was ridiculous. Spending a lot of time and effort catching an enormous fish you weren't even going to eat was actually an absurd sport, I told myself firmly. It wasn't as if I needed the excitement. Mac would provide me with plenty of excitement, I was quite certain. He always did.

I didn't speculate on what form it would take. I just sat and watched the subtle, shifting colors—all shades of blue and green, with an occasional touch of weedy brown—of the shallow water below. We were crossing the extensive Little Bahama Bank, so called to distinguish it from the even larger Great Bahama Bank farther south. There was a tiny islet or two, none as big as Walker's Cay; and then we passed the tip of the much larger island of Grand Bahama. Although big enough that only a fraction of it could be seen from the plane—the fourth largest island in the Bahamas, I'd been told—it didn't look very high,

and I couldn't help thinking that, judging by the little I'd
seen, if the whole area should sink a few feet into the sea,
there'd be nothing left but some nasty submerged reefs.
On the other hand, if it should rise just a little, there'd
be the biggest land-rush of the century, to a brand-new
subcontinent just off the coast of Florida. Undoubtedly
developers and promoters somewhere were already hard
at work on the problem of jacking up all those endless,
beautiful, lonely, useless, watery flats just far enough to
turn them into valuable real estate on which to build their
lousy little houses and golf courses.

Soon we were out over the violet-blue Gulf Stream—a
thousand feet deep, I'd been told—and shortly we were
landing at the Fort Lauderdale airport. Customs inspection
was, for U.S. Customs, surprisingly fast and considerate,
at least compared with the last inquisition to which I'd
been subjected, returning from Mexico. Maybe nobody
grows poppies or grass or coca leaves in the Bahamas. It
was nice to know that returning to your native land could
be made so simple and pleasant; but it kind of made you
wonder if it was really a worthwhile endeavor, delaying
and humiliating millions of honest, upright, martini-
drinking Americans at their own borders, elsewhere, just
to save a few people from one particular bad habit.

I guess the prospect of going back to work after a
couple of months of leisure was making me philosophical.
There were no messages for me at the Yankee Clipper
Hotel, a narrow, seven-story hostelry on a wide, white
beach that was visible from the window of my third-floor

room. I could also see a couple of sailboats far out in the blue Gulf Stream that I'd just flown over; and some powerboats closer to shore where the water was paler. The bellboy showed me the view and the TV set and the bathroom. I gave him a buck and a thirty-second head start, caught the next elevator down, and ducked into a lobby phone booth I'd spotted on my way in.

"Eric here," I said when Mac came on the line.

"Pavel Minsk," he said. "Reported heading for Nassau, New Providence Island, B.W.I. Find out why, and then make the touch. Mr. Minsk is long overdue."

"Yes, sir," I said.

2

I didn't like it. It was the usual cheapie Washington routine, trying to get double mileage out of a single agent. It wasn't enough that one of the other side's big guns, a man we'd been after for a long time, had at last been spotted out in the open where we might be able to move in on him. That didn't satisfy the greedy gents from whom Mac got his instructions, although they'd been screaming at us for years to do something drastic about this very individual—well, if it could be managed discreetly, that is.

Now that we at last had the target in view, or would have shortly, I was supposed to stall around playing superspy and learning just why he'd come out of hiding before I moved in on him. It was kind of like going after a man-eating tiger with strict orders to determine exactly which native the big cat planned to make a meal of next, before firing a shot. I mean, there was really no doubt about *why* Pavel Minsk—also known as Paul Minsky, or Pavlo Menshesky, or simply as the Mink—was going to

Nassau, if he was really heading that way. Outside his own country, the Mink went places for just one reason. The only question was *who*.

I was tempted to ask Mac why the hell the high-up people who wanted information so badly didn't send one or two of their own intelligence-gathering geniuses to handle that end of the job. They were supposed to be good at it, and information wasn't exactly my business. They could call me in to exercise my specialty when they were through working at theirs. I didn't ask the question, because I already knew the answer. Various intelligence agencies had already lost too many eager espionage and counterespionage types to the Mink. He hunted them the happy way a mongoose hunts snakes. The bureaus and departments concerned didn't want to risk any more nice, valuable, well-trained young men and women in that dangerous neighborhood. Just me.

"Yes, sir," I said grimly. "The British Colonial Hotel. Yes, sir."

"You will be briefed on the background at dinner this evening," Mac said. "Just keep the engagement arranged for you."

"Yes, sir."

"You don't sound pleased, Eric. I should think that by this time you'd be bored with inactivity and happy to have some work to do."

He was needling me gently. I said, "It kind of depends upon the work, sir."

"If you don't feel up to dealing with Minsk…"

I said, "Go to hell, sir. You know damned well the Mink rates just about as well as I do by anybody's scoring system. We're both pros in the same line of business, and if I may say so, pretty good pros at that. That means it's a fifty-fifty proposition, or was. But if I'm supposed to snoop around playing invisible tag with him for a couple of days before I make the touch, the odds in his favor go a lot higher."

"I know. I'm sorry. Those are the orders. You are at liberty to turn them down."

"If I did, you'd send some other poor dope to do the same job under the same crummy conditions, maybe Laura, and I'd be responsible for getting them killed. No, thanks."

"As a matter of fact, I did have Laura in mind as an alternate," Mac said calmly. "She should be back in this country shortly."

"Sure. And if my mother was alive, you'd use her, too."

It was a rough game we played after years of association. He'd started it; now he ended it by saying: "The British Colonial Hotel, Eric. I've told you how and when to get in touch with our local people. Minsk arrives the day after tomorrow, according to our information, which may or may not be correct. You can use the time to familiarize yourself with the city. I don't believe you've been there. And remember, we want no international incidents. Discretion is mandatory."

"Yes, sir. Mandatory. Question, sir."

"Yes, Eric?"

"Do I stop him or don't I?"

"What do you mean?"

"You know what I mean, sir," I said. There are times, even when dealing with Mac, that you've got to remember that bureaucrats are bureaucrats the world over, and you've got to pin them down. "Do I do my job before or after he does his?"

"You're assuming that he's coming to the Bahamas on official business?"

"The record says he never sticks his nose out of his Muscovite sanctuary for anything else."

Mac hesitated. Then he said, "I think it would be nice, on general principles, if Mr. Minsk's last job should be a failure. However, it is not of critical importance. Fortunately, we have no instructions to cover the point; and we are not a fine, humanitarian organization like the Salvation Army. I'll leave the matter to your judgment, Eric."

"Yes, sir."

After hanging up, I realized that I'd forgotten something I'd meant to ask him. Earlier, I'd requested a check on William J. Haseltine, the Texas tycoon who'd been so anxious for me to go fishing at Walker's Cay. I mean, it's a nasty suspicious racket in a nasty suspicious world; and when a friendly person hands you a candy bar out of the goodness of his heart, your first act, if you've been properly trained, is to check it for cyanide. Big Bill might be exactly what he'd seemed, a wealthy *Tejano* who liked to pay his debts, but then again he might not. Well, if our research people had turned up anything interesting, Mac would have told me.

Or maybe not. It occurred to me that it was kind of coincidental, my being handy in the Bahamas, where I'd never been before, at just the time Mr. Pavel Minsk decided to pay a visit to Nassau, or somebody decided it for him. I don't have a great deal of faith in coincidences like that. I warned myself that I'd better watch my step even more carefully than I normally would, dealing with a high-ranking fellow-pro, since it was possible that big mysterious things were afoot in that foreign island area just off the Florida coast; and that brilliant executive characters in Washington and elsewhere were surreptitiously shifting people like the Mink and me into striking position, like pieces on a chessboard.

At this stage of the game, if it was a game, everybody would be feeling very clever indeed, initiating supposedly infallible undercover gambits with sublime confidence. A little later, after a few unexpected reverses on both sides, everything would fall into hopeless confusion, and it would be up to the remaining pawns and pieces on the board to figure out what was supposed to be going on, and play out the contest on their own, judiciously disregarding panicky directives fired at them by rattled superiors totally out of touch with the situation in comfortable offices thousands of miles away.

I don't mean to imply that Mac ever gets seriously rattled. He's not that human. As far as I know, he never gets rattled at all. However, there are always political hacks in the upper hierarchy who have to change into rubber training-pants whenever the international going gets rough, meanwhile stammering out frantic, incoherent orders that Mac is obliged to transmit.

I was early for my seven o'clock dinner engagement, deliberately. I'd been given no indication who Mr. Jonas Starkweather was or what he looked like, and nobody'd arranged for us to wear white carnations in our buttonholes. Since I didn't know whom I was looking for, and he presumably did, I wandered into the cocktail lounge adjacent to the dining room fifteen minutes ahead of time, ordered a martini, and sat at a window looking down at the beach seven stories below, and the blue Atlantic Ocean, and the boats.

The funny thing was, I reflected a bit grimly, that I was supposed to be kind of an expert on boats these days, having stumbled through a few assignments involving watercraft of one kind or another—generally with lots of help from real sailors who happened, luckily for me, to be involved. Actually, I'd been born in the approximate center of the continent and hadn't been formally introduced to salt water until, early in my present career, I was run through a quickie training course at Annapolis designed for agents who might have to know a little about getting on and off a foreign shore.

However, you get typed very quickly in this business just as in any other. Do a good job once or twice with high explosives or a submachine gun and you suddenly discover that you're the resident big-bang or chopper expert. I had a hunch that, since my last watery assignment had turned out pretty well, I'd kind of automatically become Mac's nautical specialist, the man to be called upon whenever action afloat could be expected; and that this was at least one reason why I'd been picked for this job in the Bahamas, which are mostly water. It wasn't a reassuring thought, and I decided that if I had time in the morning before catching my plane to Nassau, I'd better hunt up a bookstore and get myself a copy of a large volume entitled *Chapman's Piloting, Seamanship, and Small Boat Handling* which, I'd been told, is the basic reference work for all aspiring small-boat sailors...

"Matt! It's been a long time!"

I looked around quickly. Two men stood above me. The one I didn't know was the one who'd spoken: a tall, thin, stooped individual with hornrimmed glasses, obviously—maybe a little too obviously—an editor bent by years of labor at desks full of manuscripts. Actually, he was probably a good man with a gun, at least a fair hand with a knife, and maybe even something of a judo or karate expert. The tweedy, intellectual look was, however, quite convincingly done. I got up and stuck out my hand.

"Jonas!" I said. "My favorite skinflint editor! What's got you buying dinner for indigent photographers?"

The man going by the name of Starkweather, for the moment, grinned. "To be perfectly honest, it wasn't my idea. I came down to arrange to do a piece on Bill Haseltine, here, and he said he'd just run into you down in the Keys, and you'd seemed like the kind of man he could work with." While I shook hands with Haseltine, Starkweather went on: "I don't know how much you know about this guy, Matt, but he's a great yachtsman and fisherman; and he just set a world's record for tarpon in the new six-pound-line class. He's got several other big-game fishing records on the books. *Outdoors* wants to do a story on him in action with a lot of color stuff… Well, let's find our table and get some drinks in our hands. Bring yours along, Matt." He ushered us toward the nearby dining room, still talking: "I don't think a tarpon is quite the fish we want for the piece, too close to shore; and tuna don't jump worth a damn. There aren't many of either available right now, anyway. Sailfish and white marlin don't run big enough as a rule, although either will do in a pinch; but a big blue marlin would be better if Bill can get one on and keep it there long enough for you to get the pictures. Let's say that, for our purposes, Bill is now trying for the world's record blue marlin on six-pound line. Of course, if it's anywhere near normal size for these parts, it will probably break that silly little thread and get away, but we can make that the point of the story, showing that the problem of setting big-fish records with this ultra-light tackle is really a matter of finding one small enough to handle." He was talking loudly enough that if anybody around didn't know the subject of the conversation, he just wasn't listening. Now Starkweather glanced at his watch and went on: "The trouble is, I've got a plane to catch; I can only stay a few minutes longer. Sorry, Matt, this just came up; dinner's on me, anyway.

I thought if I brought the two of you together you could work it out between you. You'll need a good-looking fishing boat for as long as it takes, and maybe a chase boat for a day or two, but don't break the bank, please…"

It was quite a performance. He left ten minutes later without having stopped talking once. For some moments of silence, Haseltine and I each drew a long breath of relief, simultaneously, and grinned at each other.

"Well, how did you make out at Walker's?" Haseltine asked.

"Never mind that," I said. "We can talk about fish later."

"Sure." Haseltine hesitated and spoke softly. "What do you know about the Bermuda Triangle, Helm?" he asked.

3

There are two kinds of rich Texans, the lanky cowboy type that made it with cattle, and the chunky truck-driver type that made it with oil. Scientifically speaking, the varieties are not distinct. There's been a certain amount of interbreeding, and you will occasionally find a lean Gary Cooper specimen with a pasture full of oil wells, or a massive gent with the build of a wrestler and a pasture full of cows—the pasture, in each case, being approximately the size of Rhode Island.

The Haseltine stock, however, had apparently bred true ever since the first recorded beefy roughneck of that name brought in his first wildcat gusher and named it the Lulu-belle #1 or whatever his wife's name—or current girl friend's—happened to be. If I sound a little snide it's because, although born elsewhere, I was brought up in New Mexico, a proud but impoverished state that tends to look askance at the antics of its gigantic, wealthy neighbor and the drawling, well-heeled citizens it exports in overpowering numbers. Call it jealousy if you like.

Big Bill Haseltine was at least six feet tall and weighed around two hundred and fifty pounds, not much of it fat. He had the smooth brown tan of a man who's taken pains to get a smooth brown tan; an altogether different complexion from the leathery, squinty look of the man who's actually been obliged to work outdoors and accept whatever the sun and wind dished out He had wide Indian cheekbones and thick, straight, coarse black Indian hair that retained the marks of the comb. His eyes were brown. They were friendly enough at the moment, but I didn't trust them to stay that way if the man ever got drunk, or thought that he'd been double-crossed, or that somebody hadn't treated him with the respect due the name of Haseltine.

I decided that if I ever had to take him, I'd better start when he wasn't looking and use a club. He was too big and in too good condition for me to worry about trifles like fair and unfair.

"Sorry," I said. "I was always lousy at geometry. The only triangle I can remember was called isosceles."

"It's sometimes known as the Bahama Triangle," Haseltine said. "It's also been called the Atlantic Twilight Zone, the Devil's Triangle, the Triangle of Death, and the Sea of Missing Ships. It's supposed to be haunted by sudden whirlpools large enough to suck down good-sized freighters and tankers, or immense sea monsters with hearty appetites for sailors and airplane pilots, or freak windstorms capable of totally disintegrating ships and planes, or very hostile unidentified flying objects equipped with real efficient vanishing rays. Take your choice."

"Just what are the boundaries of this lethal area?" I asked.

"Well, you were right out in it, at Walker's Cay," said the sunburned man facing me. "It kind of depends who's doing the survey, but generally speaking the line's supposed to run from a point somewhere up the U.S. coast, out east to Bermuda, down southwest to a point somewhere in the neighborhood of Puerto Rico, say, and back up along Cuba and Florida to the starting point. Some writers have put the eastern corner as far off as the Azores, and the southern one way down near Tobago, but that's stretching it a bit."

"That's a lot of water, regardless," I said thoughtfully. "If I've got the picture right, the only real concentration of land included, except around the edges, is the Bahama Islands and the Bahama Banks—if you want to be generous and call all that shallow stuff land that I flew over in the plane this morning. What's this about maelstroms and sea monsters?"

"Ships and planes keep disappearing out there," Haseltine said. "Did you ever hear of Joshua Slocum?"

"The old gent who sailed around the world all by himself, long before Chichester and the others?" I said. "Sure, I've heard of him. Vaguely."

"Slocum was a qualified sea captain, and as you say, he'd taken his little sloop clear around the world, the first man to make the voyage single-handed. You'd have to look hard to find a more experienced sailor. In 1909, Captain Slocum provisioned the *Spray* in Miami and headed for the West Indies, out in the Triangle. He was never seen again, and no trace of him or his boat was ever found." Haseltine cleared his throat. "In 1918, the collier *Cyclops* left Barbados, bound for points north by way of the Triangle, and vanished. In 1945, a flight of five planes took off from the Naval Air Station right here in Fort Lauderdale and disappeared out there, all five of them. In spite of an intensive air and sea search, no identifiable debris was ever discovered. In 1958, the highly successful ocean-racing yawl *Revonoc*, a very seaworthy yacht with a topnotch skipper, went missing in the Triangle while sailing from Key West to Miami... Am I boring you, partner?" Apparently he could switch the Texas accent off and on. "Actually, I'm just picking and choosing. Adding up all the stories I've come across, just the ones that have been reasonably well authenticated, I figure that over a thousand folks in boats, ships, and planes, have simply dropped out of sight out there, in this century alone."

He wasn't boring me, but I was having a hard time trying to guess what a supposedly jinxed patch of ocean had to do with a gent named Pavel Minsk, due in Nassau the day after tomorrow.

I said, "And what have you lost out there, *amigo*?" When he looked up sharply, I grinned and said, "Pardon me, but you're not exactly the type to do a lot of heavy research on this Hoodoo Sea without a personal interest."

After a moment, Haseltine laughed. "I reckon I should have expected you to figure that out. The man in Washington said you had brains."

I didn't know whether or not I was supposed to react to this casual mention of Mac, if it was Mac he meant, so I didn't. "Nice of him," I said noncommittally.

"He also said you were a tough, cold-blooded character, a genius with firearms and edged weapons, a terror at unarmed combat, and a hell of a fine seaman to boot. Just the man I was looking for, in fact."

It didn't sound like Mac. At least he'd never laid it on that thick, talking to me. "I see," I said.

"Look, Helm, I go first class," said Haseltine. "I use only the best. Apparently, in this case, that's you."

I said, "Whether it's true or not, it sounds nice. Keep talking."

"Do you know what the average private investigator looks like? He's a ratty little man who knows all about tailing people inconspicuously and planting bugs in motel rooms and snapping sexy pictures to go with the incriminating tapes, but show him a gun and he turns to jelly. When I heard—as you know, I've got some pretty good political connections—when I was told about the job you did over on the other side of Florida last spring, I knew you were the man I wanted. Well, I pulled some strings and was finally steered to our mutual friend in Washington. He sure doesn't go in for publicity much, does he? He was damn hard and expensive to find. Does he always sit in front of that bright window? With that glare in my eyes, I couldn't see enough of him to know him if I saw him on the street."

"Maybe that's the idea," I said.

"Anyway, I put the proposition to him," the big man went on calmly. "I showed him where it was to his advantage—a man in a job like that needs all the friends he can get—to lend me one of his best people for a week or two."

He said it quite casually, as if he'd merely gone shopping for a good fishing rod, naturally in the classiest sporting goods emporium in town. It was, of course, fairly incredible. He might as well have said that he'd talked the late Mr. Hoover into renting him a G-man for a little private job he had in mind.

That the guy would even think it was startling enough, but a lot of money tends to affect a man's mental processes, leading him to believe, more or less, that the rest of the world was invented just to serve him. The fantastic thing was, however, that Mac seemed to have gone along with the proposition, meekly agreeing to put a government agent, me, at this cocky Texan's disposal.

I didn't believe it for a minute, of course. That was the trouble. I'd never considered Mac, except for a bit of dry sarcasm now and then, as very strong in the humor department, but it was obvious that he was having a little joke at Big Bill Haseltine's expense and expecting me to go along with the gag. Something was brewing in the Bahamas or adjacent areas. Maybe the tanned gent across the table was involved in some way; and letting him think he'd hired or borrowed me was a good way for me to keep an eye on him. On the other hand, it was perfectly possible that Haseltine's problem was totally unrelated to ours; and that Mac had simply seen an easy way to spare the budget by getting a wealthy sucker to supply me with a plausible cover.

The fact that I was the guy who was going to have to duck the punches when Haseltine learned he'd been exploited was, of course, of no concern to Mac. I was supposed to be able to take care of myself. Well, the way he was setting this up, with both a cold-blooded Russian homicide specialist and a tough Texas millionaire soon to be after my hide, it looked as if I was going to have to live up to the fancy billing he'd given me, simply to survive.

I grinned. "Well, I never really bought that story about how grateful you were for all I'd done for you," I said. "So I'm working for you for a week or two?"

"Let's just say we're working together, partner," he said, surprisingly tactful. "As a matter of fact, you've been on the job for three days already, ever since you took off for Walker's Cay. I wanted you to get the feel of the Islands; and also I wanted folks there to get the impression that you're just an eager beginner at big-game fishing, panting for that first big marlin of your own, even while you're snapping pictures for this hypothetical article about Haseltine the Great dragging in a thousand-pounder on six-pound line. Nuts! Have you ever used that stuff? Hell, man, it breaks of its own weight if you let the fish take out more than a hundred-odd yards of it. If you don't have a good boat and a real gung-ho skipper who can keep you right on the fish's tail, you've had it right now." He grimaced. "How about cameras and film? Have you got enough to make it look good, wherever we wind up? If not, you'd better hit the stores in the morning and fix yourself up."

I said, "I've got a little errand to run in Nassau, Mr. Haseltine. I guess I can pick up what I need there. I've got most of it. I used to really do it for a living, you know."

"Who's sending you to Nassau, the man in Washington?" Haseltine's brown eyes narrowed and looked kind of muddy and ugly for a moment. "The understanding was that you'd be on my business full time. Maybe I'd better get on the phone and straighten him out…"

"Relax, Mr. Haseltine," I said. "Whatever it is, it's something related to your problem, just a hunch, he said, but I'd better check it out before I did anything else. I can't tell you the details because it involves some people you're not supposed to know about. After all, we've got to make some gestures toward security."

"Yeah, sure." He was still studying me suspiciously, as well he might, since I'd made up every word of what I'd said the instant before I'd said it, in the interest of millionaire diplomacy. Not that I knew that what I'd said was wrong, but I didn't know it was right, either. Haseltine relaxed slowly. "Well, okay. If you want to play secret agent a bit, I guess it won't hurt. We can get you from Nassau to wherever you need to go as soon as you're ready, no sweat. And where the hell do you get this Mister-Haseltine routine, Matt?"

I grinned. "In this racket, we're always respectful to the big brass, Bill. It makes them feel good, and it doesn't make them a bit more bullet-proof if the time should ever come that we have to shoot them."

He grinned back. We were pals—well, almost. "I wish I thought you were kidding," he said. "I bet you would shoot me if I got in your way, you elongated bastard. Aren't you going to ask what it is I want you to look for?"

"Out in that Sea of Missing Ships?" I shrugged. "Well, if you want to tell me, okay. But after the build-up you just gave me, I figure the name is Phipps, Wellington Phipps. At least he's the only person to go missing out there in a boat recently that I've heard of; and now I remember there was some mention of this Terrible Triangle legend at the time. A wealthy contractor type from the West Coast who'd brought his sailing yacht east for a season of racing. The *Ametta Too*, whatever that may mean. Vanished a while back sailing from Bermuda to Palm Beach; I saw it reported on TV. A typical disappearance like you described: no survivors, no life preservers, no wreckage at all. Bermuda to Palm Beach, that course would pass just north of the Bahamas, wouldn't it?"

He nodded slowly, unsmiling. "Okay, so you're real bright, just like your boss said. But you've got one thing wrong. I don't give a good goddamn what happened to old Buster Phipps. I mean, Buster's okay, but if it was just him and his boat, to hell with them. Only, he had his wife and daughter along. They'd flown out to job him in Bermuda after the big race. Amanda and Loretta; that's where he got *Ametta* from. Second boat of the name, *Ametta Too*. They're real cute out there in sunny California."

"Cute," I agreed. "But he could have called the second one *Loranda*, just for variety."

"I was going to marry the girl," said Haseltine. "I still am. She's alive, somewhere. I know it. Find her for me, Helm."

4

The commercial flight back across the Gulf Stream the following morning gave me time to think things over from the perspective of a new day. A jet would barely have got off the ground before dipping down for the landing, but this particular Fort Lauderdale-Nassau run—continuing on to Governor's Harbor in Eleuthera, wherever that might be—was made by a lazy old twin-motor prop plane that loafed through the sky at a reasonable altitude, giving a good view of the watery scenery below. I decided that being pulled through the air by a fan had certain advantages over being booted in the tail by a firecracker; even more so since I'm under the illusion that I know more or less how a piston engine works, while I don't kid myself I have any understanding of jets. I just hope somebody does.

"Look, I helped race that damn boat from Newport to Bermuda," Haseltine had said irritably when I asked him about the details. "She was new, she was sound, she was seaworthy as hell—actually a little too seaworthy for real racing. You've got to cut a few corners and take a few chances if you want to come home with the silver these days. The time when you could just buy a set of new sails for your family cruising sloop and hope to compete are gone forever. It's a cutthroat business now, partner, don't ever think otherwise. Business, hell! It's a science. The *Ametta* was fast, all right, but she was no skinned-out, stripped-down racing machine. And Buster was a good seaman, but—well, again, maybe *he* was a little too seaworthy for racing. He didn't really have the old win-or-die instinct, if you know what I mean. His boat and his crew came first. Oh, he'd drive us; he'd drive like hell; but if there was a question, he wouldn't gamble. He'd do it the safe, seamanlike way, and worry about getting to the finish line afterwards. Hell, look what happened in that damned race."

"What happened?" I asked.

He looked surprised. These sporting characters are all alike. They always expect everybody to know who caught the biggest fish, shot the biggest elephant, rode the fastest horse, and sailed the fastest boat.

"Well," he said, "we were in a pretty good position as we neared Bermuda, damned good in fact considering our low handicap-rating; we were right in there on corrected time. But you know that lousy finish line. Trying to find it in broad daylight in clear weather and stay off the rocks is bad enough. This was in the middle of the night with a gale blowing. And the bastards who'd set it up had made all kinds of crazy rules about what navigational equipment could and could not be used. You'd think they actually wanted a few shipwrecks for excitement. So there we were, batting around in that goddamned storm off a lee shore, well up with the leaders, and the navigator kept saying we were right on course, right on course. We just hoped he knew what the hell he was talking about. You couldn't find your fly in that weather to take a leak. Suddenly old Buster kind of wrinkled up his nose and turned to the guy, never mind his name, and told him to switch on the Omni, fast."

"What's an Omni?" I asked.

"Hell, don't ask me," the Texan said. "I was just along to pull the strings up forward when the man said pull. I get a kick out of sailing, but all that scientific crap bores hell out of me, or I'd have a boat of my own. It's some kind of fancy navigating gadget like they use on planes, I think. The ordinary RDF wasn't working worth a damn for some lousy electronic reason. The navigator objected that the Omni wasn't allowed; and Buster said goddamn it something smelled wrong, and he wasn't making a polite suggestion, he was giving a goddamned order: to hell with what was and wasn't allowed; he wasn't going to pile up his ship for anybody's crummy rules; snap to it and come up with a position *now*. A minute or so later the navigator came boiling out of the hatch with his face so pale it kind of shone in the dark and yelled get us the hell out of here we're right on the reef... Well, that was Buster Phipps, a real sailorman. Of course we were

disqualified. That's just the point. Nobody's going to tell
me old cautious, careful Buster could lose his boat in
good weather between here and Bermuda without human
intervention of some kind. Sure, he might have been run
down some night by a big ship—it happens—but I've
checked and double-checked every vessel that passed
through the area during the time that counted. No bumps
in the night, no scratches on the paint, and hell, if the
Ametta had been sunk by a collision there'd have been
some broken stuff floating around and we'd have found it.
We searched every inch of ocean from the Bahamas clear
up to Cape Hatteras, N.C., figuring the possible drift due
to wind and current." He grimaced. "Now it's your baby.
Here are some pictures."

I'd looked at photographs of the boat, a handsome
sixty-foot ketch, and of Wellington (Buster) Phipps, a
handsome middle-aged gent with tightly curling gray
hair. I'd looked at a picture of Mrs. Phipps who had once,
Haseltine said, been a big movie star called Amanda
Mayne. I'd never heard of her, but she was a good-
looking woman, and a lot of those movie girls become
big stars kind of retroactively after they marry money. I
didn't hold it against her. She looked like an independent-
minded lady who might be fun to talk with if you couldn't
do better, and she probably wouldn't allow you to do
better. Why should she? Phipps looked as if he was pretty
adequate in all departments, not only the financial and
nautical ones.

"And this is Loretta," Haseltine had said, with a funny

note in his voice that made me like him more. I mean, the girl really meant something to him.

She'd never mean anything to me. I could see that, even from a picture. She was young and blond and beautiful, and she'd obviously never had a thought in her life except how young and blond and beautiful she was. She couldn't even smile for a family snapshot without striking a glamor-pose with a lock of shining blond hair falling over one eye just so.

"They weren't handling that big sailboat by themselves, were they?" I asked.

"No, they had their paid hand, Leo, who acted as cook and steward besides making himself useful on deck when he was needed; and they had a couple of young fellows along, husky yachting characters who'd crewed in the race."

"Names?"

"Buddy Jacobsen and Sam Ellender. Here's what we've dug up on them so far." He handed me a thin carbon copy of some kind of a report. "Sam's twice had his driver's license suspended for speeding; he also tied one on in a Mexican port after one race and wound up in a local *juzgado*. Buddy got pulled in with a bunch of peace protesters a few years back. Not what you might call spectacular criminal records."

I glanced at him. "But even after racing to Bermuda with them, you had them checked out."

He grimaced. "Look, we took turns in those damn wet bunks; we didn't share them. Sure I checked them out.

The fact that a man's a good yachtsman doesn't mean he doesn't want to get rich. Hell, he might like to have a yacht all his own."

"You're thinking of kidnaping?"

"Never mind what I'm thinking," he said. "All my thinking hasn't produced any results; that's why I got hold of you. Don't let me put my ideas into your head. What I want to hear is your ideas."

I shrugged. "What about this Leo?"

"Leo Gonzales. Fifty-four, five-seven, a hundred and thirty. Dark complexion, dark hair, brown eyes. Lost a couple of fingers on his left hand—the last two—while acting as a mate on a sportfisherman before he signed on with Buster. I gather somebody was boating a big black marlin and Leo, handling the leader, got excited and took a couple of turns of the wire around his hand for a good grip, a real no-no. The fish took off, the wire came tight and, look Ma, no fingers. Must have been when he was young and dumb because he never pulled any goofs like that with Buster or he wouldn't have lasted eleven years. A tough little bastard who could hold a course in bad weather and come up with a hot meal when the boat was sailing on her ear. Buster always figured he was lucky to find a boy as good as Leo to work on board."

It occurred to me that a fifty-four-year-old member of a minority race—judging by the name—might get tired of being a good boy after eleven years; but as a transplanted Swede, by blood, I don't pretend to be an expert on anything but Scandinavians, and even there I'm kind of shaky on Norwegians, Finns, and Danes. I started to ask another question, and stopped. Any black marks on Leo Gonzales' record would be in the report I held; and the fact that Haseltine apparently didn't like the man, and was nevertheless grimly listing his virtues, only emphasized what I'd already sensed, that there were things I wasn't being told. Well, as an experienced undercover agent of a government often obsessed with security, that should make me feel right at home.

I said deliberately, "You know your girl is alive, *amigo*, but you keep referring to her daddy in the past tense. Explain that contradiction for me, please."

Haseltine frowned, his eyes going narrow and muddy again. It occurred to me that millionaire Texans with strong Indian traits constituted another minority group I wasn't really expert on.

"Don't be too damn bright, partner," the big man said coldly. Then he shrugged. "Okay. A man keeps hoping."

I said, "Not really. The fact is that you really think they're dead."

His face was hard and ugly. All he needed was some war paint and a scalping knife. "Damn you—"

I said, "Cut it out, friend. We're not the Federal Missing Persons Bureau, if there is any such thing, which there isn't. You knew that when you came to us. You paid enough snoops to pick up enough information so you could find the office and talk to the man. There isn't a chance in the world you didn't at the same time learn what kind of orders emanate from that office. And they *don't* concern rescuing beautiful maidens missing at sea."

Haseltine drew a long breath. "Okay," he said softly. "Okay, genius. They're dead. After five weeks they've got to be dead. I try to kid myself, but I know it's no damn good. Understand?"

"I understand that," I said. "What I don't understand is, if they're dead, where the hell do I come in?"

"I've just told you," he said angrily. "I've just explained, damn it! That boat didn't go down of itself. Buster Phipps didn't run his beloved *Ametta* on a reef with his cherished wife and daughter on board, no chance! He didn't let her get caught in a sudden squall with all sail up and all ports and hatches open, don't ever think so. He didn't light a cigarette in the engine room over an open can of gasoline, and neither did anybody else on Buster Phipps' boat—anyway, the bucket had a diesel auxiliary. There wasn't any gas on board. Buster wouldn't have it; too dangerous. If the *Ametta* sank, somebody sank her. If they're dead, somebody killed them. Deliberately."

"Sure. One of the sea monsters that inhabit the Lethal Triangle you just told me all about."

Haseltine gave a short, harsh laugh, like a bark. "That's a lot of bullshit," he said.

"You don't believe in that Hoodoo Ocean?"

"Do you?" He grimaced. "I bet you could take any other risky piece of water with a lot of air and sea traffic and if you started looking hard enough you could line up enough mysteries of the sea to make your hair curl. Hell, there were whole villages of Bahamians who used to make a living off wrecks less than a century ago. The old sailing ships used to pile up on those reefs like cordwood. I mean, that's a tough *sailing* area, with sudden coral heads and unpredictable currents—the way the tide runs off and on those flats is tricky as hell. The Gulf Stream doesn't help a bit, either. The sea that builds up when a cold norther blows against that north-running river of warm water is pure murder. Harry Conover, for instance, probably just tried to drive his *Revonoc* a little too hard, and she fell off one of those big, steep waves and split wide open. No, I don't believe in any sea monsters, or any death-ray-equipped UFOs, either. But I'll tell you what I do believe in."

"What's that?"

"I believe in a guy, somewhere, who read all that melodramatic bunk and decided it would make a perfect cover for putting the finger on one particular yacht in the area. He could count on nobody getting too worked up about it. Hell, it would be just another Triangle tragedy, wouldn't it?"

"What would be his motive?"

"I don't know." Haseltine spread his hands dramatically. "I've spent thousands of bucks looking and I still don't know. Buster Phipps had some people who didn't like him—nobody makes money without that—but killing enemies, no. And neither did the girls. I can't give you a clue. You'll have to work it out for yourself."

Again I had the old familiar feeling that security was rearing its ugly head, and I wasn't being told everything there was to know. Well, it was his problem. If it gave him a kick to have me solve it blindfolded—or fail to solve it—that was his choice.

"And if I find the motive, and the man?"

Haseltine leaned forward. "Don't be stupid, partner. You know what you do, and I know what you do. That's why I got you instead of some scared private eye with a tape recorder and a telescopic camera. Well, find whoever got the *Ametta Too*, and do it."

I looked up. The stewardess was telling me to buckle my seatbelt. After obeying orders, I looked out the plane window. We were coming off the blue water over a green island. At least I assumed it was an island down there, although it went on farther than I could see. There was a city down there: Nassau, New Providence Island, B.W.I. Now all I had to do was learn enough about it to deal with one of the other team's best men, quickly, so I could get to work on something truly important, like finding, or avenging, a misplaced blonde.

5

My initial impression of the British Colonial Hotel
was that the inmates, staff and guests alike, were
exclusively black. It was a great, conspicuous building
on, the waterfront in the crowded center of Nassau; a
hotel built the nice, ornate, rambling way they used to
build luxury hotels; and there didn't seem to be, at first
glance, a single paleface in the joint besides me. Please
understand, I'm not making the observation in a spirit
of criticism. People do come in varying colors, and I've
never considered the differences of great importance. On
the other hand, I'll readily admit that I'm not accustomed
to an environment in which my own particular chromatic
variation is in the minority.

   I told myself it was a valuable educational experience,
which didn't keep me from feeling slightly outnumbered,
even when I realized that there were, actually, quite a
number of white faces scattered around the crowded
lobby. Anyway, I hadn't come to the Bahamas for

valuable educational experiences. I just wanted to check in fast and take a preliminary look around the town, but this turned out to be easier to plan than to accomplish— checking in fast, I mean.

I've spent some time in the land of *mañana*, enough to get me used to—anyway, resigned to—the slower tempo of life in the semi-tropics; but at least my Latin friends were always cheerful and friendly when they kept me waiting. These hotel people seemed to resent me, which I put down to the racial difference, until I saw that they seemed to resent everybody, white or black. I suppose there's something to be said for such even-handed lack of discrimination, but I'm not really impressed by folks who act too proud for their jobs, whatever those jobs might be. Hell, even in my business, we try to render cheerful and efficient service, as I hoped to demonstrate shortly to a gent named Pavel Minsk.

I was tempted not to tip the surly bellboy who finally condescended to drag my suitcase upstairs and drop it disdainfully inside my fifth-floor room, but there was no sense in starting a feud, so I gave him a fairly adequate gratuity, and saw that I hadn't gained anything by the expenditure of government funds. I've met the same attitude in some European countries; if you're stingy, you're a rich American slob robbing the poor, proud, hardworking natives; and if you're generous, you're a rich American slob flaunting his ill-gotten wealth. To hell with all temperamental, chip-on-the-shoulder jerks, I reflected, black or white. I was tolerant. They could all proceed to the nether regions together, unsegregated, as far as I was concerned.

All the delays had brought the time well past noon, and I was hungry enough to put off my scouting expedition a little longer—quite a little longer, as it turned out. The lunch I got was not only slow, but fell considerably short of gastronomic perfection. The butter, sugar, and jam, were all served in those crummy little prepackaged, U.S.-type doses—I once had a friend who objected to this practice so strongly that he insisted on making the waitress rip open the sugar for his coffee and peel the butter for his bread, saying that he didn't eat out just to wrestle with a lot of paper and plastic, and the least they could do was unwrap his food for him if they wanted his trade. It was disillusioning to come to what was supposed to be a fancy hotel in a glamorous foreign country and be presented with the same old prefabricated hash-house garbage. My opinion of Nassau, as a pleasant luxury resort, was dropping steadily. Well, I hadn't come here for pleasant luxury.

I went out and hired a cab to take me sightseeing. Surprisingly, the driver was a cheerful black character who didn't seem to have heard that he was downtrodden by us lousy tourists. He rattled off the history of the city and the Islands as he drove me around through the left-handed, British-style traffic, showing me fine old forts that had never, it seemed, managed to keep the place from being captured by anybody who wanted to capture it—including pirates, Spaniards, and the infant navy of

the young U.S.A.—and a great old empty hotel with
once-magnificent gardens, now deserted and overgrown,
dominated by a tremendous kapok tree. I hadn't known
the stuff grew on trees.

My guide said that, when new, the picturesque hostelry
had served as a kind of headquarters for the blockade-
runners during the U.S. Civil War; the prohibition
rumrunners came later and had less classy hangouts. He
sent me up a water tower for a good view of the city and
harbor; and he had me walk down a flight of historical
outdoors stairs—I forget their exact significance. By the
time he brought me back to the British Colonial, I had
a pretty clear picture in my mind of the city of Nassau.
I paid him and added a tip carefully calculated to show
my appreciation without insulting or patronizing him.
He accepted the gift in the spirit in which I'd intended it.
Okay, so you meet all kinds, in all countries.

Inside, I picked up a paper at the hotel newsstand and
read it in the portion of the lobby reserved for drinking
purposes, over a passable martini. I learned that the
Islands were in the process of severing their political ties
with Britain. Well, that was their business. I just hoped it
wouldn't interfere with mine.

Presently, a glance at my watch told me it was time for
the next step in the proceedings. I located a phone booth
and called a number I'd been given by Mac. The voice
that answered had no distinct racial characteristics, but it
was definitely feminine. I figured that, judging by what
I'd seen of Nassau so far, the girl was probably black.

She'd almost have to be to preserve the inconspicuous anonymity desirable in a local contact. Well, I'd probably never meet her, so I'd probably never know for sure, and it didn't matter anyway. We went though a little mandatory funny-business involving signs and countersigns that somebody must have dreamed up after watching an old spy movie on late evening TV.

"Eric here," I said.

"Yes," she said. "Consignment arriving on schedule, as far as we can determine. ETA eleven hundred tomorrow morning."

"Any hint as to the identity of the consignee?"

"Not a whisper."

"Are there any guests here at the hotel who'd make likely prospects? He must have picked the place for some reason."

"He may have picked it simply because it's centrally located—most of the other big hotels, the newer ones, are farther out. We haven't spotted anybody interesting staying there. Of course, there's a tremendous daily turnover. If any promising candidates show up at the last minute, we'll try to let you know."

She sounded as if she were part of a sizable local unit, which was a welcome change. I mean, we're not the CIA or any of those other well-financed agencies with worldwide networks of operatives ready to spring into action by squads, platoons, or regiments, as required. In a foreign city we're likely to find—if we're lucky and the place is large enough—one shy individual on standby duty, experienced only in communications, useful chiefly for maintaining contact with Washington. Since this girl sounded as if she had the will and the manpower to tackle more onerous duties, I tried her out with an easy one.

"How about a car, or a car and driver, preferably the latter? Without a little practice, which I haven't got time for, I hate to tackle this backwards traffic of yours."

My unseen contact laughed. "Whether it's backwards or forwards rather depends on the way you're accustomed to facing, doesn't it, Eric? Anyway, you already have a driver. Fred will be available whenever you need him. He says you're a nice man and a generous tipper."

I was a little disappointed at learning that my guide had not, after all, been a representative specimen of local manhood. "Tell him thanks for the tour," I said. "About tomorrow, do I cover the airport in case our friend's plans change abruptly, or do you?"

"Stay in your room. We'll escort him to the hotel and see that he's checked in; after that he's all yours. Fred will let you know."

I said, "Okay, I'll wait for the word. Now, what are the chances of getting a reasonably safe connection with the top?"

"Can do."

A minute or so later, Mac came on. "Yes, Eric?" he said from faraway Washington, D.C. At least that's where I thought he was, which didn't mean he had to be there.

I said, "This vengeful *Tejano* to whom you've indentured me. How many people do I kill for him, assuming I can locate suitable targets."

"As many as necessary," Mac said calmly. "I do not believe in coincidence. We were already under orders to shift some manpower to the Bahamas when Mr. Haseltine descended on me… It is really remarkable how much a man can learn by waving hundred-dollar bills around, isn't it, Eric?"

"I wouldn't know, sir," I said. "I've never been properly equipped by my government for using that particular information-gathering technique."

"I was struck by his interest in the area to which we'd just been assigned," Mac said. "It seemed advisable to listen to what he had to say. I decided that, if the yacht with the idiotic name had actually been sunk or captured by a human agency, as our Texas friend seems to believe, it was unlikely that the incident was totally unrelated to the impending visit to the Islands of a Russian homicide artist. At least the coincidence of two apparently well-planned acts of violence being scheduled within a few weeks in the same small geographical region seemed to deserve investigation. I therefore referred the gentleman to you."

"Thanks a lot, sir," I said. "Did you get the impression that Mr. Haseltine wasn't being entirely frank with us?"

"I would say that he knows or suspects something about the disappearance of the yacht and its crew that he's reluctant to tell us."

"Considering that he's gone to considerable trouble and expense to get our help, that's kind of stupid, wouldn't you say, sir?"

"Unless he thinks there's something illegal going on involving his fiancée and her family. Drug-smuggling, or perhaps an insurance swindle of some kind. But that's mere guesswork. Of course, there could also be something illegal going on involving Mr. Haseltine himself that he doesn't care to confess to government employees like us. But in either case, why did he come to us in the first place?" There was a little pause, and Mac went on more briskly: "Regardless of Mr. Haseltine's hidden motives, I think you should operate, at least initially, on the assumption that your two assignments may well be connected in some way."

"It would be nice to know how," I said.

"Yes, it would," he agreed. "When you find out, please inform me at once. Did you have any other questions?"

"No, sir," I said. "I think that covers it for now."

"Give my regards to Pavel Minsk," he said, and hung up.

6

When the time came, it was dead easy, if you'll pardon the pun. There was, of course, a lengthy wait first, well past the estimated eleven o'clock arrival hour, but I'd been prepared for that. After all, even if the plane was on schedule, it was a twenty-minute drive from the airport; and I could count on the scrupulously undiscriminating hotel processing department not to speed up its sluggish operations for anybody, not even Pavel Minsk, alias Paul Minsky, alias Pavlo Menshesky, alias the Mink. When Fred called, it was close to one-thirty in the afternoon.

"He sent his bag up to his room—number three three four—and stayed down here to eat. You can pick him up in the dining room."

"What name is he using?" I asked.

"Menshek. Paul Menshek."

"Passport?"

"United States."

"The sneaky bastard," I said. "Clothes?"

"Palm Beach suit, white wash-and-wear shirt, flowered silk necktie, white straw hat with a flowered band. Like a country lad all dressed up for a dashing tropical vacation, don't you know? He's not very big, is he? I must say, he doesn't look very dangerous, really."

I said, "Never mind his looks. Stay away from him. That's one hundred and thirty pounds of death on the hoof, friend, and don't you kid yourself otherwise."

"And only you can handle him, Mr. Helm?" The black man's voice, over the phone, sounded faintly ironical.

I said, "That's what we're here to find out, isn't it? You stick to driving your taxi and let me worry about the Mink. If anything goes wrong, keep clear, understand?"

"Yassuh, Massah."

I said, "Okay, you big, brave, lion-eating Masai warrior, if I goof, go right ahead and try to take him. What do I care if you get dead? In the dining room, you say?"

"Yes, and you'd better get down there." Fred seemed unperturbed by my reference to his hypothetical ancestry, even though I'd probably got it wrong. "When I left to phone, he was starting to tap his foot impatiently and look at his watch."

"There's something about the local atmosphere that affects a lot of people that way," I said, and hung up.

There were no preparations to be made. I'd already made them, such as they were. I had a gun and a knife that I probably couldn't use, the way my orders read. I had two hands and a brain of sorts. They'd have to do. In addition, I had, for camouflage, a camera all done up in one of those drop-front leather union suits without which no self-respecting tourist would expose his precious instrument to the elements. As I said, it was dead easy. I was just stepping out of the elevator when my subject came by, striding angrily along the corridor in the manner of a man who's marched out of an eating place unfed, at the end of his patience, and wants everyone to know exactly how he feels about the terrible service.

Apparently I owed somebody in the dining room a sizable debt for throwing the Mink off his stride, so to speak. He'd had a long flight, he was tired, he had things on his mind—matters of life and death, particularly death—and now his concentration had been shattered by an incompetent jerk, male or female, who couldn't even perform the simple task of transporting a few pounds of food and dishes from a kitchen to a table in a reasonable length of time. It's the sort of unnecessary and meaningless annoyance that catches even the most nerveless agent off guard sometimes, causing him to function at less than maximum efficiency.

Pavel Minsk didn't even look my way as he marched by. I'd been a little afraid that he might recognize me, even though we'd never met. My picture, like his, figured in a fair number of dossiers in a fair number of countries, including his. Now that first big hurdle was behind me. If he saw me around the hotel again, and remembered me, it would most likely be as a fellow guest he'd glimpsed getting out of the elevator, not as a face in a Moscow file.

As Fred had said, he was all dolled up for the glamorous

tropics. You could tell right away that he was supposed to be Mr. Smalltown America. When a U.S. hayseed dresses for an occasion, he almost invariably buys his glad rags one size too large. His European peasant counterpart buys them one size too small; he thinks fashion should hurt, and he can't feel really natty unless his collar is choking him and his suit coat can't be buttoned except by a major effort.

But the Mink was a Yankee yokel today; and his shirt collar was loose around his skinny throat; and the pants of his ice cream suit were too long and wide for his skinny legs. He looked self-conscious and a little comical; and that was exactly the way he wanted to look, I knew. Nobody could possibly suspect this scrawny little bumpkin in his cheap vacation finery of being a very competent and deadly professional assassin. Even his hat was a little too big when he clapped it on his head, pausing near the desk to glance at his wrist watch. Then he turned and headed for the door.

I worried briefly about the possibility of a trap. Suppose he had as good information as I did. There was no reason to think he didn't. Suppose there had been a leak somewhere; there often is. Suppose he really knew quite well who I was, and was leading me out of the hotel to...

To hell with it. If it was a trap, I'd have to deal with it when it started to close. I couldn't let him disappear into the wilds of Nassau. It seemed unlikely that he was heading right out to do the job he'd come here for, so soon after his arrival, but he obviously had some appointment in town more important than lunch, and I had to make at least an effort to learn what it was. After all, I was supposed to be doing the intelligence-creeps' work here as well as my own.

The little man didn't take a cab. He just paused outside to put on a big pair of sunglasses against the glare, and strode right off up the crowded street. I followed at a discreet distance. He walked at a good pace past the inviting windows full of cheap liquor and expensive souvenirs. He was looking for street names. They're hard to find, in Nassau, but he finally located one that suited him, and swung to the right, away from the harbor. I kept on walking straight ahead. As I crossed the street up which he had turned, I saw out of the corner of my eye that he was standing on the sidewalk up there studying a street map he'd pulled out of his pocket. That is, he might have been studying the map. He might also have been waiting to see who came after him.

I didn't turn my head, of course, or break my stride. I just continued on out of his sight. The coincidence of two guests of the same hotel leaving by the same door and heading up Bay Street simultaneously wasn't really earth-shaking—anybody departing from the British Colonial on foot would naturally be heading for the nearby concentration of shops on the town's main thoroughfare. But there had better be no more coincidences. He couldn't be allowed to see me behind him again...

"Taxi, Mister?"

I looked around. There was the familiar cab—a three-year-old blue Plymouth—with my eager Masai warrior at the helm. Okay. If that was the way he wanted it, okay. I jumped in, and the car pulled away.

I said, "Fort Fincastle, the water tower, the stone staircase you showed me yesterday, or the old Royal Victoria Hotel. What's your guess?"

Fred asked, "What makes you think he's heading for any of them?"

"Anybody setting up a contact with a stranger is likely to pick one of the standard tourist attractions. Easier for him to find, and a good place to waste time inconspicuously if one party to the meeting should be delayed."

"The Royal Victoria seems most suitable. Fine spot for lovers and spies, really. You could lose an elephant in those old gardens."

I said, "Okay, we'll gamble on your intuition. The Royal Victoria it is."

When we drove into the grounds of the shut-down hotel, a Volkswagen bus with some tourists on board was just pulling away down the narrow old curving driveway that had obviously been designed for shining carriages and handsome horses back when the internal combustion engine and the rubber tire were mere mad gleams in their inventors' eyes. A small blond girl in a white linen pantsuit, with a blue silk scarf at her throat, was snapping pictures of the giant kapok tree with an Instamatic camera. The lightweight, lady-type bicycle on which she'd presumably arrived leaned against the bushes at the end of the walk. Except for her, we seemed to have the place to ourselves.

"This is the old Royal Victoria Hotel, sir," said Fred loudly, going into his spiel. "It served as unofficial headquarters for the wealthy blockade-runners back during your Civil War. A fine old place; maybe you'd like to walk around and snap some pictures, sir. That's a kapok tree, the big one there, with the platform in it. Used to have an orchestra playing up there every evening... Just take your time, sir. Look around. I'll wait right here."

I hesitated a moment; then I took out my gun and knife and dropped them on the seat beside him, having come to a decision I should have reached earlier. Well, if anything went badly haywire here, the weapons were better off with him than in my hotel room, where they might eventually cause a lot of international discussion about why a certain tall dead man had come to the Islands heavily and illegally armed. Fred glanced at me sharply over his shoulder and swept the weapons out of sight.

I got out, opening my camera case, and made my way past the bicycle, admiring the elaborate ten-speed gearshift mechanism and the shiny levers for the rim-brakes, front and rear. I guess I really had an underprivileged childhood. My bikes had all had just one lousy speed and a single, lonely coaster brake—New Departure was more common, as I recall, but Morrow was supposed to have more class.

The little white-suited blonde was coming down the steps from the orchestra platform up in the big tree. I saw that while she was small, she wasn't quite small or fragile enough to be called tiny. As a matter of fact, she was constructed on quite durable lines for her size. If she'd been six inches taller, she might have looked overly substantial, particularly in pants; as it was, she just had a cute and cuddly look, helped out by her long, shining, Alice-in-Wonderland hairdo. She gave me a restrained little smile of thanks as I stepped aside to let her pass—but her eyes, that matched the scarf around her neck, studied my face just a little too hard and too long. I thought I could read a kind of desperate question in those blue eyes: was I the person she'd come here to meet, and if not where was he and how much longer did he expect her to hang around this derelict hostelry?

It could have been my imagination, of course. I'm not a qualified reader of minds, particularly feminine minds. Still, you don't survive long in the business by disregarding hunches; and a hunch was what I had, loud and clear. I was aware of the girl glancing at her watch as, having received no satisfaction from me, she moved on toward the driveway.

I climbed the wooden steps to the weathered wooden platform supported by the thick, twisted branches of the great tree; and I went though the motions of adjusting the camera and taking a few pictures, making a kind of casual, panoramic series of shots—the box was actually loaded; we take our props seriously—the last of which caught the girl fiddling with her bike. It was a long shot for the normal two-inch lens I was using, a telephoto would have been better, but the face should turn out clear enough to enlarge if I hadn't forgotten some important technical detail. It had been a long time since I made pictures for a living.

I buttoned up the camera once more in its tourist-armor—no pro would be seen dead with one of those awkward cases—and strolled back to the taxi, trying not to make my steps too long or too fast, although I was aware of the seconds ticking away and of a small man in a sloppy summer suit getting a couple of steps closer with each tick.

"Okay, driver," I said, pulling the door closed. "Where do you suggest we go now?"

Fred started the motor. "Well, sir, you can get a fine view of the city from the water tower." He put the car into gear.

"I'm leaving the camera," I said when we were out of the girl's hearing. "Have the film processed immediately and tell them to get right to work on the blonde. Frame seven or thereabouts; the last exposure. You can fill in the description; you saw her as well as I did. Now slow down and drop me off. Then get the hell out of here and keep going."

Fred glanced at me. "Don't you want your gun?"

"I'm under orders not to cause an international incident," I said. "It's pretty hard to shoot somebody in a foreign country and follow those instructions. Or knife them, either. Whoa, right there, where she can't see us..."

Then I was standing in the driveway alone. I slipped into the bushes and worked my way through the jungle to a point from which I had a view of the enormous tree up the hill. The girl in white was back on the platform. Apparently that was the meeting place that had been assigned to her. It was a hell of a spot for a secret contact, within plain sight of anybody lurking in the thick cover below. Actually, there was only one logical reason why you'd send a girl to a rendezvous wearing target white, and arrange for her to wait conspicuously up a tree in a deserted garden...

I heard him coming before I saw him. I'd put myself in the right place, very near the spot I'd picked from above as most suitable for what he had to do—what he'd come halfway around the world to do. Okay, so I'd been wrong and he was going to take care of his job right away, within a couple of hours of his arrival here in Nassau. You had to hand it to the little man, I reflected, calmly sitting down to lunch when he found he had a few minutes to spare. No wonder he'd been mad when the food had not been forthcoming on time. It was enough to throw any virtuoso off balance, being plagued by such infuriating inefficiency just before a performance.

I couldn't hear the footsteps any longer. Then I saw him, slipping along the overgrown walk nearby, keeping well down so he couldn't be seen from above. He stopped at the edge of a little paved circular opening around an old stone fountain, now quite dry. He crouched in the shelter of the ornamental shrubbery gone wild, close to me. I heard a faint clink of metal. He'd taken two items from under his floppy pants legs and was fitting them together to form a single-shot pistol. I'd never seen the weapon before, but I'd read descriptions: a fairly new U.S. product called, I believe, Contender.

A tiny telescopic sight was already attached to the barrel. It's only in the movies that you carry the telescope separately, stick it casually onto the gun after you have your target in view, and then make a lot of interesting final adjustments—I've always wondered what the hell those movie actors thought they were supposed to be accomplishing, fiddling with those knobs and dials. In real life, when there is serious shooting to be done, you anchor the optical sight firmly and immovably to the weapon, zero it in carefully, and never dream of monkeying with it again. You just hope to God that if you leave it strictly alone the outfit will still be shooting in the right place when the right time comes. Pavel Minsk opened his firearm and slipped a cartridge into the breech. I heard a faint click as the action closed again.

Check to the tall gent trying to make himself invisible in the brush. I had a very simple choice. I had a job to do, and I could do it efficiently and safely by letting him shoot and then taking him before he could get his single-shot weapon reloaded again. Or I could be a stupid goddamn hero trying to save the life of a female stranger at the risk of my own.

I wished I'd never asked Mac a certain question. Now I knew, because I'd been told, that he didn't give a damn how many blondes got shot, or brunettes or redheads either, as long as Pavel Minsk didn't survive them by very much, say two seconds. I couldn't kid myself that maybe this diminutive wench should be preserved for some important international reason. If I saved her, it would be from pure, simpleminded sentimentality…

The Mink was rising to take aim, using both hands on the gun; the approved, modern, handgun-assassination style. The old technique of holding a pistol one-handed at the end of a wobbly outstretched arm is strictly passé for business purposes. The girl was still standing up there with her shining white suit and her inexpensive camera, waiting for the person she'd been sent here to meet— the skull-faced gent with the scythe, although she didn't know it. I heard the metallic sound of a pistol hammer being cocked; and I let out a loud yell and charged.

The yell, and the crashing in the brushes, were supposed to disconcert Minsk long enough to let me reach him before he fired, or throw his aim off if he did manage to shoot. It was a fairly primitive tactic, but it had worked for me before. But this was the Mink, and his nerves weren't vulnerable to loud noises, and he was faster than he had any right to be. If he'd had an ordinary repeating pistol, designed for fast, instinctive, close-quarters work, I'd have died right there—but in that case I wouldn't have gambled that way. With his clumsy, telescope-sighted, long-range, one-shot weapon, Pavel had to decide whether to employ his single available cartridge for a snapshot as he turned, without using the sights, or risk taking time to line up the slow and awkward optical system for a certain kill. He went the snapshot route, firing the instant the weapon swung more or less into line. I saw the flame as

I lunged forward, and even, I thought, the jump of the muzzle; and I heard the vicious crack of something more powerful than an ordinary pistol cartridge.

Something hit the side of my head a savage blow. Everything seemed to go bright red; but in the middle of the redness remained a small tunnel at the far end of which I could see the little man desperately trying to stuff a fresh load into his one-shot weapon. I went in low and caught him about the middle and carried him backward across the paved area. The redness was closing in now, but I'd made all the calculations in advance. Three long steps, and I lifted little Pavel Minsk into the air and swung him down hard, as if he were a heavy sledgehammer with which I was trying to break up the sharp stone edge of the old, dry fountain...

7

As I said, it was dead easy. At least it would have been if I'd remembered, and acted upon, Mac's very sensible remark to the effect that we in no way resemble any organization dedicated to humanitarianism and good works. As it was, having chosen to do an easy job the hard way, I woke up—well, there had been a couple of previous awakenings, but they'd been kind of hazy—in a hospital bed with a murderous headache. There were two identical little blondes in identical white linen pantsuits sitting beside my bed. It took a while, and considerable willpower, to make them fuse into one.

"Oh, you're awake," she said, seeing my eyes open. "Thank God!"

"Who're you?" I whispered. I guess I could have spoken more loudly, but with my head the way it was, I didn't want to risk cutting loose with any unnecessary volume.

"Don't you remember? In the hotel garden…"

I licked my lips. "Sure, you're the blonde with the

cheap camera and the expensive bike. Is that how you get your mail: Mr. Postman please deliver to the blonde with the cheap camera and the expensive bike?"

She laughed quickly. She was a very pretty girl when she laughed, but I kind of wished she'd curb her noisy gaiety.

"It was a rented bike," she said. "I'm Lacey Rockwell, Mr. Helm. The police told me your name. They gave me permission to wait in here. I felt so... so *responsible*. I wanted to be sure you were all right. How do you feel?"

"Great," I said. "Just as if somebody's split my head open like a piece of kindling. A nice clean split... Lacey. What kind of name is that?"

She moved her shoulders slightly. "I asked my parents that. They said they just thought Lacey sounded kind of nice... Mr. Helm?"

"Yes?"

"That man. I have to know. Was he... was he really trying to *kill* me?"

I said, "What does he say, that he was shooting blackbirds for a pie? Or did he get away after I passed out?"

Her face changed. "He... didn't get away, but I'm afraid he's not saying anything. When you tackled him, his head hit the edge of the fountain and... Well, he's dead, Mr. Helm."

I was silent for a lengthy moment. It was a relief to know that, in spite of my sentimental aberrations, the job had got done in a reasonably workmanlike manner, but of course I couldn't say that.

"Jesus!" I whispered. "My God! I didn't mean to kill the poor guy!"

"Poor guy?" the little girl said with sudden sharpness. "Poor guy indeed! You're forgetting that he was apparently trying to murder me and that he did shoot you—an inch to the side, the doctor said, and you'd be dead. I'm not a very bloodthirsty person, Mr. Helm, but I do not consider that wicked little man a 'poor guy'! I think he got just what he deserved! When you shouted, and I looked down there and saw that nasty-looking gun pointing straight at me just before he whirled to face you…" She stopped, with a shiver. "I guess I'm just a sissy, but nobody's ever tried to kill me before. I simply can't get used to the idea. *Why*, Mr. Helm? *Why* would anybody want me dead?"

It was hard to keep track of all the nuances. My mind didn't want to stay focused on her, or my eyes, either, in spite of the fact that she wasn't difficult to look at. There's something very attractive about girls—particularly small blond girls—with that clear, smooth, delicate complexion. This one even had sense enough to let it speak for herself instead of trying to improve on it with makeup. She was really a very appealing kid, and a hell of a fine little actress, and I wondered just who it was she was putting on her bewildered act for. The most logical person, of course, was me.

I licked my lips once more. "Is that another rhetorical question. Miss Rockwell?"

She frowned. "What do you mean?"

"First you ask if the guy was really trying to kill you;

and then you tell me you looked right into the muzzle of the gun, so you know damned well he was trying to kill you."

"I'm sorry." She laughed apologetically. "It's just so *unbelievable*, Mr. Helm. I have a hard time grasping it. I guess I just want you to… well, to tell me what I saw with my own eyes, so I'll know I wasn't dreaming."

I said, "Well, the little man had a gun—a funny-looking pistol with a telescope on it—and I saw him assemble it, load it, point it in your direction, and cock the hammer, if that's the correct firearms terminology. It seemed inadvisable to let him proceed to the next step: pulling the trigger. Yes, Miss Rockwell, I think it's safe to say that murder was very much on his mind, and that you were the intended victim."

"But I'd never seen him before in my life! Why in the world…"

"You didn't know him at all?"

She shook her head. "Mr. Helm, they let me look at him to make sure. It wasn't a… a very pleasant experience. But he was a total stranger to me. That's what's so mysterious, so terrifying. If you can tell me anything that will make some sense of the whole thing, I'll be very grateful."

I asked, "How can I? I didn't know him either, any more than I know you… What's the matter?"

"But you must have known him! Otherwise, why…" She stopped.

I frowned at her. Thinking was hard work, but it obviously had to be done. "What do you mean?" I demanded. "Why the hell must I have known him? I don't know anybody in Nassau except a taxi-driver I owe a few bucks for a city tour we never finished, and I can't even remember his name. Paul, or Mike, or Steve, or something. What happened was, I saw a crummy-looking punk pointing a gun at a nice-looking girl, and I decided, in my idealistic way, that something ought to be done about it." I touched the side of my bandaged head in a cautious way. "Maybe next time I'll be smart and mind my own business."

She said quickly, "I don't mean to sound ungrateful or… or suspicious. Naturally, I appreciate what you did for me. I appreciate it very much. I'm just trying to *understand*… if you didn't know Mr. Menshek, or whatever the police said his name was, why were you hiding in the bushes spying on him? Or… or were you spying on *me*?"

I stared at her for a moment. Then, again because it had to be done, I threw back my head and laughed uproariously, and stopped abruptly, and waited for the blinding pain to go away.

"Don't be so funny, Lacey Rockwell. It hurts," I whispered when I could talk once more.

"But—"

I said, "Look, doll, I'd been riding around in that cab, sightseeing. I'd had a late breakfast in my hotel room, with a big pot of coffee. The driver still had some places he wanted to show me, and I wanted to get my money's worth, and the town doesn't seem to be really loaded with sidewalk facilities like some of those practical European cities where they recognize the *limitations* of the human plumbing… So, hell, I told the guy to drop me off down there where the bushes were nice and thick and wait for me outside the gate and I'd join him in a couple of minutes. Okay? And naturally I was a little sensitive about being seen, under the circumstances, so when I heard somebody coming I just kind of stepped a little farther back into that jungly stuff hoping he'd go away, but he didn't. When I saw what he was doing, well, it just seemed like my duty as a good citizen to abort my primary mission, pull up my zipper again, and try to stop him…" I looked at her closely. "Why, Miss Rockwell, you're blushing!"

She was, too, and she had the right skin for it; it was a very pretty display. Before she could speak, the door opened and all kinds of officialdom, plainclothes and uniformed, black and white, invaded the room. In the van was a heavy, dignified-looking black man with short, gray hair, and a lean, good-looking white man with long brown hair, considerably younger. They were both in civilian clothes, but there were police uniforms behind them.

The younger one spoke to the girl, who had come to her feet facing them. He said, "That was fine. We have it all on tape. It clears things up very well. Thank you very much for your cooperation, Miss Rockwell. You're free to go now."

She moved toward the door without glancing my way. I said, "Miss Rockwell." She stopped without turning her head. I spoke to her back: "Miss Rockwell,

I'm surprised at you. You're just a lousy little blond fink. Next time I see somebody trying to shoot you, I'll help them call the shots."

"Now, now." This was the dignified black gentleman. "Miss Rockwell was just following our instructions, Mr. Helm. You should be grateful to her. She's cleared you very nicely, or helped you clear yourself."

"Cleared me of what?" I asked. "Of saving her lousy little life? I can see how that ought to be illegal, but I didn't know it was."

"Mr. Helm, please!" It was the white man, the younger one. He turned to the girl. "Go on, Miss Rockwell. Don't leave town or change hotels without letting us know, please." When the little girl had fled, he turned back to me: "What Detective Inspector Crawford means is that there are always questions to be answered when a man is killed, even when he seems to have been something of a professional gunman…"

I let my eyes widen in a startled way. "My God! A professional? What the hell have I got myself into, anyway?"

He hesitated. "Well, we're getting some very interesting information on the late Mr. Menshek. It's big and international, Mr. Helm. For some reason, certain people seem almost as anxious to get rid of that little girl who just left as they were to dispose of Leon Trotsky. At least, they employed some very high-priced talent for the job. Mr. Menshek's records seems to be long, gory, and spectacular. I have to tell you this, in case there should be repercussions."

I grimaced. "Thanks a whole lot! What you're trying to say is that I just managed to bash in the head of a high-class Commie hitman, or liquidator, or exterminator, or whatever the movie jargon is, and somebody may be real mad, is that it?"

He said carefully, "Well, it's not really very likely, sir, but I thought you should be aware of the possibility."

"It makes me feel warm all over," I said sourly. "Or cold. And what about you and your friends with your eavesdropping gadgets, are you all mad, too?"

"Oh, no," he said. "No, indeed, Mr. Helm. We are very happy. As far as we're concerned, well, you've done us a service—we don't like to have homicidal operations like that conducted under our noses, isn't that right, Inspector? If a few more brave citizens like you were to rise up and dispose of a few more nasty types like Menshek, the world would be a better place for all of us. We just had to make certain that your actions were those of a genuinely disinterested and public-spirited bystander..."

It always works. I didn't take all his protestations at face value—even with my head cracked, I can spot irony when I hear it—but at least he'd indicated that we were all going to play nice, until further notice. You can generally get by with just about anything, even homicide, as long as you're not too proud to make yourself look bad by confessing to a slightly discreditable action, like peeing in a public park.

After a while, they all went away, and I slept. Suddenly it was morning. My head was clear enough for me to take in the standard nurse-and-doctor routine. They run it just about the same with a predominantly black cast as with a predominantly white one. I got some breakfast that didn't have much taste, or maybe it was my mouth that didn't have much taste. Then the door opened, kind of sneakily, and the little blonde girl whose life I'd saved slipped through the crack. She was wearing a short, crisp, white dress, and her long hair had been brushed to within an inch of its blonde life. Obviously, she wanted to make a good impression on somebody this morning, presumably me.

"Mr. Helm—"

"Beat it," I said.

"But—"

I reached for the dingus that rang the bell and pushed the button. The service was good. Almost instantly a black nurse or aide or something—I didn't have all the Bahamian hospital ranks sorted out—came in to see what I wanted.

I said, "Get the little stoolpigeon out of here, will you, Miss. Please. She's interfering with the patient's recovery."

Lacey Rockwell departed with a reproachful look on her face. She was just as cute as the Easter Bunny, and I didn't want to lose her permanently, but I didn't really think there was much risk of that. I waited, watched the ceiling, and presently Fred came in, kind of diffidently. "Sorry to bother you, sir, but they said it was all right."

I said, "Oh, you're the driver who... Of course, you've got some money coming. I think my wallet's in the table drawer. If you'd get it out…" As he came closer, I said softly, "Careful, the place is bugged."

He shook his head. "No longer. They took it out last night, Mr. Helm. They're satisfied."

"Maybe," I said. "That white man with Detective Inspector Crawford knows more than he was saying aloud. Have we got anything on him?"

"Not much yet," Fred said. "He's not local. Somebody from London, is the word we have. A specialist, but specialist in what? He goes by the name of Pendleton, Ramsay Pendleton. The fact that he seems to be getting full cooperation is significant. With our politics the way they are right now, British officials aren't generally welcomed with open arms." Fred hesitated. "That was a brave thing you did, Mr. Helm, tackling the Mink barehanded."

I looked at him with surprise and, perhaps, a little dismay. Only an amateur worries about courage; and I don't like amateur help. I said, "The guy had only one shot in his gun. He weighed a hundred and thirty pounds. I go over two hundred when I don't watch myself. I should be ashamed of myself, picking on a little fellow like that and letting him put a crease in my skull to boot." After a moment, I went on: "Could he possibly have made contact with anybody between the time you spotted him at the airport, and the time you turned him over to me at the hotel?"

"If I'd seen a contact made, Mr. Helm, I'd certainly have let you know."

Fred's voice was cool. I'd hurt his feelings. He wasn't

supposed to have feelings, none of us are, but I'd hurt them anyway. I'd forgotten that the British have a thing about being forever brave; and that these island people, although they were in the process of discarding the colonial yoke, had nevertheless been exposed to that stiff-upper-lip tradition since childhood. Furthermore, I'd questioned his professional competence.

I said, "Relax, *amigo*. You know as well as I do that there are signals nobody can spot who doesn't know exactly what he's looking for. This thing was set up in advance, well in advance, or we'd never have had a chance to learn about it in time to make the intercept. Okay. But the Mink would have wanted to know, upon arriving, that nothing had gone haywire while he was in transit. It seems probable that somebody, at the airport, the hotel, or points in between, gave him the final green light. Maybe just a bystander blowing his nose on a dirty handkerchief, in which case we're out of luck. But the most likely candidate is somebody he'd normally have dealings with as an innocent tourist, planted somewhere along the route he'd be expected to take. The driver of the taxi he used, for instance…"

"I drove him in my cab," Fred said stiffly.

I grinned. "One possibility eliminated, then. What about the rest? Who handed him his luggage at the airport, checked him in at the hotel, took his bag up to his room, waited on him in the restaurant… Hell, maybe that slow, slow service was a signal of sorts, although it seems to be fairly standard operating procedure in that place. If you don't mind checking them all out, I'd appreciate it." He nodded, relaxing a little, and I said: "Swell, now what have you got on the girl?"

"Lacey Matilda Rockwell, twenty-four, from Winter Harbor, Maine. Unmarried. Degree from the University of Maine. Studied oceanography at Woods Hole, wherever that may be. The little lady is an expert diver, sailor, surfer… anything on the water or under it, she can do it, is the information we have."

I seemed to have an affinity for salty maidens brought up on sheets and halliards. Well, they came in handy sometimes. Maybe I could find a use for this one.

"What's she doing around here, oceanographing?" I asked.

"No sir," Fred said. "She's looking for somebody, a Harlan Enos Rockwell, twenty-two, her younger brother. Apparently an embryo singlehander, following in the footsteps of the late Sir Francis Chichester. Had a twenty-four-foot cruising sloop, the *Star Trek*—named after a TV program, I believe. He'd bought the Fiberglas hull and finished it himself, beefing it up for ocean work. Went missing at sea late this summer after heading out the Northeast Providence Channel bound for the Virgin Islands… Did you say something, Mr. Helm?"

"No," I said. After all, that was another phase of the operation—the Haseltine phase; the Treacherous-Triangle phase—and one that didn't concern Fred or his cohorts, or did it?

8

Mac said, "I have been subjected to a certain amount of criticism, Eric. Some people here in Washington are disturbed. They point out that you were instructed to obtain some information before making the touch. They feel that your action was, shall we say, a little precipitate?"

It didn't bother me, really. I mean, you don't call Washington expecting solicitous inquiries about your health—not even right after being released from the hospital—or congratulations on the success of a difficult mission. Not unless you're a naïve damned fool you don't.

I grimaced at the dark-faced pedestrians moving past the phone booth as if they were in no great hurry to get where they were going. There were some light-faced ones as well. I made a face at those, too, so as not to seem guilty of prejudice. Nevertheless, despite the standard Washington static, I was feeling pretty good. My headache was almost gone, and Nassau didn't seem like such a bad place, after all. The people looked cheerful and friendly, and the sun was shining. Maybe I'd just been in a bad mood when I arrived, looking for things to criticize. There's nothing like surviving a little brush with death to make the world look attractive just about anywhere.

"Yes, sir, precipitate," I said. "But I'm working on the information angle now."

"How? Minsk was buried yesterday."

I said, "We probably know everything the Mink ever knew about this deal: the identity and location of his target in Nassau. That was all he needed to know to carry out his assignment, so that was all the information he'd care to burden himself with. Question, sir."

"Yes, Eric?"

"How did we learn of his impending visit to this island paradise?"

"The intelligence people picked it up through one of their informants overseas, I believe. Why?"

"I don't like it," I said. "There's a funny smell here, somewhere."

"What do you mean?"

I said, "Goddamn it, sir, it was too damned easy!"

"The medical report I have says you came within a fraction of an inch of getting killed."

"I had orders not to muddy the international waters, remember? Also, I felt obliged to save a lady's life. Without those handicaps, I could have picked him off like a pigeon on a telephone wire. Pavel Minsk, for God's sake! Walking into ambush like that, like a kid on his first assignment! Take my word for it, sir, it stinks!"

There was a little pause; then Mac said: "Old professionals do get careless and overconfident after years of success, Eric. Sometimes they even get the feeling they're bulletproof, and charge stupidly into the muzzles of loaded firearms, barehanded."

I grimaced at the instrument on the wall of the booth, and said, "Yes, sir."

"However, you may have a point," he went on, without a change of tone. "I will make inquiries, but I can promise nothing. Our fellow agencies are seldom receptive to suggestions that they may have been inefficient, not to say gullible. Particularly when they were promised information from us that has not, so far, been forthcoming; information, the most likely source of which has just received a simple but Christian funeral."

I said, "We don't need the Mink any more. We stopped needing him the instant I saw where his gun was pointing."

"You may be right. But in his absence we do need Miss Lacey Matilda Rockwell."

I was glad to hear him say it, confirming my own belated realization that it had actually been very clever of me to keep the girl alive, although I hadn't been aware of it at the time. Investigating a living subject that can talk is generally easier than investigating a dead one that can't. There were a good many things we needed to know, now—or somebody did—about the unlikely little female specimen the Mink had come such a long way to kill.

"Yes, sir," I said.

"According to the reports I have, you seem to be doing

everything in your power to rebuff and antagonize the young lady. I presume you have a reason."

I wondered if Fred was sending in critical comments about my handling of the situation because I'd hurt his feelings at the hospital. Well, there's always a certain amount of friction between the people on the spot and the visiting experts they're obliged to serve—there's often the feeling, locally, that they should have been allowed to handle the job without the intervention of imported talent. Nevertheless, I kind of wished the guy had taken it up with me, if he had a criticism, instead of passing it on to Washington.

"Yes, sir," I said. "It's a matter of psychology, sir."

"Indeed?"

I said, "I had to figure out a way to keep her on ice, so to speak. If I'd just taken that police business in my stride, she could have gone off with a clear conscience, and I might have had considerable trouble finding her again, not to mention establishing a useful relationship with her. Now it should be fairly easy. She's got to come to me. As long as I persist in misunderstanding her so cruelly and treating her so rudely, she's got to hang around and try to straighten me out. She's got to convince me, somehow, that she's really a swell and sensitive person who really appreciates my saving her life; and that she only set me up for the Nassau cops and their electronics for my own good." I was watching a slim black girl in red boots, brown hose, and red hotpants. She was gone before I could complete my appraisal upward. Nevertheless, I decided that Nassau was really quite a picturesque place in spite of the hotel's plastic-wrapped marmalade. I went on: "Hell, I had to give myself a little time, sir. I had to stall until my head stopped pounding and I was out of bed and could figure out what to do next—assuming that you did want me to proceed with the assignment."

"Your assumption was correct. We took this job under certain conditions; we're more or less obliged to fulfill those conditions. How are you feeling now, Eric?"

It was nice of him to ask, after all. I said, "I'm fine, sir. The medical profession assures me no brains were spilled or scrambled. All that remains visible is a slightly oversized bandaid." At least I was a lot healthier than Pavel Minsk, I reflected, and continued: "Did you know that Miss Rockwell is in the Islands looking for a brother missing at sea out in the so-called Bermuda Triangle? No wreckage, no lifebelts, no bodies washed ashore—well, body, singular. Harlan Enos Rockwell was doing it all alone. In a twenty-four-foot sailboat. Not a hell of a lot of boat for ocean cruising, but smaller ones have made it. Apparently he didn't. At least he headed out of here several weeks ago and hasn't been seen or heard from since. It's getting to be a fairly familiar story, isn't it, sir?"

"Yes, I thought so when I heard about it," Mac said. "It certainly seems to indicate that the Minsk affair is related, somehow, to Mr. Haseltine's problem. But just what could the girl have learned, searching for her missing brother, that's dangerous enough to Moscow that one of their best men had to be sent to silence her?" He paused, and went on: "Our big trouble is, I'm afraid, that even the young lady herself probably doesn't know the answer to that question."

I said, "There are, however, two questions she should be able to answer. The first is why, having lost a brother out east in the Atlantic, she came to Nassau and hired an airplane to take her on a search in just about the opposite direction, having the pilot fly her off to the west as far as Florida in some areas."

Mac said, "Yes, I noticed that."

"The other question is: who put her up a tree for the Mink to shoot at? There's no doubt in my mind that she'd arranged to meet somebody in that garden; although she presumably didn't know the guy would have a gun. The police didn't see her waiting there, but I did. If they had, they'd undoubtedly have leaned on her harder. If we can learn how the arrangement was made, maybe we'll have a lead that'll take us somewhere."

Mac said, "I suppose that's as good a place for you to start as any. Let me know what you turn up…"

"Question, sir."

"Yes?"

"What have we got on Phipps?"

"Haseltine should have given you all the significant information."

"Sure. A wealthy contractor type with a movie-star wife, a beautiful daughter, and a yen for boats."

"You're not satisfied, Eric?"

"Haha," I said. "Don't crack such funny jokes, sir. This is serious business."

"What do you find unsatisfactory?"

I said, "You told me recently that you were instructed to shift manpower to the Bahamas. The British also have at least one agent of some kind floating around; and he's cheerfully accepted by the local authorities in spite of the fact that the Islands are busy casting off the brutal bonds of British tyranny. All this because of a missing kid in a Fiberglas tub, and a missing West Coast yachtsman with curly gray hair?" I paused. Mac said nothing. I said, "Either this Phipps gent is somebody very important in disguise, or Harlan Rockwell is, or there's somebody or something else involved nobody's bothered to mention... You spoke, sir?"

He hadn't, but he'd made some kind of a sound, a thousand miles away. Now he said, "This is confidential, Eric. Ten days ago, a sizable diesel yacht proceeding towards the Bahamas from Puerto Rico failed to make radio contact according to her prearranged schedule. She has not been heard from since: the *Wayfarer*, owned by Sir James Marcus, who was on board. Sir James is the proprietor of several English newspapers. He is considered the sixth or seventh wealthiest man in the British Isles. As I say, this is highly classified information, that I am not supposed to divulge. If the news should get out, there would be serious financial repercussions. Officially, Sir James is merely cruising for his health, incommunicado by his own wishes."

I said, "Yes, sir. It would be nice if we peons toiling in the fields were kept informed of these minor details, sir. I don't suppose an SOS or other distress signal was heard or seen."

"No," Mac said, "and no debris has been found. The search is continuing, of course."

"After ten days, the chances of anybody finding anything aren't very great, are they?" I made a face at the phone. "If it wasn't for the Rockwell kid, who doesn't seem to be particularly well heeled, I'd say somebody was starting a collection of seagoing millionaires. Well, if I stumble over any misplaced British newspaper tycoons, I'll let you know."

Entering the hotel, I had the usual sensation of being outnumbered by the mob of predominantly dark-skinned tourists that seemed to be forever checking out to catch a boat or plane. I fought my way through the bright and crowded lobby into the dark and almost empty bar, feeling the need for something to wash the hospital taste out of my mouth. As I sipped my martini, not bad as foreign martinis go, a man sat down beside me and ordered Scotch. Receiving it, he tasted it thoughtfully and spoke without looking my way.

"Thompson-Center Contender," he said. "Single shot, break action. Caliber .256 Winchester, something of a rarity. Muzzle velocity two eight ought ought, muzzle energy, one ought four ought. For a pistol cartridge, a rather potent specimen, with better than average long-range characteristics. I thought you might be interested."

"Thanks," I said. "I thought the damned thing had an unusually nasty crack to it."

"Ah," said Ramsay Pendleton, "but you are the innocent bystander chap who doesn't know what's usual and what isn't where firearms are concerned, aren't you, Mr. Helm?" There was a brief pause; then he said: "I wish to apologize."

I looked at him, but there was so little light in the bar that I couldn't make out his expression clearly.

"For planting a mike on me?" I asked.

"No, for misjudging you."

"I didn't know a judgment had been passed," I said, "let alone a misjudgment. There's been hardly any time."

"There's been all kinds of time, old chap. I knew all about you before I came here. Do you remember a man you left to die in a cave in Scotland a few years ago? Leslie Crowe-Barham was my very good friend, Mr. Helm."

There were some things I could have said to that. When I left him, the British agent in question had been dying and had known it. There had been a job for me to do while he kept the opposing forces engaged as long as he could; and I'd done it. But I saw no reason, after the time that had passed, to present the case for the defense.

"So you're one of Colonel Stark's boys," I said. "At least he was the man in charge at the time. He didn't like me very much."

"He still is, and he still doesn't."

I said deliberately, "I've left a number of men, and a few women, behind to die in caves and other places, Mr. Pendleton. Some day, somebody'll undoubtedly leave me behind to die somewhere. That's the way it goes. I'm not paid to hold people's hands while they take the big jump, and they're not paid to hold mine."

"You're too prickly, old chap," said Pendleton mildly. "I said I was apologizing, didn't I? Anybody who'll tackle a man like the Mink unarmed, merely because he's been instructed to make it look like an accident, can hardly be accused of cowardice."

I reflected that I ought to get him and Fred together and send them to discuss the subject with Mac. I said, "Obviously, it was a waste of time. Trying to make it look accidental, I mean. I didn't fool you for a second."

"No, but you made it easy for Detective Inspector Crawford to bury the case with a minimum of fuss and bother, something that could hardly have been accomplished if it had got out that agents of two foreign nationalities had battled to the death in the old Victoria gardens. What do you know about a man named William Haseltine, Helm?"

Big Bill wasn't on the classified list, as far as I knew. I always make a practice of being generous with information that doesn't cost anything.

"He's a rich, tough, petroleum-type Texan who's lost his girl friend out at sea somewhere," I said. "Mama, papa, three crewmen, and a sixty-foot yacht, are also missing, but Haseltine's concern is for a lady named Loretta, and he's willing to spend the proceeds of several of his oil wells to find her."

"Yes, I heard about the Phipps case. I understand he was turning the Islands upside down for a while, trying to locate that boat. So now he's turned to you. I wasn't aware that missing young ladies were part of your official responsibility, Helm."

"I have a softhearted boss," I said. "He was touched by the pleadings of the tearful bridegroom-that-was-to-have-been, and said for me to give him a hand."

"Yes," said Pendleton. "I've heard of that sentimental chief of yours, old chap, although not exactly in those terms." He hesitated. "What do you know about Sir James Marcus?"

"Nothing;" I said. "It's highly classified information, much too secret to be entrusted to us pick-and-shovel types."

"Yes, of course." Pendleton sipped his drink thoughtfully. "Let me ask you another question. Do you think it likely that if we should manage to find Mr. Wellington Phipps, the first recent disappearance, and Mr. Harlan Rockwell, the second, Sir James Marcus, the third, probably won't be far away?"

"Maybe," I said.

"You have reservations?"

I said, "You're assuming they're all alive. If they were killed, there would be no reason for the people responsible to go to the trouble of burying them all in the same grave, unless you want to call the whole Atlantic and its adjoining waters a single grave."

Pendleton said calmly, "We must assume they are alive, old chap. If they're dead, we're all wasting our time, and that's unthinkable, isn't it?"

"I'm also a little dubious about the intrepid young Mr. Rockwell. Why would anybody go to the trouble of molesting a penniless kid in a more-or-less homemade boat, when there are more millionaires around for the picking?" I shrugged. "Of course, we're just playing guessing games. We don't have any real leads, unless you do."

"No," he said, "but you do. You have Haseltine—"

"Who doesn't know anything, even after spending more money than you and I see in a year."

Pendleton glanced at me sharply. "Are you naïve, Helm, or are you hoping I am?"

"You think the Texan does know something?"

"I feel there's something melodramatic and theatrical about the way the man has flung money around and, apparently, even persuaded a very secret agency of his government to lend him assistance, to unravel the mysteries of what would seem, at first glance, to be a very ordinary shipwreck in an area where such incidents are common. He looks to me like a gentleman with guilt on his conscience trying to impress everybody with his innocence. And remember, he was already searching busily and noisily for his lost Loretta weeks before there had been any other incidents of the same nature. An ungenerous person might say that he knew there had been foul play involved long before there was any real reason to think so."

I looked at the Britisher with respect. He'd put into words what had been only a vague uneasiness on my part.

I said, "Okay, I'll admit the guy has possibilities, but he'll be a tough nut to crack."

"You also have another lead, Miss Lacey Rockwell, who undoubtedly does know something, or somebody wouldn't be trying to, ensure her permanent silence." Pendleton paused to drain his glass. "I am about to do something reprehensible, old chap. I am about to ask for your cooperation, in spite of the fact that, as you say, my chief does not care for you very much. I would like to be kept informed of what you obtain from these people. In return, I can promise to let you know anything we turn up, not to mention making things easy for you as long as you're here in the Islands."

I said carefully, "I have nothing against international cooperation, *amigo*; but don't overestimate my resources. Getting something on Haseltine isn't going to be easy, even assuming there's something to be got. The Rockwell girl undoubtedly does know something, and I'm certainly going to make a stab at finding out what it is, but I haven't *got* her, as you put it."

"But you're wrong, old chap," said Pendleton calmly. "You most certainly do have her. Go up to your room and see."

9

She was lying on the bed fully dressed, which was a relief in a way. I don't mean to imply that I object seriously to naked women in my bed, but one likes to meet a lady with a little originality. That nudie act has been pretty heavily overdone.

There were a number of melodramatic responses I could have made, from raping her to heaving her out into the hall, but after all, I'd made my point. The hostility routine had served its purpose. I merely stood over her, therefore, until she decided to go through the motions of waking up and discovering, to her shocked amazement, of course, that she was no longer alone. She sat up quickly. After a moment, she smoothed down the jacket of the white pantsuit I'd seen before, and pushed the long, Alice-in-Wonderland hair out of her eyes. She was really quite a pretty girl, in a bouncy, blue-eyed sort of way, and I had all the normal impulses I was supposed to have, finding her like that, but I repressed them firmly.

I said, "You're a persistent little bitch, aren't you, Miss Rockwell?"

She licked her lips, looking up at me. "I am," she said, "a scared little bitch, Mr. Helm."

"What scares you? Paul Menshek was buried yesterday, I'm told."

"You know that's not the end of it, not for either of us," she said. "If Menshek was a paid assassin, as they claim, that means somebody hired him, doesn't it? And if somebody hired one killer, he can hire another, can't he? And if he's mad enough at having his homicidal plans interfered with, he might even hire two, or give his one gunman a few extra bullets to use on you."

"The word is cartridges, doll."

"What?"

"A bullet by itself is just a small, inert hunk of metal, of no use to anyone. For homicidal purposes, it requires gunpowder to drive it, a primer to fire it, and a brass case to hold it all together until the time comes—in other words, a complete cartridge. I don't know too much about firearms, but I do know that much."

She said stiffly, sitting there: "You're making fun of me."

"Who, me? Make fun of an innocent girl who's merely trying to scare me out of my pants, or get me out of them by other methods? Now, I wouldn't do a thing like that, ma'am, not me!" She licked her lips once more, and didn't speak. I went on: "Frankly, if there is a homicidal mastermind at work here, which hasn't been proved, I figure he's got too much sense to take on every casual citizen who happens to get involved in the action. Whether Menshek was just hired for the occasion, or was a permanent fixture on some Communist payroll, as the police seem to think, I have a strong hunch he was considered expendable and nobody's likely to feel obliged to avenge him in spite of the fact that everybody's trying to frighten me to death with the possibility, for one reason or another."

"Everybody? Who else—"

"That friendly Mr. Pendleton used just about the same line. I figure he hoped that if he got me scared enough, I'd be more likely, wanting police protection, to spill my guts. He made just one slight miscalculation. I don't have any guts to spill. Just as you're miscalculating, Miss Rockwell. It's no use your trying to seduce me or terrify me. I haven't got what you want, either."

She was on her feet, facing me. "Really! If you think I came in here to—" She stopped. I didn't say anything. After a moment, she blushed very nicely and give a half-embarrassed, little-girl giggle. "Well, at least I wasn't obvious about it. I did keep all my clothes on, didn't I?" I still said nothing. She said, "I'm being followed, Mr. Helm. Everywhere I go, there's a man behind me."

"Probably the Nassau police, making sure nobody takes another crack at you in their bailiwick. It should make you feel nice and safe."

"He doesn't *look* like a policeman." After a moment, she said, "You said you didn't have what I want. How do you know what I want, Mr. Helm?"

"Hell, it's obvious," I said. "You want a unique combination of Hercules and Einstein, the former to protect you and the latter to figure out what to protect you from. You've more or less indicated that you're even willing to go to bed to get it. Well, I appreciate the offer, doll, but I'm just a plain old camera-journalist, and I don't accept the work if I can't deliver."

She said, "You don't have to be crude!"

I grinned. "Who's crude? You didn't find me draped invitingly over anybody's bed, did you? There's also another principle involved. I never take a job if I can't trust the client, Miss Rockwell. Now, if you don't mind, I'd like to take a shower. There's something about a hospital—"

She said, "You're still mad about those silly microphones, aren't you? What was I supposed to do, in a foreign country, tell all those foreign policemen to go to hell?"

"What was I supposed to do, in a foreign country, tackle a professional foreign gunman with my bare hands, for a girl I didn't even know?"

Her tongue made the round trip of her lips once more. "You didn't know he was a professional gunman when you did it!" she snapped. Then she went on quickly: "I'm sorry. You did a brave thing and I shouldn't belittle it. I'm grateful, Mr. Helm, I really am!"

"Sure," I said. "You just picked a funny way of showing it."

Anger flared in her eyes once more. "You're supposed to be a respectable photo-journalist. I checked. So why are you so sensitive about policemen? What I did didn't hurt you a bit!"

"I could ask you the same question," I said. "Why are you so sensitive about cops, Miss Rockwell? Sensitive enough that you were willing to betray a heroic chap who'd just got shot saving your life, merely to stay on the right side of the fuzz?" Her eyes wavered, and I went on: "Could it have something to do with this missing brother of yours that you're supposed to be looking for so hard?"

"Supposed to be? I *am* looking for Harley—"

"Cut it out," I said. "Your brother's boat was last sighted a couple of hundred miles to the east and south, still doing fine. If he foundered or was sunk by a freighter or a whale or something—the funny thing is, several yachts have been sunk by whales recently, did you know that?—it happened well out in the Atlantic. But you've been flying around in a hired airplane, I'm told, all over the Bahamas, places where Harlan Rockwell couldn't conceivably have sailed, drifted, swum, or crawled from his last reported position in any reasonable length of time."

"I've been looking for a white light."

Her voice was very soft, almost inaudible. I stared at her for a moment; then I shrugged, and said scornfully: "Sure, the great white light of understanding."

"Or a white lighthouse. It's something Harley said over the phone, long distance, just before he shoved off from Nassau. He said, if anything should happen to him, I should check around the white light or lighthouse. Afterwards, I couldn't really remember exactly…

Mr. Helm, do you know how many white beacons and navigation lights there are in the Bahamas and up and down the Florida coast?"

I said, "It sounds screwy to me. If you think you're going to intrigue me with some mysterious gimmick out of the late-late show—"

"I can't help being a real lousy heroine," she breathed. "I always wanted to be brave and strong but... It was just too much, Mr. Helm. I'd almost been murdered, I'd had to look at one man with a smashed head and another with blood all over his face, I'd been badgered by policemen and told that if I just cooperated a little maybe we'd learn something that made sense of this... this crazy attack on me... She stopped, and made a defeated little gesture, and let her hands fall. "Help me," she said.

I looked at her bleakly. "That was really very good, doll," I said. "Very good indeed. The despairing gesture, the tears you put in your voice—lovely, just lovely. No, damn it, don't cry. We'll just assume that you cry real pretty, too." I paused, and went on slowly, "And we'll assume that I'm just a sucker for a crying woman. I mean, as they say in the law courts, we'll postulate that for the record, so we don't have to waste time going through it all in detail... Just what the hell do you expect me to be able to do for you, anyway?"

There was a long silence. At last she smiled faintly. "You're a brute, Mr. Helm," she said.

"And you're a phony, Miss Rockwell," I said.

"Of course I am," she said. "But Harley really said that

about the light. And I really am scared. And there really is a man following me; and if you take me to dinner at the Café Martinique, I'll show him to you..."

10

Older descriptions of Nassau refer to Hog Island, the lengthy offshore strip of land that forms and shelters the city's harbor, but you'll find no geographical feature by that name on current maps. The developers got hold of it, had a tollbridge built out to it, and... well, you can't expect people to invest several million dollars in a hunk of real estate named for pigs, can you? It is now referred to as Paradise Island. One of these days I suppose we'll see Cape Cod—Codfish Cape, for God's sake, how unromantic can you get?—renamed Perfection Promontory, or Angel Point.

For a short bridge, the toll was steep, two bucks, but the black taxi driver, who wasn't Fred—I had Fred engaged in work unrelated to transportation—assured us that this entitled us to get off the island as well as onto it.

"The casino is right up the hill there, sir, just a few steps through the trees, if you and your lady would care for a little action after dinner," he said as he pulled up before an impressive mansion. "Even if you're not gambling folks, it's worth seeing, and you can pick up a taxi easier up there than you can down here."

"Thank you, driver," I said, and gave him an adequate tip with the fare.

"Thank *you*, sir."

I turned to escort Lacey into the place. She looked prettier and more fragile, having changed into a dress— the same abbreviated, sleeveless number I'd seen one morning at the hospital. Nevertheless, small as she was, she was still far from giving the impression that the first breeze would waft her away. Inside, a dignified white gent in a somber suit led us to our reserved table in the main dining room of the converted old luxury residence. Lacey had wanted me to ask for a spot out on the porch that overlooked the water of a nearby canal or inlet. She'd described it as very pleasant and picturesque, and I could now see that it was, but I'd pointed out to her that in view of her fears it wouldn't really be very smart of us to make targets of ourselves outdoors, unnecessarily.

I was relieved to see that the clientele of the place, like the head waiter, was predominantly white. It was not a question of intolerance, quite the contrary. I simply needed a rest. It's exhausting to be so very damned careful not to use a single word or phrase that could possibly be misconstrued as prejudice, particularly since they all seem to have convinced themselves that all slighting or fearful references to darkness or blackness in the English language are of racist origin, forgetting that fear of the black and hostile night, as opposed to the bright and friendly day, is basic to a lot of primitive cultures and some not-so primitive. Hell, I used to be scared of the dark, as a kid, long before I ever saw a man with a black skin.

Among these light-skinned tourists I could relax and be my rude, crude self once more. "What do you think they are?" I asked my blond companion as we waited for our drinks. "Schoolteachers from Indianapolis, or millionaires from Miami Beach?"

She didn't smile or answer the question. "Did you see him?" she asked instead.

"The guy in the Volkswagen, behind us? Sure I saw him. What makes you think he's not just a cop keeping a friendly eye on you?"

"Friendly? That thug? And would he make himself conspicuous with that long hair, if he were an undercover cop?" She wrinkled her nose to indicate distaste. "I think it's really a mistake for men to wear it long, even if it's considered very fashionable in some circles nowadays. They either look too pretty, like fairies, or they just look repulsive, like him. I mean, that enormous man—I saw him on foot yesterday, and he's almost as tall as you and a lot wider—with that tough, tough face and those flowing damn locks! He gives me the creeps every time I see him!"

Our drinks had arrived. I said, "To hell with his flowing locks. Drink up and tell me about Harlan Enos-Rockwell, known as Harley. And his boat. Start with the boat."

She said, "Well, it was actually designed as a kind of daysailer and weekender, you know, with a big cockpit

and a rudimentary cabin and galley, but Harley got a
bargain he couldn't afford to pass up—the company
was going out of business—so he bought the shell and
fixed it up the way he wanted it. Actually, it was a solid
little sloop with good sturdy lines, not one of these
light-displacement, fin-keel, spade-rudder monstrosities
they're building nowadays to sail so fast, fast, fast; and
it takes three strong men at the helm to hold them going
downwind in a breeze because they've got no directional
stability whatever—"

I grinned. "Okay, doll, you've impressed me. Light
displacement directional instability, yet! I can guess at
fin keel, but what the hell is a spade rudder? It sounds
like a naughty ethnic term to me... So he took what was
essentially a sheltered-water boat and beefed it up."

"That's not quite right, Matt. Harley saw that the basic
design had good deep water possibilities, although of
course the rig was too light and the cockpit was much too
big—one boarding wave and goodbye, particularly since
there was no bridge deck and the main hatch originally
fitted was a big, flimsy affair that could easily give way
and let the whole ocean below to swamp the boat in really
heavy weather..."

I listened to a lot more of this, understanding a bit here
and there, although I'm even less expert on sailboats than
I am on motorboats. It was fun just the same. I mean, a
pretty girl discoursing seriously about centers of effort and
centers of resistance and storm trysails and sea anchors
is always fun. If you simply have to acquire a nautical

education, I can't think of a nicer way to get it. The gist of her lecture was that her young brother, an experienced offshore sailor, had done everything possible to redesign and rebuild his little bargain vessel to be as strong and seaworthy as its size, and his finances, permitted.

"He wasn't quite happy about the outboard motor he had to use for auxiliary power, but *Star Trek* wasn't designed for an inboard installation, and he couldn't afford it, anyway," she said. "But otherwise she was a very sound little ship, Matt. And Harley was a fine seaman. I mean, really. If you're thinking of a crazy, reckless kid heading offshore in a totally unsuitable cockleshell... It wasn't that way at all. He'd studied all the others, from Slocum on. He'd planned the voyage for years. He had everything worked out to the last drop of drinking water and scrap of canvas..."

The local ocean seemed to be full of expert, missing sailors. Probably, when we got the inside dope, we'd learn that the vanished Sir James Marcus, or his hired captain, was also a meticulously careful seagoing genius.

"Description," I said.

"What?" She looked at me over her glass. "Oh. Well, Harley was blond and good-looking, not very tall but well built, with blue eyes. Very sunburned, of course. He'd been months outdoors working on the boat in the yard in Connecticut where he'd been helping out in return for the use of their space and tools. He'd brought *Star Trek* down the Intracoastal Waterway and spent the last few weeks at the Faro Blanco Marina down in the

Keys running the final tests before… What's the matter?"

"*What* did you say?" I asked, staring at her.

"I said he'd spent the last few weeks in the Florida Keys making sure everything—"

"No," I said. "That marina. What was the name of it?"

"Why," she said, "it was called Faro Blanco, whatever that may mean…" She stopped, her voice trailing off into silence. I didn't say anything. Lacey licked her lips. "Have I been stupid, Matt? Blanco means white, of course, but it never occurred to me… Faro is a card game they used to play in the old Wild West, isn't it? I… I figured it meant a white ace or joker or something. I guess I never really thought much about it."

I said, "Faro is Spanish for lighthouse, Miss Rockwell."

"Oh, dear," she said softly. "Oh, dear! If I bend over will you kick me hard? Very hard? Right out into the middle of that canal, please? When I think of all the money I paid that pilot to fly me around looking at all those silly buoys and beacons—"

"Just exactly what did your brother say in that last phone call?"

She paused to think back. "Well, he'd called from Nassau to say goodbye," she said at last. "He was finally shoving off on the first leg of the great adventure. Everything up to that had been just preparation and practice. Now he was going to head offshore for real. His first stop, he said, would be Charlotte Amalie, on St. Thomas, in the Virgin Islands. There are easier ways of getting there, like working down the Bahamas first, in

relatively sheltered waters, with harbors handy in case
of trouble, but he was going to head for open water and
to hell with the prevailing winds; it would be a final test
of the boat, not to mention his navigation." She drew a
long breath. "I didn't really worry at first. I mean, it's a
thousand miles from Nassau down to the Virgins; and the
breezes all blow the wrong way. Working a small boat
to windward you could easily cover more than twice
that distance and maybe not average fifty miles a day. At
least... at least that was what I kept telling myself, Matt."

"Your brother had no radio?" I said.

"He had a good transistorized receiving set working
on flashlight batteries for weather reports and news and
entertainment, but no transmitting equipment. I told you,
he used a little outboard for auxiliary power; he had no
way of keeping a storage-battery charged... When it got
into fall and the hurricane season, I began getting anxious.
I knew he'd planned to be out of the Caribbean, heading
for the Panama Canal, by that time. Finally... Well, I just
quit my job in New York and came down here. I had a
little money saved up—"

"Let's go back to that phone call," I said. "He told you
he'd call from this Charlotte Something-or-other place?"

"Charlotte Amalie, on the island of St. Thomas. Yes.
He said he'd call if he could; if not, he'd certainly write.
He was about to hang up; and then he hesitated and
said..." She frowned, and went on after a moment: "I'm
trying to remember just how he put it. I think he said that
he'd run into something funny he'd better not talk about

over the phone, but that if anything should happen to him, I might do a little checking around the white light—" She spread her hands helplessly. "He stopped right there, as if he'd changed his mind. Afterwards, trying to remember, I couldn't be sure whether he'd actually said lighthouse, or if I'd just got the impression that was what he'd intended to say. Anyway, he was silent for a bit; then he went on: 'Ah, forget it, Sis. I'm probably just imagining things. I'll call or write from St. Thomas. Be good.'" She drew a long, ragged breath. "Harley was always telling me to be good, as if he were the older one instead of me."

There was a little silence. At last I said, "He was really planning to sail clear around the world?"

"Yes. Through the Panama Canal and down into the romantic South Seas full of beautiful dancing girls with grass skirts... No, damn it, I won't make fun of it, and I won't let you make it sound foolish, either! Hundreds of small boats have done it since Slocum, why shouldn't he? Would you think it smarter if he'd stayed on shore and fulfilled his dreams with marihuana or heroin?"

"No criticism or ridicule was intended," I said.

This wasn't quite true, of course. I mean, after all, the damned world is twenty-four thousand miles around. In a small sailboat jiggling and rocking and splashing along at fifty miles per day, or even a hundred, that's not a voyage, that's practically a career. My Scandinavian ancestors may have been seafaring folk, but that was a long time ago; and while I enjoy fishing, I'm not all that crazy about water. As far as I'm concerned, when you've seen one ocean you've seen them all.

Lacey didn't speak. I said, "Okay, so much for the lesson in seamanship and navigation and boat-building and stuff. It's been very educational; and I guess we'd better plan on taking a look at that Faro Blanco place. However, that's a couple of hundred miles away, back across the Gulf Stream in the good old U.S. of A. Before we leave Nassau, it seems to me there's a bit of unfinished business we'd better attend to. Something you've been very careful to avoid mentioning either to me or to the cops; and a snoopy journalistic character can't help but wonder why."

She didn't look at me. "I… I don't know what you mean."

"Sure," I said. "You just rented a bike and took your camera and went sightseeing. You just happened to be in a certain place when a certain unsavory character just happened to wander by with a gun…"

"It was a phone call," she said. "A woman. She called me at the hotel. She asked if I was the young lady who'd lost something at sea. She said if I was interested in getting it back, I should be on the orchestra platform in the Royal Victoria gardens at two o'clock the following day. She said for me to put on something white with a blue scarf—I could wear that any way I liked just so it showed—and somebody would get in touch with me. She said… she said the relative about whom I was concerned had got into serious legal difficulties down in the Caribbean, and if I ever wanted to see him again,

I'd better be careful not to call his predicament to the attention of the local authorities any more than I'd already done by my blundering inquiries." She hesitated, and went on: "That was why I was willing to do, well, practically anything, Matt, to keep the police from asking me any more questions… The woman never gave me a name. I don't see how we can trace her. I'm sure I'd never heard her voice before."

"Was it a British or a Yankee voice?"

"I'd say American, but refined. Eastern seaboard, maybe a little south but not very. What do you think we ought to do?"

"Well," I said judiciously, "right now I think we should concentrate very hard and decide what wine goes best with this roast duck with oranges they've got listed on the menu…"

The food, when it arrived, restored my faith in the culinary abilities of the Bahamians; and I added the Café Martinique to my list of such establishments as Stallmästaregården in Stockholm, Sweden, and La Louisianne in San Antonio, Texas; the ones where even an ignorant meat-and-potatoes type like me can luck into a superlative meal. Afterwards we had coffee and brandy—well, she had something sweet and ladylike—and it was time to go.

Outside, it was very dark. There were no cabs in the tree-lined driveway.

"I'd better go back in and get the doorman to call one," I said.

"No, let's walk up to the casino and see what it looks like," she said. "The taxi-driver said there were plenty of cabs up there, remember?"

I said, "Look, sweetheart, you're the little girl who came to me for protection. My opinion, as a not-very-expert bodyguard, is that midnight strolls through the woods are not recommended; and as a matter of fact, just standing out here under these damned lights isn't really the brightest idea in the world—"

"Now you're being stuffy and tiresome," she said. "Come on."

I shrugged, and followed her up the paved path through the trees, toward the large, lighted building up the hill, that seemed to serve as a sizable hotel as well as a gambling joint. Lagging a little, I could see her white dress ahead of me in the dusk.

"Matt—"

Her voice was interrupted by a shrill, warning whistle from among the trees. Expecting it, I threw myself flat. Lacey was turning, her hand drawing something small and shiny from her white purse, and pointing it at me. I rolled aside, and the little pistol followed me, steadying. I brought up against the bushes at the side of the path and had nowhere else to go, and nothing to do but wait for her shot. Then a heavy firearm opened up from the darkness to the left and cut her down.

I drew a long breath, picked myself up, and walked forward slowly, brushing myself off. There was a rustle in the bushes. I looked that way. Black men have it all over us light-faced gents when it comes to operating in the dark. I could hardly make out Fred standing there. A large revolver, rather oddly proportioned by American handgun standards, gleamed in his hand: a husky old .455 Webley, at a guess.

"Okay, Eric?" he whispered.

"I'm okay," I said, "but what's the matter with you, buck fever or something? You cut it damned close. The whistle was okay, but the gun was way slow. The next time, please let me know that you have qualms about burning down pretty young potential murderesses; and I'll get somebody to cover me who doesn't!" He didn't speak. I drew another long breath, still not quite steady, and said, "Excuse it, please. I spoke in the heat of the moment. Forget it. Now you'd better beat it before the mob arrives. Oh, take this with you." I knelt and freed the little automatic pistol from the fingers of the fallen girl and handed it to him. "Ditch it deep," I said. "It never existed. Report to Washington right away and check with me later."

"Yes, sir."

The exaggerated respectfulness indicated that he disapproved of me or my orders or something. Well, I wasn't very happy with him at the moment; he'd damn near let me be killed. He was good in the dark, though; I had to hand him that. He simply vanished. One moment he was there; the next, I was looking at nothing but shadowy bushes and trees. I could hear voices both above and below as people milled around asking each other where the loud noise had come from. The white, small figure on the ground stirred painfully.

"Matt?" she whispered.

"Right here, doll," I said, kneeling once more.

"Damn you," she breathed. "Oh, damn you, damn you, damn you! Morgan will get you. And if he doesn't, there'll be somebody else, somebody who's wanted you dead for a long, long time!"

"Morgan," I said. "Is that Sir Henry or old J.P.?"

"You make jokes, but he'll hunt you down," she whispered fiercely. "And there's an old, old friend of yours who'll laugh and laugh when she hears you're dead. She's the one you've really got to thank. She spotted you this summer and got in touch with us. She calls herself… No, I won't tell you. You knew her by a different name, in a different place. She's been waiting a long time for the chance to strike back. You shouldn't leave vindictive women behind you alive, Matt."

"Whoever she is, she'll have to take her turn with the rest," I said. "The line forms on the right. But just one shot per customer, doll."

"You didn't even give me one."

"Okay, so I'll let your friend Morgan have two. That's the big guy with all the hair?" I thought I saw her nod. "And he was supposed to take me out on that porch where you wanted us to have dinner, but I insisted on eating indoors so you decided you'd better handle it yourself. But why did you rush it? You had a fancier plan all worked out, involving that mysterious white lighthouse in the Florida Keys—"

"It wasn't going to work. You were being too damned sweet and attentive; and at the same time too cautious. I knew you were beginning to suspect."

"Tell me one thing. Where's the real Lacey Rockwell?"

"I don't know." Her voice was getting very weak. "They never found the brother, although a boat went out to try to intercept him so he couldn't interfere. But it's a big ocean, and they never saw a sign of him. I really don't know what they did with the girl after letting me talk with her enough so I could play the part…" Pain hit her suddenly. I heard her gasp. The excited voices were drawing closer from both directions. The girl whispered, "I'm dying, aren't I?"

"I should hope so," I said. "If not, we'll have to send my associate back to marksmanship school."

After a shocked moment, she managed a little ghost of a laugh. "Thanks," she gasped. "Thanks for not feeling obliged to lie unconvincingly and tell me I'm going to be fine, just fine."

"That bullshit is for amateurs," I said. "We're all pros here, aren't we?"

"Yes, but how did you know?" she breathed. "I thought… I thought I was doing… very well. But all the time you knew, damn you. How?"

"It was too easy, doll," I said. "You were good, you were great, you were cuddly and cute, I wanted to believe in you with all my heart, but it was just a little too damned easy all the way."

I stopped talking. There was nobody left to talk to.

There was just a white dress with blood on it, and a pair of white shoes, and a white purse, and some other inert material. People were running up at last, and it was time for me to become a helpless sort of photographer chap all broken up by the shock of having a sweet and innocent young girl foully murdered right before his very eyes…

11

It was daylight before I finally made it back to the hotel after putting on my dramatic performance for several interested audiences, including the Nassau police and Mr. Ramsay Pendleton. I took the elevator up to the right floor, dug out the right key, and started to enter the room in the heedless manner of an innocent citizen bone-tired after a tragic, sleepless night. Then I thought better of it and took a few precautions as prescribed by the book. It was just as well.

"I'm glad to see you're being careful, Eric," Mac said from the chair by the window.

I looked a bit grimly at the familiar figure in its familiar gray suit; and the familiar face with its heavy black eyebrows, beneath the familiar crisp gray hair. Like a school kid looking up to see the principal standing over him, I wondered what the hell I'd done wrong now. He gets out of Washington now and then, but not so often that we're really hardened to falling over him in the middle of an assignment.

I said, "I might as well set up a cot in the airport waiting room, for all the privacy I get around here." I closed and locked the door. "Welcome to Nassau, sir."

"How did you make out with the authorities?"

"Well," I said judiciously, "I won't say everybody believed me implicitly, but nobody called me a liar out loud. Officially, everybody's looking for a mysterious longhaired gent, who was following the poor girl around and scaring her to death."

"I received a report on the situation from our local people, but there were some gaps. I'd like you to fill them. There was also a complaint."

I reflected that it was funny the way people who seemed quite reasonable face-to-face could turn into real pains when they were no longer in your presence and had phones in their hot little hands.

"Yes, sir," I said. "He really keeps burning up those airwaves, doesn't he?"

"Fred's a good man."

"Nobody's questioned his manhood, that I know of," I said. "It's his marksmanship I was criticizing; or rather, the time he took getting around to exercising it."

"He's claiming prejudice, Eric."

I looked at Mac grimly. "He's perfectly right, sir. I'm prejudiced against guys who let me play target while they're making up their cotton-picking minds whether or not to pull their triggers."

"I believe what he had in mind was racial prejudice." Mac spoke without any noticeable expression. "He claims you were abusive last night; and that previously you'd spoke to him in a derogatory fashion, calling him a big, brave, lion-eating Masai warrior, if I remember correctly."

"I apologized for blowing my stack last night," I said. "Even though I had a certain amount of provocation. As for the rest, I'm sure the Masai will be surprised to hear that it's derogatory to call a man a Masai warrior. No derogation was intended, in any case. I'll be happy to make that a formal statement, if you like. Freddie's a great guy. He's just godawful slow on the draw."

"How slow?"

"Well," I said judiciously, "if we'd been dealing with an old pro like Minsk instead of a relatively young and inexperienced female agent, I'd have absorbed a full clip of short 9mm stuff before Fred got around to discharging that overgrown Webley once. Jesus! His instructions were to signal *and* shoot the instant he saw a firearm displayed."

"I'm informed that he only waited long enough to make absolutely sure the girl really intended to—"

"Who the hell asked him to make sure of anything?" I demanded sharply. There was no sense to this. It had been a private matter between Fred and me. I would have let it stay that way; but if he simply had to unload his sensitive soul, well, I had a sensitive soul, too. I drew a long breath and went on: "I explained it to him very carefully ahead of time. It was a perfectly simple proposition. If she had a gun, she wasn't Lacey Rockwell. Innocent young oceanographer ladies don't smuggle illegal firearms into foreign countries, not even when they're looking for missing brothers. Even in the unlikely event that they should want to, they'd be scared to try, with all the hijacking precautions the airlines are taking nowadays. Therefore, if she had a gun, she was a phony, and a dangerous phony. Therefore, if she had a gun and showed it, he was to shoot her down instantly. To hell with his making sure. It wasn't his job to make sure. Of anything. Except that I stayed alive and unperforated. *That* was his responsibility, his only responsibility; and the only way he could be certain of carrying it out was to fire the instant he saw a glint of metal in her hand. The rest of the responsibility was mine and none of his goddamn business—"

I was interrupted by a knock on the door. I didn't really mind. I'd said more than I'd intended. It was a remarkably stupid intramural argument, and I had to admit to myself that it had apparently been triggered by my careless, kidding remark early in our relationship that had apparently given Fred the notion, although he'd hidden it well, that he was dealing with a confirmed racist. The knock was repeated. I looked at Mac.

He said, "I took the liberty of ordering breakfast for both of us."

If he was planning to break bread with me, as the old phrase goes, he probably didn't intend to reprimand me very hard; although we both knew I'd made a professional goof. It's the job of the agent in the field to get along with the local people and utilize them only within the limits of their capabilities. With the big boss's eye on me, and the situation mildly strained, I made a real secret-agent production of getting the door opened safely. It was a waste of time. Outside was a genuine waiter with a genuine breakfast tray. At least the man didn't attack us and the food didn't poison us.

The distraction served to switch us onto other subjects; and by the time we'd finished eating I'd filled in the gaps in Mac's factual information and was embarked, upon request, on a resumé of the theoretical background.

"As I said before, it was just too easy, sir," I said, walking to the window with my coffee cup and looking down at the sunny lawns and the beach and the people, mostly dark-skinned, mostly young, and mostly wearing very bright beach clothes. I went on: "I mean, for instance, the way the Mink just happened to come striding by, looking neither right nor left, just as I happened to emerge from the elevator that first day, for God's sake! At the time, I had an uneasy feeling it might be a trap. I should know better than to ignore my uneasy feelings. All I had to do was fall into step behind him, determine the way he was heading, figure out his most likely destination in that direction, and beat him to it—to find a pretty girl pacing back and forth impatiently and glancing at her watch in an obvious way! It was just too damned good to be true."

"As you describe it, it implies a considerable amount of organization, Eric." Mac's voice was neutral, expressing neither belief nor disbelief.

"Oh, they had organization, all right," I said. "Fred's people have come up with a waiter in the hotel restaurant who has the right connections—or the wrong ones, depending on your point of view. There must have been somebody else upstairs here, keeping an eye on my room, maybe the man she called Morgan, ready to pass the word down that I was heading for the elevator and it was time to give Minsk the signal to slam his napkin on the table and march out indignantly. Our local geniuses are also running a check on the cabdriver who took the girl and me to the Café Martinique last night. His little speech about the casino up the hill with its readily available taxis could have been a coincidence, of course, but it made a very handy excuse for her to lead me up the dark path to be shot, maybe a little too handy—"

"That's all very well, but you seem to be ignoring the fact that Minsk died at your hands, Eric," Mac said. "Is it your theory that the plans went wrong, or that he was sacrificed deliberately?"

"I have a hunch it was a little more than just a sacrifice play, sir," I said. "We've had them feed us agents before who'd come to the end of their usefulness. My feeling is that Pavel, although he didn't know it, was actually one of the two main objectives of the exercise; the other being, if you'll pardon the lack of modesty, me."

"You're guessing," Mac said.

"Yes, sir," I said. "But the girl indicated that somebody'd spotted me loafing around the Keys this summer and passed the word. Apparently plans were laid to take me, discreetly. Just as we laid plans to take Pavel discreetly the minute we learned he was coming—as they knew we would. He was the ideal bait; we'd been after him for years; now they were going to let us have him. All they had to do was move him into my neighborhood, let us know where he was heading, and they could pretty well count on your getting instructions to point me in that direction immediately. Pavel was undoubtedly told there'd be a backup man to help him take care of me when I showed myself. That was why he left himself wide open in such an uncharacteristic way. It was part of the overall plan, the way he understood it. Remember, he'd always been a great one for setting traps for agents deluded enough to think they could tangle with the Mink and live."

"In other words, you think his associates double-crossed him."

"I think the whole plan was an elaborate, official double-cross, sir," I said. "Minsk was probably told that somebody like the longhaired Mr. Morgan would be waiting behind me with an accurate rifle or other suitable weapon, ready to take me out before I could do any real damage. Only Morgan, if he was the assigned sniper, had secret instructions that Pavel didn't know about, and stayed home."

"We've had no indications that Mr. Minsk's services were no longer appreciated," Mac said slowly.

"As far as I can see, on this job our sources, whoever they are, have been passing us only information deliberately leaked to them by the opposition. I think you might suggest to the intelligence boys that a slight shakeup is in order." I grimaced. "It would be a carefully

guarded secret, anyway, wouldn't it, sir? You wouldn't
want to risk letting a guy like the Mink get wind of the
fact that you were planning to get rid of him—and how do
you dispose of a guy like that, anyway? It's kind of like
the aborigine trying to throw away his old boomerang.
You could lose a lot of valuable young agents, trying to
remove one experienced old assassin who'd outlived his
time. Much better to let the other team do the job for you."

There was a little pause. Mac glanced at me rather
sharply. "I can see that you've given the matter a great
deal of thought, Eric."

"Not a great deal, sir," I said, poker-faced. "But some.
I thought of it particularly last night when friend Freddy
was so damned slow on the trigger."

Mac rose to the occasion, as I'd thought he would.
"I can assure you," he said calmly, "that if the time ever
comes that you must be removed, I will assign the task to
a first-rate operative of ours, and not trust to the fumbling
and inefficient efforts of the opposition."

I grinned. "Thank you, sir. Flattery is always appreciated."

He went on without changing expression noticeably:
"Your theory is, then, that Moscow was killing two birds
with one stone: using you to remove Minsk, and at the
same time using Minsk to set you up for the young lady."

"Yes, how could I suspect her when she'd apparently
almost got killed, herself, by that dreadful Commie
gunman?" I shook my head quickly. "And of course I had
no suspicions at first. But, well, in spite of what I told her
when she was dying—there was no need to rub it in—she

really wasn't very good, sir. I mean, psychologically the character she wanted me to believe in was a mess. Hell, she was positively vicious about Pavel Minsk after he was dead, to take just one example. Now, you know that a nice young university liberal with an assortment of bright intellectual degrees would never, never come out in favor of violence, even if said violence had saved her life. She'd feel morally obliged to express all kinds of mushy regrets about the terrible incident that had resulted in a man's death, even if it had prevented hers. But this particular young lady *had* to say nasty things about Minsk, alive or dead—or felt she had to—so nobody could possibly suspect there was a connection between them."

Mac didn't say anything. I watched a boat heading out of the harbor; a big, sportfishing boat with tall outriggers. As I watched, the mate started lowering one of the long poles into fishing position. I wished I were on board, with nothing to worry about except sailfish and marlin, and maybe a small bonito or two.

I said, "And then, of course, there was that business of cooperating with the police to put me on the spot, even though I'd risked my life for her. Again, she just didn't dare antagonize them and maybe have them digging into her background and discovering she wasn't the real Lacey Matilda Rockwell—but it was hardly proper behavior for a young Maine lady with a stern New England sense of obligation." I turned away from the window to look at him where he sipped his coffee at the small table by the wall. "It didn't come to me all at once, sir, but it kept adding up.

When she went into that corny white-lighthouse routine, it got to be a little too much to swallow. Waiting for her to change for dinner last night, I sat down and refigured the situation on the basis of her being a complete phony, and saw that everything added up much better that way." I waited for Mac to speak. When he didn't, I said: "I guess that just about wraps up the job, unless you want me to carry on with the Haseltine business just to keep fifty million dollars happy. Or is it five hundred million?"

Mac looked up, surprised. "We can hardly call it wrapped up, can we, Eric? After all, there's still that Florida marina named after a lighthouse to be investigated. I'm informed that the place does exist and that it is part of a well-known and very pleasant and respectable resort complex in the town of Marathon, on Key Vaca, about midway between the Florida mainland and Key West. And then, of course, there's the person who put the finger on you in the first place, who must be dealt with—"

"No, sir," I said.

He regarded me closely. I was pleased to see, that he had to squint a little. For once I was the one with the bright window behind me.

"Explain yourself, Eric," he said.

I said, "We both know the name of the person involved. At least I do, and your memory is usually at least as good as mine. Hell, I don't have so many vindictive females in my past that I can't spot one who (a) is knowledgeable about boats, and (b) speaks with a refined American accent, east and a little south. The fact that the female in question is supposed to have drowned in Chesapeake Bay when she deliberately ran her eighty-foot schooner aground one night in the tail end of a hurricane is irrelevant. No body was ever found; and that lady wasn't good drowning material, hurricane or no hurricane."

Mac said, "You are assuming that the girl really received a telephone call sending her to that deserted hotel; and that she described the voice of her caller correctly."

"Why not? Everything indicates that they staged this whole thing very carefully, why not a real phone call? And why not describe a real voice? I have a hunch that phase two of the original plan involved leading me to the Keys with that lighthouse story and getting me interested in the mystery lady in question, so my little blonde girl friend could lower the boom while I was looking the other way. Something like that. Only something I said or did tipped her off that I wasn't quite happy with her, so she tried to rush the job."

"That's not airtight," Mac said, "but assuming I accept it, how does a knowledge of boats become significant?"

I moved over to fill my coffee cup again. I said, "I was entertained all through dinner with a long lecture on nautical subjects. The girl, whatever her real name was, had all her terms perfectly straight, as far as I could determine by reference to my own limited seagoing vocabulary. Okay, she was impersonating Lacey Rockwell, and she'd have done a certain amount of homework; and okay, she'd even talked to the real, captive Lacey Rockwell enough to get a feeling for the character she was to play; but that salty jargon is hell to master, sir. Somebody had really drilled it into this kid but good."

"That somebody being the mystery lady you think you can identify?"

"Our girl never got all that stuff out of a book, or a frightened girl prisoner, either. Somebody had learned a lot about Harlan Rockwell and his boat—just about everything about them—and passed it along. Well, the boy spent several weeks in the Keys preparing for his round-the-world jaunt. I figure he made the acquaintance of a nice lady down there—maybe a nice lady with a boat in the same marina—who could talk his sailor-language like an expert; and who listened to his plans and dreams and nautical problems, and gave him advice and encouragement. She may have had nothing sinister in mind at the time. Later, however, after young Rockwell had sailed away, she spotted me hanging around the Keys making like a fisherman, and remembered her old grievance. She got in touch with her former associates, I figure, if she hadn't been in touch with them right along. When a plausible cover story was needed, she remembered the vanished *Ametta Too* and all the recent publicity about the deadly Bermuda Triangle. She remembered the boy and his boat; maybe the sister—the real Lacey Rockwell—really gave her the idea by turning up in the area making inquiries about her brother, missing at sea. Our ingenious, vengeful lady saw how all these elements could be combined into a story I'd be likely to swallow—"

When I paused, Mac said, "You are, of course, thinking

of the Michaelis case. The lady's name, as I recall, was Mrs. Louis Rosten. As you say, she was officially declared dead—after some pressure was exerted by her husband who, as you undoubtedly recall, had very good reasons for wanting her dead."

"Yes," I said, "like a busted face, a broken arm, and a million-odd dollars, now legally his, I suppose. Well, I guess Louis earned it the hard way. That black henchman of his wife's really worked him over that last night. Nick, that was the big guy's name. I don't suppose she's forgiven me for Nick or any of the rest of it."

"Obviously not, or she wouldn't be trying to have you killed—if your assumptions are correct, and Robin Rosten is actually the person you have to thank for it."

"She's the one," I said definitely. I stood there for a moment, remembering a big schooner roaring through a stormy night with a dark-haired woman at the wheel and a black giant stalking me through the rigging… I shook my head quickly. "To hell with it," I said. "It was just the old cobra reflex, sir. I cost Robin Rosten a great deal. She was a fine society lady living on a great estate; and on account of me—well, her own behavior had something to do with it; but she'd disregard that—she wound up a nameless fugitive crawling ashore on a dark coast with nothing but the wet clothes on her back. So she spotted me and took a crack at me, or had somebody else take a crack at me, so what? We got Pavel Minsk out of the deal; a guy we'd been wanting a long time. Actually, she did us a favor. To hell with Robin Orcutt Rosten, whatever she's calling herself these days. Let her sit in the Florida Keys and wonder when I'm coming after her. Forever, as far as I'm concerned."

"Eric—"

"Goddamn it, sir," I said, "I can take care of myself. There are quite a few folks who'd like me dead, and you, too, sir; are we going to track down every one of them? Unless she's threatening the safety of the country in some way, and I've heard nothing about it, for God's sake leave the dame alone! I've seen enough dead females to hold me for a while; and if you send me after this one I'll probably wind up having to arrange for her death in some devious, Machiavellian way—"

"I see," he said, regarding me thoughtfully.

"Yes, sir," I said. "I'm just another sentimental, chivalrous slob like Fred. The only difference is that I wait until they're dead before I commune with my goddamn conscience."

"I'm afraid," Mac said slowly, "that you are going to have to disregard your goddamned conscience here, Eric."

"Why?" I demanded. "It's all over. It was a very simple Moscow deal to eliminate two agents they found embarrassing: one of ours, me, and one of theirs, Minsk. It's finished."

"There are three important personages still missing—"

"That's got nothing to do with this," I said. "We were wrong in thinking there was a connection—except insofar as a missing boat, and the general reputation of the area, gave the Rosten and her associates the notion of cooking up a disappearance of their own involving a poor little girl searching for her lost brother, just the right sucker bait for the notoriously susceptible M. Helm."

"You feel quite certain that it was a coincidence, Eric? That Moscow has nothing to do with the other disappearances?"

"Well, one stimulated the other, as I just said," I told him, "but I'd be willing to bet a large sum that the people who kidnaped Lacey Rockwell so another girl could take her place haven't the slightest idea what happened to the two millionaire yachts..." I stopped. "Wait a minute! Young Rockwell wasn't all that important, except to his sister. You said three *important* personages?"

Mac nodded. "Yes. We just got word that a private plane flying a wealthy French politician to Martinique has failed to arrive. We can't be certain, yet, that it's another Phipps and Marcus case; but there were no radio messages of distress, although the fuel would have come to an end several hours ago, so the plane must be down somewhere." He paused, and went on: "All governments involved are seriously concerned, Eric. Washington has congratulated us on disposing of Pavel Minsk; but he is now a minor detail—"

"Sure, we're all minor details when we're dead," I said sourly.

"The fact is that we—you—seem to have a finger on one feeble thread that might, just possibly, lead to an explanation of all these disappearances."

"My hunch, and I'm a pretty good huncher, is that

it won't," I said. "Okay, so somebody is apparently, as I said before, making a collection of seagoing—and airgoing—millionaires, but Lacey Rockwell wasn't one of them, and neither was her brother; and the collector isn't Robin Rosten."

"Then Mrs. Rosten is in a very unfortunate situation," Mac said smoothly, "because she will soon be questioned intensively by people acting on the assumption, not really as implausible as you make it sound, that she *is* connected with these disappearances. And the minute she is investigated, her true identity will come out, and no matter what else happens, she'll be brought back to Maryland to face several old charges including, I believe, one that reads accessory to murder." Mac paused significantly. "That is, of course, unless the interrogation and investigation are conducted by somebody more or less sympathetic to the lady's cause."

I drew a long breath, regarding him grimly. "I don't believe it," I said. "I hear it, but I don't believe it, sir. You are actually trying to blackmail me into doing a job that's really none of our concern by threatening a woman who tried her damndest to kill me?"

Mac said dryly, "One must work with what one has, Eric. And if what one has is a self-styled sentimental, chivalrous slob—"

12

The Florida Keys are an ecological disaster perpetrated, or at least initiated, by a gent named Flagler who had the crazy notion of running a railroad—Flagler's Folly, it was undoubtedly termed at the time—a hundred miles out to sea, island-hopping his rails from the Florida mainland all the way out to Key West. His project, after actually functioning for a while, was wiped out in a hurricane, but the eager-beaver highway builders, always looking for places to spread their sticky asphalt, promptly followed his lead.

As a result, a string of lovely tropical islands has been transformed into what may be the longest motel-and-filling-station blight in the world, very similar to what you'll find leading into, any big city, except that there's water on both sides of it. At least that's the view from the Overseas Highway, so-called: a long, rough, suicide strip interrupted by endless narrow bridges that serve, I suppose, the worthy purpose of helping to reduce overpopulation in the area to a slight, bloody degree.

Off the dismal, crowded highway, however, there are still quite a few pleasant green pockets of privacy more or less untouched by the greasy fingers of progress. (Actually, as I'd learned staying here with Laura earlier in the year, the best part of the Keys is getting off them in a boat—the farther you get from them, either on the deep Atlantic Ocean on one side or the shallow Gulf of Mexico on the other, the better they look. When they're barely visible on the horizon, you can imagine what this oceanic paradise was like before the dredges and concrete mixers and paving machines moved in.)

The Faro Blanco Marine Resort, to give it its full name, was such a palmy waterfront enclave in a hostile, hamburger-and-hotdog environment. It was a big, parklike place on the Gulf of Mexico side of Key Vaca—the north side—with guest cottages scattered at random under the shady trees. Stopping outside the office, I got out of the rented car that had been waiting for me at the Marathon airstrip, where I'd been deposited by the small plane that had first dropped off Mac at the Miami airport to catch a flight north.

"Be careful, Eric," he'd said as we parted. "On the record, that's a fairly dangerous woman."

"I hope so, sir," I'd said. "I'm counting on it, in fact."

Well, he was halfway to Washington by now, if he'd made his connection; and I was here, about to renew my acquaintance with a lady who'd twice almost managed to have me killed. I went into the motel office to register.

"Mr. Helm?" said the pretty brunette girl behind the desk. "Oh, yes, here we are. Matthew L. Helm. You have cabin 26. Just follow the driveway around behind the office and you'll find it on your right, about halfway down to the marina."

"I was thinking of doing some fishing," I said. "A friend of mine recommended a guide here named Robinson. A lady guide, he said." I laughed. "Anyway, it'll be a new experience, if she can take me out. How do I get in touch with her?"

The girl said, rather stiffly: "And why shouldn't a woman be able to locate fish for you as well as a man, Mr. Helm?" Then she laughed quickly. "Ouch, I guess my Women's Lib is showing. You'll probably find Cap'n Hattie down on one of her boats, either the open twenty-two-foot *Mako* tied up near the dockmaster's office—that's the building like a lighthouse, out on the pier—or the forty-footer she lives on; the first boat in Charter Row, just across from our bar and restaurant. She's got a sign up: the *Queenfisher*, Captain Harriet Robinson. You can't miss it."

I didn't miss it; but first, after tossing my suitcase into my cabin and turning on the air conditioning because the place was stuffy, I drove down and checked on the dockmaster's office built like a lighthouse, out of curiosity. It was just that: a tall white tower out on the pier, with a revolving blue beacon on top. Inside was the usual marine-store collection of fishing tackle, charts, boat supplies, sunglasses, guidebooks, and sunburn lotions, plus a tanned gent in a yachting cap who pointed out Cap'n Hattie's two boats to me.

He said he thought she was on board the cruiser, but I stopped to inspect the empty, smaller vessel first, since I had to walk right by it. It was a good-sized craft for an open boat, about as big as they come, aside from Navy workboats and such. Instead of placing the helmsman and windshield up forward, runabout fashion, it had the arrangement currently popular in boats built for fishing, with the controls located on a console amidships. There were two comfortable pedestal chairs behind the console. The rest was just wide-open cockpit with plenty of walk-around space for casting, or fighting a fish standing up. If you were the lazy type who preferred to battle sitting down, the starboard chair had a rod socket, or gimbal, for the purpose.

Across the stern, forming a bench seat ahead of the motors, were the built-in bait-well and fish-box. There were gaffs, outriggers, a radio antenna, an auxiliary gas tank for extended running, and neatly furled awnings fore and aft that could, presumably, be erected to protect the paying guests from hostile elements, wet or hot. There was also a slender Fiberglas pushpole about fourteen feet long held in clips along one gunwale—a common sight on small fishing boats plying the shallow waters of the Gulf of Mexico and Florida Bay, where the fish are often stalked silently by poling, but unusual on a craft this big.

On the transom, tilted out of the water, were two large Johnson outboard motors marked a hundred horsepower each. My amateurish estimate was that this amount of power, assuming for the moment that the markings were correct, would put the top speed close to forty knots, which is moving right along on the water, as I'd learned recently in the much smaller vessel of a very similar type which had been assigned to me for my previous job in these parts. I frowned down at the big, tilted motors and exposed propellers, wondering just how far the similarity extended…

I shook my head quickly. Guesswork was a waste of time when the answers to all questions were close at hand. I strolled along the waterfront to where the big charter fishing boats were docked. The first one in line was a shiny white craft with the customary outriggers and flying bridge. The deckhouse, under the flying bridge, had blinds drawn against the sun and seemed to be air-conditioned. The hatch in the cockpit was open for access to the twin engines; and a narrow figure in khakis was prone on the deck, reaching down to work on the machinery below.

I said, "Captain Robinson?"

There was a small space of silence; then a female voice I remembered said: "That's me. Hand me that wrench, will you, Helm?"

I stepped down into the cockpit and, rather cautiously, placed the only wrench in sight into the slender, grimy hand that reached up for it.

"What's the problem down there?" I asked.

"What do you care?" asked the familiar voice that

brought back memories, not all unpleasant, of a distant time, and a place far north. "You didn't know much about boats the last time we met. I don't suppose you know a hell of a lot about motors, either... Now the screwdriver, please. Thanks. That's got it."

She backed herself up and out, and sat on her heels to look up at me. I saw that she hadn't changed very much. She'd always been a slim, handsome, dark lady with a style all her own, and she still had it, even in well-worn khakis with grease on her hands and a smudge on her cheek.

"Alone?" she said.

"How many does it take?" I asked. "Particularly now that you haven't got Nick to help you."

Her eyes narrowed. "Why remind me of that, darling? You'd never have got Nick if you hadn't been using a goddamn club—"

"And all he had was about fifty pounds extra weight, and you at the wheel doing tricks with that damned schooner to help him while we fought it out. Poor Nick. And poor Renee... Oh, yes, we traced her, finally, the kid you just sent after me, or had sent after me. Renee Schneider, alias Lacey Matilda Rockwell. Where's the real Lacey Rockwell, Mrs. Rosten?"

"Don't call me that," she said, rising. She looked at me hard. "I don't know how you do it, Helm," she said. "You're not very smart, not really. You're not very strong; Nick could have broken you in two. You're not very attractive. And you're a lousy seaman, if it matters. And still, damn it, you always come out on top." She shrugged.

"Well, to hell with it. Let me wash my hands and—"

"Robin," I said, as she turned toward the closed and shuttered deckhouse.

"What?"

"Don't," I said.

She frowned. "I don't know what—"

"Whether you're planning to take a handful of barbiturates, blow your brains out dramatically, or dive out a porthole, don't do it," I said. "And don't try to blow my brains out, either. You'll never make it. Renee tried, and she was a trained agent, and I'm still here. At blowing out brains, I'm a pro, and you're just a lousy amateur. At least, before you do anything drastic, wait until you hear what I have to say, please."

She studied me for another second or two. "My apologies," she said quietly. "Maybe you are half-smart after all. Okay, darling, I'll wait. But you'll never put me in jail. You know that."

"Nobody's said a damned thing about jail except you," I said. "Wash your hands and let me buy you a drink across the road and speak my piece. After that, if you want, you can slit your throat and welcome. I've got a nice sharp knife in my pocket. Be my guest."

The place across the road—actually one of the paved driveways of the extensive resort complex—was a pleasant restaurant with a bar in the shadowy back corner. We picked a table nearby and had the drinks brought to us. She was a bourbon girl, as befitted a former native of Maryland.

"Okay," she said. "Talk."

"I've got a deal for you," I said. I'd had time to do some thinking on the flight from Nassau; and I thought I'd figured out a way this wild-goose chase on which I'd been sent to keep Washington happy could be made to show a profit. It involved a lot of guessing and a lot of luck, but then, most operations do.

Captain Harriet Robinson, to give her her local name, sipped her whiskey thoughtfully. "What's in it for me?" she asked.

"Forgetfulness," I said. "A total lapse of memory on my part and that of my chief. Robin Rosten's bones remain buried in the silt at the bottom of Chesapeake Bay. Captain Harriet Robinson carries on with her Florida fishing-boat business undisturbed. That is, of course, assuming she can control her homicidal impulses in the future."

The tanned woman facing me drew a long breath. "It seemed like a good idea at the time, but now… How many years has it been, Matt? Too damned long to keep a good hate going. Okay, that's what I get out of your deal. What do you get?"

"Five things," I said. "Lacey Rockwell. Wellington Phipps and his daughter Loretta. You can throw in the wife, Amanda, if you're feeling generous. Sir James Marcus. Baron Henri Paul Lavalle."

There was a lengthy silence. Cap'n Hattie closed her eyes tightly and opened them again, drawing another lengthy breath. "I'm a fool," she said. "Of course you have to tease the captured animals a bit. I should have expected it; but I really thought you were serious. I thought you really intended to give me a chance—"

"I do." After a moment, I said, "You're not denying that you do know something about Lacey Rockwell, are you?"

"I'm not denying or admitting anything right now, darling."

I said, "We know the brother, Harlan Rockwell, spent a good deal of time right here at this marina getting his sloop, *Star Trek*, ready for a round-the-world jaunt. He wasn't really flush, and from time to time he made a little money by helping out on the local charter fishing boats. He worked on your big boat several times when you had a party to take out and your regular mate had tied one on and couldn't drag himself out of bed. Our information is that you became quite friendly with the boy, gave him advice and help on matters nautical, and maybe slept with him a few times, or maybe not. On this point, our intelligence is a little shaky."

"Don't be delicate," said the lady across the table. "Of course I slept with him, why not? But only once. He was too damned respectful; he made me feel old as the hills. Who the hell goes to bed to be *respected*, for God's sake?"

I grinned. "I'll keep that in mind," I said. "Anyway, at last the boat was ready and Harlan Rockwell shoved off on his great voyage. Weeks passed. Suddenly a little blonde girl with long hair turned up, concerned about her brother, who apparently hadn't filed a flight plan with her. It seems that communications between Rockwell brother

and sister weren't really as good as I was led to believe in
Nassau. They led pretty separate lives; the girl was busy
at her job up north; she'd only known Harlan was staying
here from a casual postcard. Then she got another card
from Nassau saying the circumnavigation was finally
underway, and he'd drop her a line next time he hit terra
firma. Followed a long time of nothing. Getting worried
at last, and feeling guilty, I suppose, about not having
looked after her kid brother more carefully, the girl had
taken leave from her job and come down here to see if,
before leaving, he might have told somebody the detailed
plans he hadn't confided to her. She was steered to you.
The two of you were seen together. Okay?"

"Yes, the girl was here. I talked with her on board my
boat. As you say, she was worried about her brother. I told
her as much as I knew of his intentions."

"Which was plenty," I said. "And at this point, things
get kind of complicated. Following the trail of her
missing brother, Miss Lacey Rockwell leaves the Florida
Keys. Miss Lacey Rockwell appears in Nassau, only
it's not the same Miss Rockwell at all. Well, we know
what happened to Female Rockwell Number Two, the
imposter. She's buried in a Nassau cemetery, terminated
by a slug from a big old Webley .455 just as she was trying
to put a nasty little 9mm projectile into me. The question
is, where did Female Rockwell Number One get to, the
genuine, original article? Obviously, she was taken out
of circulation somehow, so the imitation Rockwell would
have a clear field. I'm hoping she's still alive. If she isn't,

you're at least an accessory, and we'll have it that much harder keeping the cops off you, assuming you give us a motive for trying."

There was another silence. At last the woman facing me said: "The girl is alive. I may even be able to get her released. I don't think she's been allowed to see or hear enough to make trouble for anybody except Renee Schneider, who talked with her; and Renee, as you say, is dead. But why, darling, are you interested in a fairly boring little blonde who, aside from her brother, can't seem to think or talk about much of anything except saving the oceans of the world from pollution. I'm not knocking it, but I shouldn't think it was one of your major interests."

I laughed. "To be honest, Hattie, aside from a sort of general, kindly humanitarianism, I'm not really concerned about the fate of Lacey Rockwell. However, the fact that your associates couldn't find the brother and his boat out there in the Atlantic and take him out of circulation, too, doesn't necessarily mean he's dead. It's a big ocean. The kid may still turn up and come looking for his sister. You're the last person known to have been seen with her. For your own sake, I think it would be a lot smarter if you did get her turned loose, eventually."

"Eventually?"

I said, "Well, right now I'll admit Miss Rockwell would be kind of an embarrassment, complaining hysterically to the authorities about her mysterious kidnaping and cruel imprisonment. She might even make some trouble for you if she's halfway bright. At the moment, I wouldn't like that. I need you trouble-free. Or, let's say, the only troubles I want you concerned with are my troubles. So just tell her jailers to keep her well fed and blindfolded until we get the rest of these people taken care of."

"That's a pretty callous attitude, isn't it, Matt?"

"Callous?" I said. "Hell, who's holding her prisoner, you or I? Who had an innocent young girl kidnaped in the first place, so a substitute could impersonate her in Nassau and commit cold-blooded murder on a fine, upstanding government agent named Matthew Helm? Or was she supposed to decoy me here so you could do the job? Anyway, don't talk callous to me, Captain Robinson."

"Well, I'm not actually *holding*—"

"Now you're quibbling," I said. "Anyway, as I've said, I'm not really worried about Lacey Rockwell except in a vague, sentimental way. I just brought her up so we'd have all the cards on the table. You and I both know that the girl and her brother have nothing to do with the rest of this business. We know that those two kids were just part of an independent, murderous plot dreamed up by you—with the help of some interesting friends—after you saw me here in the Keys and decided your vengeance had waited long enough. The only connection between your endeavor and all these other vanishings is that you may have got your idea, in part, from the Phipps disappearance. So, let's put Lacey Matilda Rockwell in the hold file for the moment. What we want to concentrate on is two or three Phippses, one Marcus, and one Lavalle. How about it?"

Harriet Robinson shook her head quickly. "You've

just answered that yourself, darling," she said. "You just admitted that the Rockwell angle is the only one I know anything about. I read about Phipps when he turned up missing, of course, and you may be right that it gave me some ideas, but this Sir James and Baron Henry—all right, *Onree*—I never even heard of."

"It's been kept quiet," I said, "while search-and-rescue teams churned the oceans to froth, without success."

"If they failed, how can you expect me to find—"

I leaned forward. "They don't have the connections you have," I said harshly. "And they don't have the motive you have."

"Motive? What motive?"

"Survival, my sweet," I said.

"You're blackmailing me to help you—"

"Wonderful! I'm gradually getting through to the lady!" I sneered. "You're goddamned right I'm blackmailing you, Captain Harriet Robinson. I've got a lousy job to do, and I've been sent down a dead-end street to do it, and you're going to find a way out for me, or you're going to jail! Is that clear enough for you, doll?"

"But how—"

I said angrily, "Damn it, don't pull that helpless act on me! This is Matt, honey, the guy you just tried to have killed for the second time. I know you're just about as helpless as a cobra, a very bright cobra. Get the old reflexes working, doll. If I fail, you're sunk; get that through your head. So get hold of the same people you called in when you had this brilliant notion of having me murdered. If they don't have the information I need, they can get it, I'm sure. They know whom to ask and how to get the answers. At least they can get enough that we can figure out the rest, you and I, with the help of your special knowledge."

"Special knowledge?" Her eyes were narrow. "What special knowledge?"

I said, "Hell, you know boats and the sea, don't you? This is a seagoing caper, but nobody seems to have really studied it from the nautical point of view. You'd think, the way folks talk, that all these people had vanished from the New York Thruway instead of the Atlantic Ocean."

She seemed relieved. "Well, if you think a little seamanship will help, I'm perfectly willing to—"

"And then," I said deliberately, "there's that very, very specialized knowledge you've got that should be of great assistance to us: your knowledge of the only place in this part of the world where they can possibly be if they're still alive. The place you were planning to go if things got too hot around here."

There was another extended silence. Harriet shook her head quickly once more, and her voice was flat and hard when she spoke at last: "I don't know what you mean."

"I saw the boat, doll," I said. "It's lying right over there by the phony lighthouse. That big, innocent-looking, shoal-draft fishing boat, with a mere two-hundred horsepower on the stern—only it's actually three hundred or more, isn't it? Three-hundred-odd horses and fifty-odd knots; and when you open her up wide, which you're careful not to do where anybody can see you, there isn't a boat around short of the all-out ocean racers that can catch her, is there? An eighteen-gallon auxiliary gas tank in the cockpit in addition to the standard fifty-gallon job under the floor—"

"Sole."

"What?"

She said quietly, "Boats don't have floors, darling, at least not the kind you walk on. You may properly refer to it as the deck, but technically it's known as the cockpit sole. And the main tank under it holds fifty-*one* gallons."

I regarded her with respect. She was still in there pitching; she hadn't forgotten her nautical duty to the human race. They're all alike, these seagoing, geniuses. There isn't a one who'll ever let you get by with *calling* any part of a boat by the wrong name, even if the world is coming to an end, and they've got to keep St. Peter, or the other guy, waiting a little longer while they set you straight.

"Have it your way," I said. "Cockpit sole. But you really don't need a hell of a lot of extra gas for a one-way trip, do you? It's only a little over a hundred miles from here to Cuba, isn't it? Why aren't you there already? Why didn't you point that nautical buzz-bomb south the minute you heard your friends in the Bahamas had failed and I was still alive?"

13

Afterward, I walked her back to her cruiser. We'd spent some time over our drinks, and it was getting dark. We were friends once more, or reasonable imitations thereof; and I was taking her out to dinner. She stopped at the short gangplank bridging the gap between the concrete seawall and the big boat's varnished mahogany transom. Turning, she held out her hand.

"Just give me time to get into some civilized clothes," she said. "Matt?"

I held her hand for a moment, and released it, feeling that I'd missed a cue. I should have bowed over it and kissed it. Even in her mannish Cap'n Hattie costume, she was that kind of a woman.

"Yes?" I said.

"You were guessing, weren't you? Guessing, and bluffing like hell."

"Sure. Some of it was guesswork and some was bluff. I didn't really *know* you'd had those motors souped up.

Only, I remembered a little boat my chief provided me with not long ago. Eighty-five horsepower it said on the motor cover; and when I cracked the throttle we practically went into orbit. He'd had them switch the markings on a one-twenty-five. It seemed like a logical thing for you to do, under the circumstances."

"They don't really put out three-hundred horsepower," she said. "Only about a hundred and forty apiece, which was about as much as you could get out of them reliably when I got them; you can do better than that now, but I figured it was enough. She'll do over fifty knots in calm water; real knots, not Madison Avenue miles-per-hour. The real souped-up deep-vee jobs will pass her, but not much else."

I said, "Of course, partly I merely exercised that cold and remorseless logic for which I'm renowned."

She smiled. "Well, I never did like modest men," she said. "It's too bad."

"What is?"

"I've had such fun hating you all these years. It's not very nice of you to turn out to be just an ordinary, conceited, male human being after all, instead of the devil with horns. Don't forget to bring the charts."

"Aye, aye, Skipper."

I left my rental car where it was, parked at the waterfront, and walked the short distance up the paved driveway to my cabin, feeling pretty good. I mean, it was one of those times when the world and the people in it seemed totally predictable and I had the whole thing all figured out and knew exactly what everybody was thinking, and what they'd do next and why...

They jumped me from the trees, just across from the bungalow with the right number. There were two of them. They grabbed my arms, one from each side. I went limp between them instantly, dropping to the ground. It brought one down on top of me, still hanging on. The other let go and stepped back. Fortunately, the arm that was still in hock was the left, not the right; the knife was in my right-hand pants pocket. I'd got it back from Fred in Nassau, who still didn't like me. There seemed to be a lot of such people around. I'd also got my gun back, but this wasn't the place for a lot of noise.

I flicked the knife open one-handed, usually a show-off stunt, but convenient here. The flash of the blade towards his face caused the man on top of me to release his grip and roll away.

"Look out, the crazy hombre's got him a shiv—"

The standing man stepped in and aimed a kick to disarm me and missed. Then I had his foot. I made a neat surgical incision in the proper place, just above and behind it. The keen edge didn't hurt very much, not enough to elicit a scream, just a gasp of surprise.

"Goddamn it, he cut me—"

He didn't get any farther with that sentence, falling flat on his face. He'd put his weight on the foot in question, but there was nothing to hold him up with the Achilles tendon out of business. The other man was scrambling to his feet and starting to run; but I wasn't any slower getting up, and my legs were longer. He wasn't very big. I caught him just around the corner of my cabin and threw myself into him, slamming him against the building. I had my arm across his throat, and my knife-point in his back before he could recover.

"Who?" I panted.

"Listen—"

I was mad. My neat little all-figured-out world had fallen apart. Nobody was supposed to be laying for me here, now, in this clumsy fashion. The only man I was supposed to have to worry about was Morgan, the dead girl's friend and possible avenger; and Morgan, if he came, would come alone, and like all avengers, he'd want to talk before he struck. I'd miscalculated somehow and I didn't like it. I didn't like it at all.

"You have three seconds from the time I stop talking," I breathed. "The name of the person who sent you or comes it four inches of steel. Talk!"

"Listen, you-all cain't get away with—"

It was just too damned bad. He'd used up his time; and will they never stop telling people with knives or guns what they can't get away with? The blade went in easily, all the way. I felt a little blood, not very much, warm my knuckles. The man I held pinned against the cabin started to gasp, scream, protest, curse, or otherwise indicate his disapproval of my crude behavior. He stopped and was very quiet instead.

"Hell, I warned you," I said in his ear. "Now give me the name, fast, or I'll twist the goddamn thing around in there."

His voice was a shocked whisper. "Haseltine. Cabin 7A. The sonofabitch. He didn't tell us he was sending us after a pro. Go... go easy, partner."

"Haseltine?" For a moment, I couldn't even remember where I'd heard the name. Then the whole thing began to make some kind of sense, if you could call it sense. "Oh, Christ," I said to nobody in particular. "Oh, Jesus, how stupid can you get? Be brave, now, little man, it's coming out." I gave a quick jerk and the knife came clear. The man groaned and went to his knees, resting his forehead against the cabin wall. I said, "Stay there. Don't move. Tell your partner to stay where he is. Somebody'll be coming for you in a minute..."

There was a light in cabin 7A. I heard somebody get up at my knock and walk to the door, a big man by the sound. The lock rattled.

"Okay, bring him in," said Big Bill Haseltine's voice.

I kicked the door hard as it started to open. Haseltine jumped back to avoid catching it in the face. Then I was inside with the door shut behind me. We stared at each other for a moment or two. His gaze shifted to the red knife in my bloody hand, and stayed there.

"Tell me," I said softly.

"What?"

"Tell me I can't get away with it," I whispered. "Tell me what a big man you are and how many umpteen million dollars you've got and how you can send your cheap oilfield roughnecks to drag anybody you want anywhere you want any time you want them. Tell me, Mr.

Haseltine. Tell me all about it. Shit!" I tossed the knife into the air, caught it the other way, and drove it into the table by the door, like an icepick. It quivered there. We watched a little blood run down the blade to form a tiny pool around the imbedded point. "You dumb *Tejano* bastard!" I said.

"What happened?" His voice was flat and dead.

"You've got one punk who needs crutches, and one who may be in the market for a coffin if he isn't lucky and doesn't get patched up soon. What the hell kind of a juvenile game do you thing you're playing, you half-ass Comanche?"

"You were supposed to be working for me," he said in the same flat voice. "You were supposed to be working for me, Helm, not getting shot up playing secret agent in the Bahamas, or having cozy drinks with a handsome babe who runs some crummy boats down in the Keys. The deal was, you were working for *me*!" His big hands closed into tight fists at his sides.

I grinned at him nastily. "Come on, Big Boy. Teach me a lesson. Teach me to respect the great brainless Haseltine. Slap me around. You'll have five .38 Special slugs in your belly before you ever touch me, but come right ahead, give it a try. Just don't tell me I can't get away with it. Your punk said that, and he's out there in the dark with a leaking liver, or maybe it's a kidney. My knowledge of anatomy just isn't what it ought to be. Sorry."

"Damn you, Helm, they were just going to—"

"Just going to grab me from behind. Just going to

rough me up a little. Just going to haul me in here and dump me at the feet of their imbecile boss so I'd know whom I was working for. Christ, Haseltine, do you think a guy in my line of work survives by stopping to ask people who jump him whether they're really planning to hurt him or just muss him up a little?" I drew a long breath. "Okay, that's enough histrionics. Get in your car and drive around to my cabin and pick up anything you see lying around. Be sure to kick dirt over any blood you spot; we don't want people asking a lot of questions, come morning. I'll go to the office and make a phone call from their public booth. Stop in front and I'll join you. I assume you do have enough sense to hide all casualties from sight. Okay, on your way."

He hesitated, obviously about to start an argument about who was giving, and who taking, orders around here. Then he thought better of it, which was too bad. After the rude and disrespectful way I'd addressed him tonight, I'd probably have to deal with him sooner or later, and I'd happily have got it over now while I still had a good head of steam up. But he turned and marched out. I heard his car pull out of the parking space alongside the building. I yanked my knife out of the table, went into the bathroom and washed it off, and my hands, and brought some toilet paper to wipe off the table, and flushed that down the john. I went to the office and made my phone call. The big sedan pulled up alongside while I was still in the booth.

"Well?" he said when I came in to him.

"Pull out to the highway and turn left, toward Miami. Drive slowly. A white Ford station wagon will pass you in about ten minutes. Florida plates." I gave him the number. "Speed up and follow it, not too closely. It will turn off somewhere and stop in a nice private place. You'll transfer your passengers, clean up your car, and join me and a lady for dinner at the Tarpon Lodge, about a mile east of here."

He said, with a hint of belligerence, "Look, Helm—"

I said, "Make up your mind. You got them knifed; do you want to fix them yourself, or do you want us to do it?"

"Okay, but—"

"I know, I know," I said. "One of these days. Sure. Now roll it."

He started to run up the power window, and stopped. "You got one thing wrong, Helm."

"What?"

"I'm not a half-ass Comanche. I'm a quarter-ass Kiowa."

I watched the car drive away, wait for an opening and join the traffic on the crowded Overseas Highway, disappearing from sight to the east. Well, anyway, the big guy had a sense of humor, for what it was worth.

14

The Tarpon Lodge was another lush green pocket of quiet and relaxation off the busy, noisy, honky-tonk highway strip. The dining room was located well down towards the shore, but it looked out on a lighted swimming pool instead of the dark Gulf of Mexico. I suppose it proves something about Florida that with all that lovely open water just lying around out there, they still have to pump the stuff, filter it, chlorinate it, heat it, and package it in tile and concrete before they'll condescend to swim in it.

I parked the rental car in the designated space under a couple of palms, which always makes me uneasy. One thing they haven't managed down there, yet, is to stop those trees from doing what comes naturally and producing coconuts. I'm sure they're working on the problem, but in the meantime you're in the target area any time you're under one. I don't suppose the chance of being beaned is much greater than that of being struck by lightning, but in a high-risk business one prefers to avoid all the avoidable dangers. Nevertheless, I screwed up my courage and walked politely around the car to help my companion out like a real gentleman, coconuts or no coconuts.

She'd changed to a long, flowered skirt and white silk shirt that made her skin look very brown in the darkness. Her hair was done up the way I remembered it, smooth and ladylike. I escorted her into the place. It wasn't crowded: a fairly high-class-looking restaurant with a dignified hostess who greeted my companion by name and title and showed us to a booth at the side of the room. A waitress took our drink orders.

"Cap'n Hattie," I said, when we were alone once more. "Cap'n Hattie, for God's sake!"

Harriet Robinson laughed softly. It occurred to me that she'd always had trouble with names. She'd never been the elfin type I normally associate with the name Robin; and she certainly wasn't the staid New England spinster I visualize when somebody says Harriet.

"I'm a local institution, darling," she said. "I'm their tame lady skipper. If you don't treat me with respect, a dozen salty charterboat captains will come for you with gaffs and billy clubs."

"How did you manage it?" I asked. "That's close to a hundred grand's worth of air-conditioned sportfisherman you've got in that slip; and maybe ten grand's worth of outboard over at the other dock, counting the radiotelephone and other electronic gear."

"Just about," she agreed. "I'm not a fool, Matt. I knew I was getting mixed up in something that could backfire badly, up there on the Chesapeake, and I took a few precautions. I hear my dear husband had me declared legally dead."

"So I'm told."

"I'm afraid it didn't make him quite as rich as he'd hoped. Oh, he's got enough to get by on; maybe enough that he never even noticed there was any missing. A head for business was not his strong point, if he had one. In all our years of marriage, I never found one, even in bed. God knows why I married him... Well, that's kind of irrelevant, isn't it? Anyway, I'd put quite a bit aside where I could get at it under another name, if I had to run for it. As I did, thanks to you." There was a little silence. The waitress put our drinks on the table and went away. Harriet glanced at the long cylinder of rolled-up paper I'd brought with me, and said: "Well, break out your charts and let a nautical expert look at this problem of yours."

I shook my head. "Not yet. We're going to have company. I don't want to have to go over it twice."

"Company?" Harriet frowned quickly. "I don't know that I like that very much, Matt. Does this 'company' know—"

"About your colorful past as the rich and subversive Mrs. Louis Rosten?" I shook my head again. "No, and he won't if you follow my lead. Just look beautiful and mysterious like the time you greeted me in a filmy negligee late at night—and slipped me a Mickey just when things were getting interesting."

She laughed; and we compared notes about those

bygone days; and I told her what she needed to know about Big Bill Haseltine, including a brief sketch of the evening's stupid activities, which she found highly amusing. I was glad to see it. When I'd known her before, she hadn't been a lady to be shocked by a little gore, and I was relieved to find that the years hadn't softened her noticeably.

"Here he comes now," I said, glancing toward the door.

She looked that way, and whistled softly. "That is a *big* man!"

"So was the dinosaur big," I said sourly. "With a brain the size of a golf ball, located mostly between its hind legs... I think the resemblance is very close. Captain Robinson, Mr. Haseltine. Harriet, Bill. You've got to watch this guy, Hattie. If he disapproves of you, he'll send his big, dangerous goons after you."

"Lay off, Helm." Haseltine sat down, glanced appraisingly at the handsome woman beside him, and looked at me. "How much does she know?" he asked.

"Enough," I said. "You can talk freely in front of her... Hattie."

"Yes?"

"Tell him, please. Recite the list of people I wanted you to help me look for, if you don't mind."

"Of course, Matt. The names were: Marcus, Lavalle, Rockwell, Phipps, and Phipps."

I looked grimly at Haseltine. "Just to settle the question of whom I was working for here in the Keys, and why I was having drinks with the lady. Our problem, you see, has got mixed up with a bunch of others. I had a hunch it might be easier to untangle the whole mess from here, and I wanted Hattie's help. She's got some special qualifications we can use, never mind the top-secret details. And if you see her behaving in a way that doesn't seem to make sense, will you please ask a few questions before you have her beat up? There just might be a logical explanation, you know."

He said, "Goddamn it, Helm, I asked you to lay off. Maybe I was a little out of line, but you kind of overreacted, didn't you? Sticking a knife in a guy's back just because he gave you a little lip, for God's sake!"

I said, "*Amigo*, except for a few special individuals of interest to the organization I serve, all anybody's ever had to do to stay perfectly safe and healthy in my neighborhood is leave me alone. Your thugs chose not to. Once they opened that gate, I figured I was at liberty to walk as far in as I chose. That's how far I chose. Anyway, the guy wouldn't have talked if I'd given him time to think about being strong and silent."

"Goddamn it, the boys weren't armed! All they were going to do—"

Harriet put a warning hand on his arm. "Here comes the waitress, Bill. What do you want to drink?"

"What… Oh, bourbon and branch water, thanks."

She passed the message to the girl, who went away. It was time to stop the bickering, which had served the purpose of distracting him, keeping him from asking too many questions about the newest and most attractive member of our team.

I grinned, and said, "Okay, so we're both bastards, Bill. Maybe I ought to tell you how I got that way, so you can make allowances." He was still glowering at me, and if I'd had my way I'd have taken the rich, dumb ox out into the middle of the Gulf Stream and drowned him, but I wasn't here to indulge my private preferences. I went on quickly, before he could interrupt: "It was in college, the first college I went to, a real gung-ho place. It had a kind of ornamental pool, called the Lily Pond, although it was mostly muck and weeds. The upper classmen, if they disapproved of the behavior of a lower classman, had the cute habit of descending on him in force, dragging him out to this glorified mud puddle, and heaving him in. It was kind of an old school tradition…"

I waited while the waitress put Haseltine's drink in front of him. He tasted it sulkily and said nothing. I went on.

"Well, one day the grapevine let me know I was next on the dunking list. I'd been expecting it. I'd been planning on upholding the school honor in such individual sports as fencing and rifle-shooting, but the seniors had decided I ought to go out for basketball because of my height. I'd told them frankly that if there was anything that turned my stomach, it was team sports of any kind, particularly the ones that became college religions. That hadn't gone over real big, if you know what I mean. Well, I just didn't feel like an involuntary bath that evening, so I laid out a hunting knife and wedged a chair under the doorknob of my room. It was a fairly feeble old chair and the back was cracked, but nobody knew that but me. I just wanted some evidence that they'd actually broken in. There weren't any locks in that dormitory that worked. It was a real togetherness institution. You weren't supposed to want privacy, ever. That was considered antisocial and un-American."

I grimaced, and took a sip of my drink, and glanced at Harriet to see if I was boring her. Apparently I wasn't. Her eyes were bright with interest. She was really kind of a bloodthirsty bitch, come to think of it, but I found it a refreshing contrast to the phony, mechanical humanitarianism currently fashionable.

"Go on, Matt," she said.

"Well, they came," I said. "There was the usual loud-mouthed, beery mob. They yelled at me to open the door. I called back that I hadn't invited them, and if they wanted in, they knew what to do. They did it. The first one inside after they'd smashed the door open was the big school-spirit expert who'd given me the pep-talk about how I didn't want to let the college and the basketball team down. He was very brave. He told me not to be silly, I wasn't really going to use that knife, just put it down. I told him when he put a hand on me, I'd cut it off. So he did; and I did. Well, not all the way off. I understand they sewed it back on and he got some use out of it eventually. Nevertheless, the immediate result was a lot of groans and gore, very spectacular. I told the rest it was a sample, and I had plenty more if anybody wanted it. Nobody did."

I looked at Haseltine. He reacted beautifully, right on cue. "Jesus Christ, Helm, those boys were obviously just tight and having a little fun—"

"Sure," I said. "And they could have gone and had their tight little fun anywhere they damned well pleased, except in my room at my expense. I made that quite clear to them before the action started. They chose to ignore the warning. That made it open hunting season by my way of reckoning. I figured... I still figure that anybody who invades my domicile by force is mine if I can take him. Anybody who lays hands on me without my permission is fair and legal game. Anybody who opens the door to violence has simply got no legitimate beef if a little more violence walks in than he bargained for. As far as I'm concerned, people can either stick to polite, civilized conduct, or I'll give them jungle all the way."

"What happened then?" Harriet asked curiously. "What did they do to you? The school authorities, I mean?"

I grinned. "It's strange that you should ask," I said. "What makes you think they'd do anything to *me*? I was the aggrieved party, wasn't I; the victim of unprovoked aggression? I mean, there I was in my room, studying hard and minding my own business like a good little freshman. A bunch of hoodlums breaks in and, outnumbered though I am, I defend myself bravely... Wouldn't you think I'd be in line for a hero medal, or something?"

"Hell, you didn't have to use a *knife*!" Haseltine protested.

"Of course I had to use a knife. Or a gun," I said. "What was I supposed to do, beat up a dozen older boys, including some outsized football types, with my bare fists? Superman, I'm not. To stop them, without actually killing anybody, I had to do something swift and bloody and dramatic to show I meant business right at the start. I did just about the least drastic thing that could get my point across... They threw me out of that school, of course. Having a weapon in my room, was the official excuse. The broken chair, proving they'd forced their way in, saved me from being sued or arrested for assault, but nobody ever did anything about any of the others besides a sort of token reprimand. And at that point, *amigo*," I said, looking at Haseltine, "I realized I was just a little out of step with the rest of the world, a world where you're supposed to let people heave you into fishponds any time they happen to feel like it. I decided I'd better look around, once I'd finished getting my degree elsewhere, and see if I couldn't find at least a few characters marching to my kind of music. After a while, I found them; or they found me."

There was a little silence. I could see Haseltine getting ready to give me a big argument. There wasn't any doubt whose side he'd have been on in that old college hassle; and I found the old anger coming back that always hits me when I meet that kind of a guy, the kind that broke into my room that night, the kind that's always pushing people around and always gets terribly, terribly shocked and self-righteous when he runs into somebody who's willing to die, or kill, rather than put up with his overbearing nonsense.

"Oh, I almost forgot," I said, just as he was starting to speak. "There's a kind of epilogue that might interest you, Bill. Three years later I read in the papers that there was a big scandal at that school. You see, another bunch of arrogant seniors had got hold of another poor dumb freshman whose behavior wasn't to their liking; and they'd given him the old school heave—only, it turned out, there was some kind of a rusty drainpipe out there in the muck that nobody'd ever noticed. He landed right on it. The last I heard, he was still alive, if you can call it living. He can blink his eyelids once for yes and twice for no, or vice versa. And every time I think of him, I remember my old hunting knife with much affection. If it hadn't been for those six inches of cold, sharp steel, that human vegetable might have been me."

Haseltine licked his lips and didn't speak. After a moment, Harriet said brightly: "Haseltine. Haven't I heard that name recently? Of course, you're the man who landed a world's record tarpon off Boca Grande last spring…"

Good girl. They were off; and I had to listen to lures and lines and rods and reels and striking drag and fighting drag and all the rest of the saltwater-angling routine. At the moment, it didn't interest me greatly, but it carried us through dinner; and by the time we got to our coffee, Harriet had wheedled our tame Texas millionaire into a pretty good mood.

"Okay," he said at last, condescending to acknowledge my presence once more, "okay, now let's hear about this hunch of yours."

I said, "You tell him, Hattie."

"Matt thinks the place you want is somewhere along the coast of Cuba," she said.

Haseltine frowned. "Cuba? Hell, that's clear over on this side of the Bahamas, way south and west of the *Ametta*'s course. What makes you think they're in Cuba?"

I said. "Assuming they're alive, and not at the bottom of the Atlantic, they couldn't be anywhere else, if you did any kind of a job looking for them.".

He bristled. "Damn it, man, we checked every scrap of land in the upper Bahamas—hell, the whole Bahamas— and every patch of water. And the authorities were just as thorough; although they didn't carry their search patterns out quite as far as we did."

I nodded. "That's just the point. You all looked, and looked hard, in all the plausible places, figuring the yacht's course and the prevailing winds and currents. Apparently, at that time, you were thinking in terms of a natural disaster of some kind, or a seminatural one like a collision with a ship. Then, Bill, for some reason you decided you were dealing with a criminal endeavor instead of an accident or act of God, and got me involved. I'd like to know what changed your mind."

He hesitated, and shrugged. "I guess you'd call it the process of elimination. Collision, fire, explosion, foundering… in any of those cases there'd have been something left floating and we'd have found it, like I told you before. Anyway, Buster Phipps wasn't that kind of a skipper, like I also told you. Therefore it didn't just happen. Somebody made it happen; and I want the guy who did."

It was plausible enough; but he didn't look at us as he

said it. This was no time to play boy detective, however, and I said: "Sure. Either somebody sank the boat and then hung around and carefully policed the area to make sure nothing drifted away to betray him; or he captured it and took it somewhere. Well, there have been two significant disappearances since the *Ametta Too*. Both involved rich individuals of some prominence, the kind who are generally considered more useful as living hostages than dead corpses. We can therefore at least hope that they, and the people from the *Ametta*, are all being held somewhere alive, for some purpose. We can also figure they were brought to this place, wherever it is, by the means of transportation they were using when captured. In other words, we can figure the kidnappings were inside jobs."

Haseltine started to speak, maybe to remind me that he'd had all the *Ametta*'s crew checked out without finding anything really damaging. He stopped.

It was Harriet who asked: "What makes you so sure of that?"

"Sure?" I said. "Who's sure? I'm just guessing wildly. Maybe we're dealing with a homicidal seagoing maniac who's got a murderous grudge against anybody with a bank account exceeding five figures. But if we're not, if we've got a series of kidnappings to solve, then they're most likely inside jobs because one involved a plane. And while taking over one boat from another on the high seas has been done since the ancient days of piracy, capturing one flying airplane from another isn't really practical under most circumstances—at the best, it would involve a serious risk of alerting nearby ground stations with a lot of melodramatic radio chatter. Well, if the plane was an inside job, a hijacking carried out by somebody on board, it seems likely that the boat disappearances were, too. Certainly it's the method involving least equipment. Instead of armed pirate ships and planes, all you need is a few enterprising individuals with guns. So we have to find a place to which all the hijackers could sail or fly fairly quickly, a place where they could hide a couple of big yachts and a sizable airplane. And considering how hard everybody seems to have looked everywhere else, it's likely that spot is in Cuba, the one island within reach that nobody can search without becoming the target for a lot of Castro firepower…" I stopped, as the waitress approached the table. "Yes, Miss?"

"Are you Mr. Helm? There's a phone call for you. Over there, sir."

I went over there and talked a while with Mac, who, it seemed, had missed his flight to Washington or taken another back. I returned to the table.

"Your boys are going to be okay," I said to Haseltine. "Everything seems to be under control, medically speaking. However, I'm afraid I'm going to have to split, as the cats say, and take Hattie with me. There's a new lead we have to look into—"

"I'll come with you."

I looked at him wearily, reminding myself that he was after all a taxpayer, the man who paid my salary, such as it was.

"Don't give me a hard time, Bill," I said. "You got hold of me because I was supposed to know what I was doing, didn't you? Well, just relax and let me do it. I'll be in touch. In the meantime, as soon as you can, charter us a good-sized seagoing powerboat, something around thirty feet, say, that'll really burn up the water, say thirty knots; the fastest thing you can lay your hands on large enough to carry a dozen people without getting low and slow in the water. Cruising radius, four or five hundred miles—"

"You're dreaming, *amigo*," Haseltine said. "There aren't any fast thirty-footers around with that kind of range built in, unless you want to mess around with a lot of spare fuel-drums in the cockpit. You'll have to get something bigger to go that far."

I said, "Okay, you're the expert. Pick what you figure we need and get it ready for a long haul. Your story, if anybody asks, is that you're heading for the marlin grounds somewhere to do this hypothetical story of ours—"

"Off Yucatan, maybe? Cozumel? That's better than a four-hundred-mile run from Key West. It would explain the extra fuel." Now that he was being consulted, he was flattered and cooperative.

"Now you're cooking," I said, and we left him there.

Outside, I asked Harriet, "What the hell is a Cozumel?"

She laughed. "Like the man said, it's off the south coast of Yucatan, over on the other side of the Gulf of Mexico. A Mexican resort island with a lot of fish around it... Matt?"

"Yes?"

"Maybe I shouldn't bring it up, but I do have a fairly fast cruising boat with plenty of range. I mean the *Queenfisher*, not the outboard. She won't do thirty, but she'll cruise all day at twenty, and hit twenty-five in a pinch."

"Sure," I said. "So let's keep him busy and happy scrounging up another. He can afford it, and maybe it'll keep him out of my hair. Besides, what the hell makes you think I'd trust any boat and crew of yours any farther than I have to? Incidentally, where is your crew? You can't run both those boats yourself, and a mate was mentioned; but I haven't seen anybody around."

She glanced at me sharply as we stopped at the car. I thought she was about to make an angry retort, but she laughed softly instead.

"That's better," she murmured. "That's much better! I thought you were being just a little too trusting and forgiving. Yes, I do have a captain and mate for the *Queenfisher*, but I let them take off for a couple of weeks. I didn't want them hanging around just now, if you know what I mean. The outboard I handle myself when I've got a client for it."

"I bet it's fun, poling that big job across the flats. Well, get in. It makes me nervous as hell, standing around under these damn loaded palm trees."

She was laughing again as I got in beside her. "You're really something else, Matt, as they say nowadays. First you casually put two roughnecks into the hospital, and then you worry about getting conked by a stray coconut." She hesitated. "Are you permitted to tell me what you learned over the phone, darling, or shouldn't I ask?"

I grimaced. "Well, to be philosophical, it's the great modern dilemma," I said as I started the car and drove us out of there without a single heavy object bouncing off the roof. "It would be so simply marvelous if the human animal weren't aggressive by nature, so a lot of people figure they can stop it from being so just by having everybody pretend it isn't so. The only trouble is, they won't sit down and calculate what's going to happen if the prescription doesn't work on everybody who takes it."

"Yes, Professor," Harriet said obligingly, "and what is going to happen, please?"

"Exactly what has happened," I said. "Bunches of arrogant thugs—like those college creeps who came for me—shoving people around, serenely confident that none of their brainwashed, nonviolent fellow-citizens will be willing to, or able to, lift a hand in effective self-defense. Once you start raising whole generations on the lovely, unrealistic principle that the use of force is always evil and unthinkable, that you should be willing to endure any indignity and pay any price rather than spill a little blood, why, you've set yourself right up for them, haven't you?"

"For whom, darling?"

"For the intimidators," I said. "For the people who haven't the slightest qualms about using force or spilling blood. For the ones on whom the pretend-we're-all-nice medicine didn't work. All the bullies and dictators and little-league Caesars. *And* all the kidnapers and hijackers and political-action fanatics who've suddenly discovered the wonderful leverage we've given them by our terrified modern attitude toward violence. They've learned that the way to intimidate the whole tender-hearted world and make it do their bidding is just to wave a weapon at somebody, anybody. Just flourish a knife or a gun under the nose of one pretty airline stewardess and just like that you've got yourself a whole airplane and a million-dollar ransom..."

"I suppose there's a point to all this," Harriet said dryly.

I grinned. "I always say, there's nothing like a woman making a man feel big by hanging breathlessly on his every word. Sure, there's a point. That's what this is all about, all these mysterious disappearances. To hell with the Voodoo Sea of Missing Ships. Just as we were guessing, it's another lousy hostage-for-ransom deal; and why they spread the operation over a couple of months remains to be seen. I don't know the details yet, or just what payment is being demanded or who's demanding it, but there's a man meeting us in my cabin who'll brief us..."

15

It was a beautiful, cool, quiet, Florida fall evening with plenty of stars but no moon. That is, it was beautiful and quiet once we turned off the garish Keys highway and headed down past the Faro Blanco office along one of the treelined resort drives. My cabin was dark when we reached it. I kept on driving. Harriet stirred beside me.

"I thought you had Number Twenty-six," she said.

"I never told you that," I said. "You've been snooping. If you know so much, maybe you can tell me why the light isn't on."

She laughed. "Don't overdo the secret agent bit, darling."

I said, "A gent named Ramsay Pendleton, a fine, upstanding British operative, was supposed to be waiting for us in my place, with the light on. My chief knows I don't like meeting people in the dark when I don't have to, even people I know; and there's no reason for us to be mysterious tonight. Well, the light isn't on. Can you offer an explanation?"

Now she was angry. "Damn it, of course I can't, Matt. How the hell could I?"

"I don't know; I was just asking," I said mildly. "After all, I never did learn just how the Mickey got into that drink you served me all those years ago, either." I pulled onto the grass at the side of the driveway and grinned at her in the darkness. "Relax, I was just needling you. But this is for serious: wait here. You're not dressed for prowling through the bushes, and it isn't safe. That cabin of mine seems to have a fascination for unsavory and unfriendly people tonight; I've already been jumped there once. Maybe I'm imagining things, but as far as I'm concerned, once I'm out there, anything that moves is hostile and I'm going to shoot hell out of it. I'll be sorry if it turns out to be you, but my abject apologies won't do you much good if you can't hear them. So please don't set foot outside this car until I get back. Okay?"

I took the short-barreled Smith and Wesson from under my belt; and slipped out of the car, eased the door closed, and made my way back through the maze of trees and cabins and little concrete walks. Out here I could hear the occasional sounds of voices and television sets, but the small, dark, white building in which I was interested was almost silent. The windows were all closed, as I'd left them. The air-conditioner was running, making a small whirring sound, that was all. I remembered turning it on earlier. Well, maybe Ramsay Pendleton hadn't got here yet; the question was why. Mac's scheduling usually works as planned; he'd have made a good train-dispatcher.

Maybe our British associate had been here and left, and again the question was why.

There was no easy way of doing it. There was only one door. I had to pass through it. It took me longer than it normally takes a citizen to enter a room he's rented for the night; but once I started to go, I went a lot lower and faster. On the floor inside, gun ready, I waited in the chilly, air-conditioned dark for greetings, hostile or friendly. None came.

I got up, switched on the light, brushed myself off, and checked the little kitchenette and bathroom at the rear of the place, feeling, as always after taking a lot of unnecessary precautions, like a melodramatic damned fool. Well, it's a better feeling than dead, or so I'm told.

Harriet looked around quickly as I slid into the car once more. "Well?"

"Nothing," I said. "No booby traps, no splintered furniture, no bullet-holes in doors or walls, no pools of coagulating gore. I think the resort office was closed when we drove by just now. Where's another phone booth?"

"On the dock, right next to the *Queenfisher*," she said.

I started the car. "*Queenfisher*. I've been wanting to ask: what kind of a name is that?"

"Well, if there's a kingfisher, there ought to be a queenfisher, oughtn't there? It's only fair." She hesitated. "You say this Pendleton person is a *British* agent?"

I said, "Don't be snoopy. Just take what information comes your way and be grateful for it—or ask your friends; they can probably tell you more about my business than

I can. Great international wheels are turning and we are all just helpless human cogs in the immense machinery. Here we are. Stay put again, cog."

In the phone booth, I called the Miami number I'd already used once before tonight. The same man answered and said resignedly: "Oh, no, not again! Hell, the boys just scrubbed out that station wagon. How many this time?"

"You're going to have to look for this one," I said. "The allied troops didn't make the rendezvous. Our friend hasn't called in with excuses, has he? Maybe he couldn't find his old school tie and didn't feel like appearing in public improperly attired."

"Just a minute, let me check." There was a pause; then his voice came again. "Eric."

"Right here."

"I say, old fellow, shouldn't be too hard on the foreign chap, don't you know?" said my unseen contact slowly. "Particularly since he's dead."

I drew a long breath. "Details?"

"Hold on. Somebody wants to talk with you." Then Mac's voice came on the line. "Eric."

"Yes, sir."

"Report."

"No light. No Pendleton. No signs of a struggle. Where was he found?"

"In his car, at the side of the highway some distance from your motel. The report just came in. Body warm. Car engine warm."

"Well, they would be. Hell, even now, it hasn't been three-quarters of an hour since you called me at dinner and sent me to meet him."

Mac said, "I spoke with him an hour before that, by phone, asking him to drive over and brief you on the latest developments. He was in Islamorada at the time, with about thirty-five miles to go."

"He must have run into something not too long after he hung up," I said thoughtfully. "Maybe on the way, but that's a crowded road to commit murder on. Most likely somebody was laying for him in my place when he got there. Or laying for me; and Pendleton bought the treatment instead. It would have to be that way. The air-conditioner was running."

"Explain."

I said, "I don't know what kind of weather you're having up in Miami, sir, but it's a cool fall night down here. I forgot and left the machinery turned on when I went out to dinner. Things were pretty chilly by the time I got back. A legitimate visitor would have switched the gadget off before settling down to wait. Why freeze unnecessarily? A would-be murderer, on the other hand, would have resigned himself to shivering a bit rather than take a chance of warning me by changing anything in the place. So it looks as if Pendleton walked in on the killer rather than the other way around. Not that it really matters." I hesitated, and said slowly, "He told me, the one time I really talked with him, that he used to be a good friend of Leslie Crowe-Barham—you remember the late

Sir Leslie—but that he wasn't holding any grudges on that old account, mainly because he admired the brave way I'd charged the Mink's gun. They have some quaint, old-fashioned ideas over there, don't they?"

"Yes, but it's kind of irrelevant now, isn't it, Eric?"

"Yes, sir," I said. "Irrelevant."

"I have to drive down into the Keys," Mac said. "I have to make sure the case is handled discreetly by the local authorities in charge."

"Yes, sir," I said. "Discreetly."

"Then I'll come by and bring you up to date myself," he said. "If the lady is available, keep her that way, please."

"She hasn't been out of my sight for three hours," I said. "But I'll hang onto her. Just knock before you enter, sir. No telling what I may have to do to keep her entertained until you arrive."

Harriet had the radio on when I got back to the car. She switched it off as I got in beside her. "A girl hates to complain, but it's not the most exciting evening I ever spent in my life," she said dryly.

"It's the most exciting evening Pendleton ever spent," I said. "At least, he'll never be able to top it."

She was silent for a significant interval, while I got the motor started. "He's dead?" she asked then.

"Apparently very."

"How?"

"Somebody was waiting for him in my cabin, we figure. A pro. I never learned our British friend's exact qualifications, but he'd been in the business at least long enough that it would need a real pro to take him without even mussing the rug."

"I'm not a pro," Harriet said quietly. "Not really. Not unless you're talking about boats and fishing. Where killing is concerned, I'm just a lousy amateur, you said so yourself. Anyway, we've been together since seven-thirty. If that's the way your mind is running."

I grinned. "That's the way a lot of minds are running. The last thing my chief said to me before I came down here to see you was that I should be careful because I was dealing with a very dangerous lady."

"I didn't murder your friend."

"He wasn't my friend, just a guy I knew slightly. And I know you didn't kill him. As you point out, I'm your alibi. Very convenient, isn't it?"

She shook her head quickly. "I didn't have him killed, Matt."

I shrugged. "Okay, so you never told anybody to go murder you a Pendleton. But you might have asked somebody to murder you a Helm. After all, it wouldn't be the first time, or even the second."

She drew a long breath. "No, it wouldn't. And don't think the thought never crossed my mind. But it happens that I didn't do it. And now, unless I'm under arrest, I think since we're here I'll just say goodnight and go aboard my boat—"

I said, "I've got instructions to keep you available in my cabin until an important gent can join us, the same guy who thinks you're a dangerous lady."

She hesitated, and said in a tentative tone of voice, "I've got friends here, Matt."

I grinned. "What are you planning to do, rip your blouse and scream rape? Sure, all those salty seagoing friends of yours will come running with those gaffs and billy clubs you mentioned earlier, and your picture will be in all the papers…"

She laughed softly. "Blackmail! Actually, I was bluffing, darling. I'm the only one who lives on board, until you get down the line to the private boats. There's not much of anybody around Charter Row at this hour of the night. So I guess we'd better go up to your place and take a look at those charts you've been dragging around all evening. Unless, of course, you have something else in mind…"

16

Regardless of what I did or did not have in my lecherous mind, we were soon knee deep in maps and charts, spread out on the cabin floor. Some day somebody's going to have to take me aside and whisper in my ear the facts of cartographic life like, for instance, what the hell is an oblique Mercator projection. The maps were more colorful than the charts; but the charts had more cute little numbers on them. Did you know that there's a spot in the Caribbean south of Cuba that's over four miles deep?'

It was the north coast of the island that mainly concerned us, however. At least I had a hunch that was the most likely area, and Harriet agreed with me. Here there's a sort of three-way watery crossroads between Florida, Cuba, and the Bahamas—well, actually the Great Bahama Bank. The Old Bahama Channel cuts between these immense shallow flats and the north coast of Cuba; and then joins the Florida Straits carrying the Gulf Stream around the southern tip of the United States.

Right at the intersection, like a safety island at the junction of two boulevards, is the small, triangular Cay Sal Bank, pronounced Key Sal Bank.

Kneeling on the rug, Harriet pointed out this and several other features, yanking her long skirt aside as she moved from chart to chart.

"You don't know a hell of a lot about geography, do you?" she said. "Politics being what they are these days, I'd think Cuba would be a place you'd have learned something about, in your business."

"I've been there," I said. "A plane put a couple of us down in a hole in the jungle in the middle of the night, some characters with peculiar Spanish accents—the Cubans don't seem to murder their Castilian quite the same way the Mexicans do—pointed us in the right direction and led us back again when we'd finished our job; and the plane came back for us, again at night. As a sightseeing jaunt, it was a bust."

"I won't ask what the job was," she said. "Exactly where did you say all these boats and planes disappeared?"

"The last reported positions are all marked on the big map over there."

She shifted her anchorage a fathom to port. "Damn this skirt," she said, rearranging it once more. Then she studied the map for a while, and went on: "It's plausible. That ketch with the cutie name might have hit a few head winds steering that far south of her course; but I gather she was a fast, weatherly boat with good auxiliary power, so it shouldn't have slowed her up much. She could have slipped through any of these passages below the Great Bahama Bank without being seen. Even if Haseltine was already searching for his blonde beauty by the time the boat got there, I gather it didn't occur to him to look that far south that early in the game."

"How did you know she's blonde and beautiful?" I asked.

"All you have to do is look at the man and you know the kind he'd pick," Harriet said calmly. "Anyway, there were more pictures of Loretta Phipps and her movie-star mother in the papers at the time, than of her rich and important father. As a matter of fact, as far as pictorial coverage was concerned, the poor man ran a bad fourth behind the boat, if I remember right."

"What about that diesel yacht out of Puerto Rico?" I asked.

"Sir James Marcus, you said his name was? He was the closest; he was practically there. The plane heading for Martinique is the big question. Even assuming it had enough gas…" She frowned at the brightly colored islands on the blue paper ocean. "Was it a seaplane or a landplane, darling?"

"Land," I said.

"Of course, they could have ditched it in the water and had a boat standing by to take them off." She shrugged. "That's probably the way they did it. Landing strips still aren't too common along that coast, I gather, particularly landing strips unknown to the local inhabitants and the Castro police."

I said, "My hunch is that these people have an arrangement with the Castro police; they'd almost have to have one. That's why I figure one of your politically oriented friends won't have too much trouble getting the information for us. It should be available to anyone knowing the right people in Havana." She didn't say anything. I went on: "Now, where's *your* harbor of refuge on this Communist shore?"

She glanced at me sharply. "You can't expect me to tell you that, darling. I mean, maybe I'm willing to use my contacts to help you with this lousy job of yours, to save my own skin, but I'm not going to betray them to you."

I said, "I don't go around slapping down Reds just because they're Red. Tolerant, that's me."

"Maybe," she said, "but I'm still not going to tell you. It's not my secret; and it's got nothing to do with your problem. There's no airfield and no secret harbor to hide a couple of hijacked yachts. It's just a little fishing village on the coast; and when the time comes, if it comes, I'll run in there and ask somebody to take me to Señor Soandso; and somebody'll bury the boat for me; and I'll be safely on my way to the workers' homeland. Ugh."

"Tsk, tsk," I said. "That's a hell of a Marxist attitude."

"They've used me and I've used them," she said. "We have a working relationship, darling, but there never was a meeting of political minds, if you know what I mean. Why do you think I'm living here finding fish for people too stupid to find their own?"

"I was wondering about that," I said.

"Because I'd rather do that than be part of their regimented paradise." She grimaced. "Actually, I guess I'm kind of a nature girl at heart. I like working outdoors; I had a model dairy farm once, up in Maryland, remember?"

"I remember," I said. "The government put a highway through the middle of it, and you declared war on the United States of America."

She laughed. "Well, I lost, so let's forget it. But the fact is I'd rather run my own boats and lie awake nights figuring out the weather and the tides and the fish, not to mention the clients, than be part of their society of the future with a bunch of their stupid bureaucrats telling me what to do. If it's a choice between that and jail, I'll go; but not until I have to. And don't tell me I'm inconsistent. Who isn't?"

There was a little silence. It was time to change the subject; and I looked down at the map.

"Just one more foolish question," I said. "What are all those funny little blue and red arrows for?"

"They indicate prevailing winds and currents," she said. "As you can see, heading from here south to Cuba you'd better bring plenty of gas because it's all uphill; everything's against you. On the other hand, the refugees from Castro's Communism have it easy once they're past the patrols; everything blows and drifts from Cuba toward the land of liberty, if you'll pardon the term. That chief of yours is taking his time, isn't he? *If* he's coming here at all. I only have your word for that."

I grinned. "Don't go ingénue on me, Hattie. You're a

grownup girl and I'm sure you can take care of yourself, if you really want to."

She sighed theatrically. "But that's just the problem, darling. I can't decide whether or not I really want to take care of myself, as you so delicately put it. After all, we do have some unfinished business between us."

"That's not my fault," I said. "I was doing my best to finish it, as I recall, when your knockout drops took effect…" I sighed, and said more briskly, "Saved by the bell. Here he comes now."

Having recognized the footsteps that preceded it, I wasn't too careful about answering the knock on the door; and it was Mac all right. His appearance hadn't changed greatly since I'd left him at the Miami airport that afternoon. I closed the door behind him.

"Watch where you step, sir. We've got half the Caribbean spread out on the rug."

He'd stopped in front of Harriet, who'd risen. He studied her for a moment without speaking, seeming particularly interested, for some reason, in her neat, smooth, dark coiffure. At last he glanced at me.

"You're absolutely certain she hasn't been out of your sight this evening? It's very strange."

"What is?" I asked.

"There was some interesting evidence clutched in Pendleton's hand. The police allowed me to borrow it temporarily. If you have a sheet of white paper…"

I produced a piece of motel stationery from the table drawer. He took an envelope from his pocket, spread it open carefully, and with the point of a mechanical pencil drew out and arranged on the paper several long, dark hairs.

17

After a moment, Harriet laughed. She reached up deliberately and separated a couple of filaments of her own hair from the rest. With a quick little jerk, she pulled them free, wincing slightly. She laid them across the other end of the sheet of white stationery.

"Human hairs are supposed to be different," she said. "You're welcome to check."

"We have," Mac said calmly. "These hairs are from a man. A man with hands considerably larger than yours, Captain Robinson. He knocked Ramsay Pendleton unconscious with a blackjack, and then choked him to death, leaving distinctive marks on the throat. Do you happen to know a long-haired man with very large hands?"

Harriet laughed again. "Drama!" she murmured. "What was I supposed to do, panic at the thought that I was a murder suspect and blurt out the name of the real killer to save myself?"

Mac shrugged. "It was worth a try."

"Hardly. Even if I knew the man, which I don't admit, I've already told Matt, here, that while I'll allow myself to be blackmailed to the extent of using some of my contacts for your benefit, I'm not going to betray them to you. Find your own long-haired murderer."

"The man's name is probably Morgan," Mac said imperturbably. "He was seen in the Bahamas, where he is wanted for a murder I'm afraid he didn't commit. A terrible miscarriage of justice. However, he seems to have eluded the Bahamian authorities; apparently he is now in the Keys; and he does seem to have committed this crime, apparently by mistake or accident, since there is no good motive known for him to kill Mr. Pendleton. He apparently had another victim in mind. Mr. Helm was told by a dying young woman that Morgan would get him; and that if Morgan didn't, you would."

Harriet faced him defiantly. "If you know all this, why the play-acting?"

"A great deal may depend on you, Captain Robinson," Mac said. "I am trying to determine how far you can be relied upon."

"And I'm supposed to sell out this Morgan, whoever he may be, to prove my good faith?"

Mac shook his head. "No. You're supposed to refuse to sell him out to prove your good faith. As you have just done."

Harriet glanced at me, and made a wry face. "If you work for this one, darling, I don't envy you one bit. Does he ever make sense?"

Mac said, "If you were planning treachery with the help of your Communist associates of long standing, you'd most likely have got permission to throw us a bone or two—a bone named Morgan, for instance—to allay our suspicions. Since you instead have exhibited commendable loyalty to these people, I feel there is a fair chance that you may give us the same loyalty. I never trust traitors, Captain Robinson, no matter how noble their proclaimed motives may be. A man, or a woman, who'll betray once, will betray twice."

"So I passed the test," Harriet said dryly, unimpressed. "Goody for me. Now what do we do?"

"Just a minute," I said. "Before we get down to other business, let's finish with Morgan. Talking about making sense, he doesn't."

Mac frowned. "What do you mean, Eric?"

I said, "Figure it out, sir. Here Morgan was, long hair and all, hiding in the closet or kitchenette or whatever, waiting to kill me. A stranger walks in and spots him—Pendleton, a pro, would check out the place as a matter of routine, before settling down to wait. Okay so far. But then what happened? Pendleton, unfortunately, wasn't really expecting to find anybody hiding in the closet; he was just going through the standard motions, more or less off guard. Morgan caught him by surprise and knocked him out. Still nothing remarkable. But what happens next? Why, Morgan grabs him by the throat and strangles him to death—and takes off, for God's sake, lugging the limp body away with him!"

Harriet asked, puzzled: "What's the problem? Do you think he should have stuck around—with a dead man at his feet?"

I said, "Precisely. That's exactly what he should have done. Otherwise, why kill?"

"I don't get it," Harriet protested. "What are you trying to say, darling?"

"Simple," I said. "If he was going to flee anyway, once a stranger stumbled onto the scene, why did Morgan bother to commit murder? I mean, all he had to do was whack the intruder on the head—as he apparently did—and split before the guy regained consciousness. Even if he didn't recognize Pendleton as an agent, and he'd probably seen the guy in Nassau, he could assume that anybody visiting me secretly at night wouldn't make a public outcry about being sapped in my room. Once out of here, Morgan would be free and clear. On the other hand, if he was set on staying to finish the job he'd come to do, *then* killing Pendleton would have been quite logical—killing him, and hiding him in the bathtub behind the shower curtain or something. That way, grimly determined to go through with his original plan, Morgan would be sure Pendleton wouldn't revive at the wrong moment and interfere. Either way, it would have made some sense. But to first go to the trouble of committing a quite unnecessary murder, and then to give up on the murder he'd come here to do, and run—taking the body with him, for God's sake!—is professional idiocy."

Harriet said, "Maybe this hypothetical Morgan,

whoever he may be, simply lost his head, and his nerve."

"I hope so," I said. "If he's that shaky, he should be fairly easy to cope with the next time he tries for me. But I saw him in Nassau, and he didn't look like a man who'd normally blow his cool in a crisis. If he did crack under great pressure, who or what was exerting it?"

"Darling, maybe you're overestimating the human race, at least where homicide is concerned. We aren't all cold, calm, calculating automatons like you, remember? If somebody blundered in on *me* when I was waiting to kill somebody, I'm sure all my actions would be strictly illogical."

I grinned. "That's what you say, but I don't think I'd care to bet my life on it."

Mac glanced at his watch. "Mr. Morgan is interesting, but he is not the subject I came here to discuss." He gestured toward the stuff on the floor. "Have you come to any conclusions about our problem, Captain Robinson?"

"Not yet," she said. "There really isn't too much to go on. Matt has a theory, and it's not too far out; but even if it's correct it covers a lot of ground, and water. Cuba's a big island with lots of coastline suitable for hiding pirated boats. After all, the old buccaneers used all the Greater Antilles for approximately the same purpose for years, very successfully."

"The Greater Whats?" I asked.

She laughed. "You really are a geographical innocent. The Greater Antilles are the big northern islands, from Cuba as far down as Puerto Rico, I believe. The Lesser Antilles are the rest of the Caribbean chain, the Leeward and Windward Islands and all that small stuff off the coast of South America."

Mac said, "The point is that Cuba is the only island within reasonable sailing or flying distance of these disappearances, as close as we can place them, that has not been, and cannot be, searched very carefully. We have not been permitted to risk an international incident there, at least not yet. Satellite reconnaissance hasn't been very helpful, and speculative scouting expeditions and over-flights have been strictly forbidden. If we find the hiding place, we may be allowed to act against it, but we will be given only one chance, and our action must be successful. Apparently, delicate negotiations of some kind are in progress somewhere; and too many people remember the Bay of Pigs. There must be no more fiascos in that area."

"Well, Bahia de Cocinos is clear over on the south coast of Cuba," Harriet said. "It's hardly the same area, but I see what you mean."

There was a small pause. I took advantage of it to shove a chair forward for Mac. He waited politely for Harriet to sit down on the bed before seating himself. I took the couch at the side of the room. I didn't bother to offer drinks around. It wasn't exactly a social occasion.

Mac studied the colorful map of Cuba at his feet for a moment, and looked up, addressing Harriet: "Considering your rather questionable security status," he said, "you will forgive me if I omit certain classified details. The basic problem seems to be this: Recently a certain small island in the Caribbean—down in the Lesser Antilles, since we're making the distinction—declared itself a free and sovereign nation, as others have done. There was no real opposition at the time. The European nation that formerly exercised sovereignty over St. Esteban, as we'll refer to it, wasn't greatly concerned about the loss of a piece of fairly impoverished real estate, and everybody else was happy—everybody except the St. Estebanites, or Estebanians, or whatever they should be called."

"What was their gripe?" I asked.

Mac made a wry face. "It turned out that there were two factions striving for power, and once they no longer had a foreign government to hate, they promptly started hating each other. Frankly, I have been unable to determine the exact basis for disagreement. The races and language groups involved seem to be fairly evenly divided between the two sides. It seems to be an obscure family quarrel no outsider can really comprehend. The fact is that one group has managed to drive the other out of the capital city of St. Esteban, which we will also call St. Esteban, and bottle up its active, armed members in a mountainous corner of the island. The rebels, as they are now called by the faction that controls the seat of government, have struck back, quite simply, by seizing fairly prominent hostages from three major nations with Caribbean interests. All three governments have just been formally notified that if military aid is not forthcoming to help these downtrodden people regain their 'rights,' the hostages will die."

I whistled softly. "Jesus!" I said. "Those airplane

hijackers are pikers, with their lousy little half-million-dollar ransoms. These characters think big. What they want is the United States Marines, Her Majesty's Gurkhas, and the French Foreign Legion, if I have the titles and outfits correct."

"You haven't," Mac said. "As a matter of fact, I believe two of the military organizations to which you refer no longer exist in an effective way. But the principle is correct."

Harriet asked, "If it's not classified, what's the official reaction?"

"Whose official reaction?" Mac shrugged. "The British have their reaction and the French have theirs. In Washington, I would say the message at first evoked equal parts of incredulity and dismay. The dismay remains. The incredulity soon faded when it was established that these people do in all likelihood hold the hostages enumerated; and that they probably mean what they say. Apparently, they are logical men and women in their primitive way, and reason that a nation that has never seemed reluctant to hand over a large sum of money to ransom an airplane and a few obscure passengers, isn't going to hesitate to provide an armored regiment or two in return for a number of reasonably important citizens and their expensive nautical and aeronautical toys." He paused, and went on: "The message also states that it is no use for us to try to locate the hostages, as they are being held in a place where we couldn't touch them even if we found them. This could, of course, be a ruse to keep us from looking too closely at a certain corner of the island of St. Esteban, but it could also mean that Mr. Helm is on the right track. The Cubans may well have been persuaded to extend unofficial hospitality to a project guaranteed to embarrass a number of capitalist nations, including the United States of America."

I said, "I suppose there's a time limit."

"We have five days left," Mac said. "In the meantime, orders have actually gone out to certain units of the Marines; and suitable transports are being ostentatiously prepared in Key West. What the final decision will be, if the hostages are still hostages at the end of the allotted time limit, nobody knows; but it was thought best to go through the motions to keep their captors happy while other responses are being considered."

"Like us," I said. "One question, sir. Satisfy my curiosity. Has it been established that there actually was an Estebanian, or whatever they're called, on each of the craft involved?"

"The inhabitants of the island are noted for being excellent sailors and fishermen," Mac said. "When they leave St. Esteban, they often find work on board yachts and sportfishing vessels. The *Ametta Too* carried a paid hand, Leo Gonzales, who was born on St. Esteban. It is thought that one of the two American college youths on board was also sympathetic to the rebel movement; at least he'd spent some time in the area before independence."

So much for the clean bill of health given the crew, albeit reluctantly, by Haseltine. I wondered if he'd known the truth, and if so, why he'd held it back.

"What about the others?" I asked.

"Sir James Marcus's yacht employed two crewmen from the island; and Lavalle's plane carried a very attractive black Estebanian stewardess, I'm told," Mac said. "One of the Baron's companions, Adolfo Alire, is known to have commercial connections in the island, maybe significant, maybe not. I think we can take it that the crafts were not captured by open enemy action; they were seized by people already on board, and sailed or flown to the place we're trying to find." Mac looked from me to Harriet and back again. "Any more questions? No? Then I'll take my leave. I was supposed to be in Washington six hours ago." He glanced at me. "Come out to the car, please, Eric. There is something you'd better see before I leave; something confidential. If you'll excuse us, Captain…"

18

It was a big sedan, almost as big as Haseltine's; and there was a driver waiting patiently and silently behind the wheel. Mac stopped beside the vehicle and turned to face me.

"I brought you out here under false pretenses," he said. "I have nothing to show you."

"Yes, sir," I said, to be saying something. He was obviously just making up his mind about what to tell me, or how to tell it to me, now that Harriet was no longer present.

He said, "Inside, I said that the decision how to handle this situation had not yet been made. That is incorrect. As a matter of fact, two decisions have been made. One applies if we cannot locate the kidnapers and their prisoners. The other becomes effective if we can. In neither case do we pay the ransom demanded."

"I see," I said. "Do our allies go along with this?"

"They have to," Mac said. "Neither of them has manpower or shipping available locally in the quantities required. They are unable to act unilaterally even if they wish. It's up to us, either way; and for various diplomatic reasons it is absolutely impossible at the moment for us to intervene in this Caribbean family squabble with military force, or even with weapons and supplies. I am assured by those who know that it is politically unthinkable. Even if we wanted to submit to this ambitious blackmail scheme, we couldn't."

"Because of those delicate negotiations you mentioned inside?" I said. Mac didn't answer. I went on: "If we don't locate the hideout, what happens?"

He moved his shoulders slightly. "The hostages will presumably be killed. If it happens, it will become our duty to track down and remove every man and woman involved. The word must get around—unofficially, of course—that we will not submit to this kind of extortion; and that anyone who tries it, dies."

I drew a long breath. "That'll be one tricky manhunt, sir," I said. "How the hell are we going to identify a bunch of obscure Estebanian *paisanos* once they throw away their guns and go back to their fishing nets, or their sugar cane or maize or whatever they grow on that lousy little island, which probably isn't even called St. Esteban, at least I don't recall seeing the name and I've been looking at maps till I'm cross-eyed."

"It isn't," Mac agreed. "If it becomes important, we'll try to obtain the real name for you. As yet it has not been entrusted to me."

I said, "Security! Everybody going hush-hush about

something I could find out in an hour by getting on a phone and tracking down the birthplace of this Leo Gonzales who worked for Wellington Phipps. Or I could make it real simple and ask Haseltine; he probably sailed with the guy enough to learn where he was born. If everybody wouldn't waste so goddamn much time trying to hide stuff from us—"

"The real location isn't significant right now, is it?"

I said, "With all due respect, sir, how the hell do I know what's significant right now and what isn't?" I Shook my head quickly. "Okay. So we let them die and avenge them; that still won't get Haseltine back his lost Loretta. He won't like it."

"A great many softhearted people won't like it," Mac agreed. "Our allies don't like it very much. But the feeling in Washington, at least at the moment, is that the time has come to put a stop to the growing hostage industry. This is a good test case, since it doesn't balance money against human lives. Even the most dedicated humanitarian idealist isn't going to be able to point out a great many humanitarian advantages to saving the lives of one group of people by sending the Marines to slaughter another, and probably larger, group."

I wasn't really interested in the philosophical gymnastics of a bunch of Washington *politicos*. "And what if we do find the hiding place, sir?"

"Then we will be given a certain period of time in which to effect a rescue," Mac said.

"And deal with the so-called rebels?"

"That will not be required," he said. "At the end of the time-period allowed us, regardless of the territorial rights involved, and regardless of who is or who is not still on the premises, there will be a rather spectacular explosion at the predetermined latitude and longitude. The fireworks will, of course, be nonnuclear and quite inexplicable. We will all be properly horrified at the deaths of all those poor people, innocent and otherwise. But such things happen when relatively primitive, untrained islanders try to cope with modern weapons and explosives they don't understand.'

There was a brief silence. "Wow!" I said softly, at last. "Somebody's getting real tough. I wonder why."

"There are reasons," Mac said. "Unfortunately, it won't last. The Germans tried getting tough once, with those Arab terrorists at the Olympics, remember? Of course, they mismanaged the job atrociously—their marksmanship was hopeless—but the principle was quite correct. Nevertheless, they were severely criticized for even making the attempt, in spite of the obvious fact that the only way to deal with these incidents on a permanent, long-term basis, is to make it absolutely clear that there is no longer any profit, political or financial, to be gained by this type of operation; and that instant and certain death awaits anyone who thinks he can intimidate society as a whole by threatening a few individuals."

I said mildly, just to be arguing: "It may be obvious, but it's apt to be kind of tough on the threatened individuals."

"Of course," Mac agreed, "but in the long run more lives will be lost by yielding to these blackmailers and encouraging others to emulate them, than by putting an end to the racket now by acting instantly and ruthlessly regardless of who gets hurt." He shrugged. "Well, that is theory. In practice, in this particular instance, because of the highly classified political and diplomatic complications involved, the ruthless approach will be used, but in these sentimental times I don't really expect it to set a popular precedent. Unfortunately."

"Yes, sir," I said. "I'm sure that if it were clearly established that any airliner that's hijacked will simply be shot down on the spot, passengers and all, that would cure the disease pretty quickly."

"Precisely," Mac said calmly.

I'd been more or less kidding, but he was perfectly serious. Sometimes he manages to surprise me, even after all these years. On the other hand, come to think of it, he did have a solution that would work if people were willing to pay the price, which was more than anybody else could say…

"So much for international theory," I said. "As far as strictly local practice is concerned, I think I'm going to need Morgan, preferably alive."

Mac frowned. "He may be difficult to produce. Even if we should catch up with him, the local police may feel they have priority, since he has committed murder here."

"Don't tell them," I said. "Just pass the word along the official underground. Haste is imperative. Find him but don't touch him; and tell me, not the cops. I really want him taken alive; and that's a job I guess I can't wish on anybody else, big as the bastard is."

"Very well." Mac hesitated. "Eric. One more thing."

"Yes, sir."

His voice had changed. I wouldn't say it had softened; that would be an exaggeration. But there had been a hint of a change, let's say, in that general direction; and I had a sudden cold feeling somewhere near the diaphragm, because it's a direction in which he seldom moves.

Mac said slowly, "This is a private matter. I'm afraid I have bad news." He stopped, and went on: "A man in my position sometimes has to decide whether or not to maintain the efficiency of an agent in the field by witholding adverse information of a private nature, but... Ah, to hell with it."

Now I knew it was serious. He hardly ever resorts to blasphemy, unlike some people in the organization. I reviewed the possible private matters about which he might have received adverse information.

"Lorna," I said. "She was supposed to be back shortly, you said the other day. She didn't make it."

He nodded. "I was notified earlier this evening. I'm sorry."

"How and where?" I asked.

He shook his head. "You don't want to know."

He was right. I didn't want to know. In our work, it happens in all kinds of places, in all kinds of ways, none pleasant. It was better just to remember a tall woman walking out to board a plane without looking back.

"Thank you for letting me know, sir," I said. "I'll be in

touch when I have something to report."

I stood there for a moment after the big car had driven away. Then I started for the cabin, but stopped. I drew a deep breath and rearranged my face to look, I hoped, cheerful and maybe even a little expectant, like, the face of any man rejoining an attractive woman in a motel room late at night...

19

Harriet had cleaned up the place, neatly rolling up all my charts and maps and snapping around them the rubber band I'd used to hold them before. The long paper cylinder lay on the table by the door. The lady herself, propped up against a pillow, reclined on the sofa in the corner with a partially filled motel glass in her hand.

"I found your bottle," she said, "and there's ice in the kitchenette refrigerator. I'd have made a drink for you, but I wasn't sure you'd trust it, considering what happened the last time I plied you with liquor."

I grinned. "What's the difference? You could have spiked the whole bottle with cyanide while I was outside." I went back into the kitchenette. When I returned, armed with glass and contents, she tucked her long skirt closer around her legs to make room for me on the sofa beside her. "Well, it's been a long time," I said, sitting down.

"That's a cold man you work for," she said.

I said, "Don't change the subject."

She smiled. "All right, Matt. It *has* been a long time. I... sometimes I've kind of wished..."

"What?"

"That I hadn't been quite so fast with those knockout drops that night."

I regarded her for a moment; and took a long drink from my glass and set it aside; and looked at her again. She was a hell of a good-looking woman, with her smooth dark hair and her tanned skin contrasting nicely with the white silk blouse. In some respects, if you considered women as types instead of individual people, she was a lot like another tall woman I'd known recently; but that wasn't a thought I wanted to dwell on tonight. After all, I had serious work to do. Duty called.

"I know what you mean," I said. "I've had some disturbing thoughts along those lines myself, from time to time. I knew damned well you hadn't drowned. You dove overboard before I could tie a brick around your neck. A lead brick."

"You say the sweetest things," she murmured. "I do love men who aren't afraid of a little sentiment."

Smiling, she held out her glass to me, and I set it carefully on the floor beside mine. She held out her arms, and I accepted the invitation and kissed her hard. We both knew where the noses went, and it was really quite a respectable performance. Anybody watching would have sworn there was real passion involved; and maybe there was. It comes in a wide range of flavors, both natural and artificial; and after things progress beyond a certain point it's hard to tell one from the other.

"All right, darling," she whispered at last, "all right, all right, just go turn out the light like a good boy, please, while I... No, damn it, you'll tear... I'll do it, just get that goddamn light!"

Then the light was out and the time for idle chatter was past. I wasn't really a good boy, and she wasn't a good girl, either; and there was apparently a lot of violence in both of us that needed, and found, an outlet. Afterward, we lay for a long time catching up on breathing that had got far behind schedule. Presently she managed a small, rather ragged laugh.

"Oh, dear," she gasped, "oh, dear, and all my life I've tried so hard to be a real lady!"

She moved a little, indicating a desire for freedom, and I let her go. After a moment, the light came back on. I'd rather have remained in the dark. I was feeling slightly ashamed of myself, realizing that I'd done my best to pay her back for that long-ago seduction that had misfired; I guess I'd also been punishing her for something that was not at all her fault—a private grief, and a feeling of guilt because I'd been here doing this instead of paying my respects to the departed in a sober and sincere and conventional way, preferably in church.

I was relieved to see that Harriet seemed to have taken no damage. She was standing, slender and brown and naked, in front of the mirror. Apparently she did her sunbathing nude, since there were no bikini marks in evidence. I had an intriguing mental picture of her fishing boat drifting idly out in the Gulf Stream while the lady charter captain took the sun on the flying bridge without a stitch on. I watched her pull the remaining pins out of her moderately disheveled hair, and shake it loose about her shoulders.

"Well, are you satisfied?" she asked without looking around. "Did you get it out of your system, whatever it was? What did he tell you out there, anyway? You looked like sudden death when you came back in with that frozen grin on your face." When I didn't answer, she said, "Matt."

"What?"

"It's a lousy goddamned game. Can we stop playing it now, please?"

Everything was very quiet. For a moment, I hated her. I mean, we'd been doing fine. It had been a great act, the clever, clever, secret agent laying, in the line of duty, the bright, bright female with useful enemy connections; each principal to the sordid bedroom drama full of devious motives far removed from sex... Well, as far removed from sex as possible. Now she'd gone and spoiled it.

I looked at the slim woman standing there without any clothes on, patting the strands of her loosened hair into place, apparently totally unselfconscious, but nobody was that unselfconscious.

I said, "Harriet, if you're trying to be smart, cut it out. Everybody's been quite smart enough in here tonight, already."

"That's what I mean." She still hadn't turned to look at me. "Your chief coming in here and making elaborate speeches about how he's going to trust me because of my loyalty, for God's sake! That man doesn't even trust himself unless he's standing in front of a mirror where he can keep an eye on himself! Trust, hell! What does he think I am, a child?"

I reached for some garments I'd mislaid. I said, "Nobody's going to think that until you at least put your shirt on, doll."

"Oh, stop it!" she said irritably. "You're not all that virile. At the moment, I'm sure you don't give a damn whether I'm nude or wearing overalls. Why pretend?"

"Okay, I'll stop," I said, "when you stop pretending you're totally unaware that you're standing there raw and there's a man watching you who's just made love to you."

After a moment, she laughed, and turned at last to look at me. "All right, darling, that's a point for you. Toss me that stuff on the floor, will you, and then go make us another drink while I put myself back together…"

When I came from the kitchenette with two reloaded glasses, she was sitting on the edge of the sofa, fully dressed once more, combing her hair. She put the comb away in her purse, took the glass I offered her, and patted the space beside her.

"Games!" she said bitterly as I sat down. "That man's playing games, and you're playing games, and maybe I'm playing games, too, but I'm tired of it. Can we stop it? Who's first? Who grits the teeth and makes with the truth for a change?" When I didn't speak at once, she said, "All right, I'll start. It's a deep, dark plot and you're the plottee. Well, you and a man named Minsk, but you took care of him, so now there's just you."

"Who are the plotters?" I asked. "Besides you, I mean."

"You know who they are. They're some folks who've got word from a long ways off that people there, important people, are tired of keeping a dossier on a skinny gent named Helm. He's taking up too much space in the files. They want to be able to pull the folder and stamp it TERMINATED. Well, there was another termination to be attended to simultaneously, as I just said, and that worked fine, but you managed to slip out from under; and you know how bureaucracies are. Even if the job isn't very important—and I don't suppose all Moscow is trembling with fear of one Matthew Helm—they can't afford to admit failure, once they've started. So Plan Number Two was put into effect, with me as the bait instead of Minsk. Actually, it's just a variation of Plan Number One, the only difference being that originally that little bitch, Renee Schneider, was supposed to gain your confidence and, if required, share your bed here in the Keys, while I was to act the dark villainess you were both trying to bring to justice—until she saw a good chance to lower the boom on you. Now, with Renee out of the picture, I take over the glamor spot, persuading you that I'm just a poor misunderstood lady—really a very lovable type—until I can set you up for a quick, clean kill. There! How's that for letting the hair down, literally as well as figuratively?"

It was fun to watch her work. The theory, of course, was that if she told me how she was planning to kill me, I'd think she was going to stop trying, although that wasn't what she'd said at all.

I said, "Yes, that's about the way we had it figured."

She looked slightly disconcerted. "You did?"

"Why else would you hang around here after the Nassau fiasco, when either of your boats could have had you safe in Cuba in a few hours? Obviously, you were waiting for me. And I'll admit my instinct was to just let you wait and to hell with you; but the powers that be said otherwise. And of course that's why you made a point of letting me know—early on, as Pendleton would have said—that poor little Lacey Rockwell, the real Lacey, was being held alive somewhere. If I started getting too tough you could trot her out as a hostage. But I kind of confused you by not getting tough at all, didn't I? And by springing on you a lot of irrelevant kidnappings you'd had nothing to do with and knew nothing about? But now that you've had time to think, and consult with your secret friends, you've all realized that I'm playing right into your hands, haven't you? All you have to do is tell me where these people are that I'm looking for, and be sure there's a good strong trap awaiting me when I get there. And in the meantime, of course, my suspicions are to be lulled with equal parts of sex and frankness…"

I heard her draw a quick, sharp breath beside me; then she laughed softly. "Oh, dear! When somebody says stop playing games, you really stop, don't you? Well, all right, it's your turn. Say we're going to trap you if we can. What are you going to do about it? Tell the truth now, darling. I did."

"Do?" I said. "I'm going to do what I came here for, of course. Why else would I visit a dame—even sleep with her—who's already tried to kill me twice? I'm going to let myself be trapped."

There was a brief silence. She spoke without looking at me: "You're still being clever. I'm disappointed in you, Matt. I was honest with you."

I said, "Hope to die, Hattie, that's the truth. I've got to find these lousy *ricos* who've gone and got themselves snatched by a bunch of crackpot revolutionaries fighting among themselves. If I have to stick my neck out to do it, well, so be it."

"But you've got some kind of an ace up your sleeve you're not telling me about."

"Sure," I said. "Don't you? If you, and your friends, want to see my hold-out cards, and show me yours, tell me where to go. Not some deserted mangrove key off the Cuban coast, but the real hideout inhabited by the real kidnapers, or at least the real kidnapees. And to make sure you've gone to the trouble of finding the right place, through your Cuban contacts, and aren't just exercising your imaginations at my expense, I'd like to see a little something in the kitty. Tell the boys they're going to have to ante up to see my hand. Let's say Loretta Phipps. One of the others would do, I suppose, but she'll get me off the hook with Haseltine, so I'd rather have her."

"They won't go for it," Harriet said. "It's too simple and straightforward and stupid; they'll be sure you're playing an elaborate trick on them."

I said, "Don't be silly, of course I'm playing a trick on them. I'm tricking them into giving me what I want, the information I need, the information I can't get out of Cuba but they can. And, of course, when it comes time to make the payment, my neck, I'm going to do my best to renege on the deal. I'm kind of fond of my neck and I have every intention of keeping it intact if I can. I mean, that's elementary, doll; they'd know it even if I hadn't told them. The only confusing element is that in this atmosphere of mutual honesty, I did tell them, through you. But okay, suppose I sweeten the kitty a bit, too. Suppose I throw in Morgan, to match Loretta Phipps. Will they go for it then?"

"You've got Morgan?"

"That's what the man took me outside to tell me," I said untruthfully, hoping it would become true before I was called on to produce. "That, and a few other things you weren't supposed to hear."

She hesitated. "Well, you were more or less right in what you said about Morgan," she said slowly. "He went completely haywire when that dumb little girl was killed in Nassau. They were kind of worried about his behavior even before he pulled this crazy, pointless murder tonight. They may be willing to make some kind of a deal for him, just to get him out of circulation before he makes trouble for everybody. I'll try it on them, anyway." She drew a long breath. "I... I hope you know what you're doing, Matt."

"Do you?"

She glanced at me sharply, and laughed. "No, I suppose I really don't. What I really hope is that you're just a cocky, conceited, secret-agent type who thinks he's simply too good to be caught in anybody's traps."

I said, "Set your deadfall and see, sweetheart. The bait is Loretta Phipps. Show me the blonde and I'll follow you anywhere."

Harriet rose and brushed at her skirt and turned to look at me. After a moment, she said: "Matt?"

"Yes?"

"You couldn't possibly be working on the assumption that I'm the ace up your sleeve, could you? That when the chips are down and your life is really in danger I'll come through for you because of what we've been to each other tonight? You couldn't be so fatuously stupid, could you?" She smiled thinly. "No, of course not. Stay here. If you get hungry, have your breakfast at the café up by the road and come right back here, so I'll know where to find you."

I watched the door close behind her, and grimaced at my reflection in the mirror across the room, because of course I could be just that fatuously stupid. It was, after all, one of the only two real cards I had to play: a woman who hated me, and an explosion that would occur at a certain hour at a certain place, if we could find the place.

20

It was a bright, sunny, Florida morning with hardly any wind; a good day to go fishing, I reflected. Leaving my cabin, I wondered how the weather was down along the Cuban coast. I wondered where Harriet had got to and what she was doing there, and with whom. I wondered where Morgan was and how soon somebody would spot him for me and how hard he'd be to take. I wondered if the roadside café associated with the resort—the fancier restaurant down by the water was only open evenings—served any food worth eating.

A moment after entering the joint, I spotted my millionaire Texas playmate perched on a stool at the counter just like an ordinary human being. By the time I saw him, it was too late. He'd already seen me. I couldn't back out quietly and go find a place where I could breakfast undisturbed; besides, Harriet had told me to be here if I wasn't at my cabin. Haseltine waved me to the stool beside him, with a royal flourish.

"I've got the boat you wanted," he said as I sat down. "She's over by Key Largo, a thirty-six-foot express cruiser with diesels you wouldn't believe. The man says she'll do forty with a light tail wind. She cruises all day at thirty-five, but of course she's pretty thirsty at that speed. If you slow her down about ten knots, however, she'll cover four hundred and fifty miles between drinks—just a goddamn floating fuel tank. I have a hunch the designer had a little illegal import-export business in mind when he drew her up. Okay?"

"That's great, Bill," I said. "Can you handle her yourself?"

"Handle, sure. In clear weather, in daylight, I might even be able to find Cuba. But when it comes to all that complicated stuff on board—loran, radar, RDF—I'm lost. A compass and depthfinder are about the extent of my instrument education, *amigo*. Sorry."

"You and me both," I said. "Well, we'll have to scrounge up some kind of a navigator." I hesitated. "Oh, there was a question I wanted to ask you, about Leo Gonzales. Did you ever happen to hear where he was born?"

"Leo?" The big man's brown eyes had suddenly become less friendly, but his voice remained hearty and cheerful: "Gosh, Matt, I don't think I ever did hear where that *hombre* came from. Is it important? I can have it checked… Somebody wants you."

I looked the way he was looking, and saw the pretty girl from the resort office beckoning me to the door. I told Haseltine I'd be right back, and went over.

"I saw you come in here, Mr. Helm," she said. "There's a call for you on the pay phone in the office."

I walked across the way with her, and went into the booth and closed the door behind me. I picked up the instrument with the kind of tenseness you feel when things are getting ready to break and you can't help wondering what the hell's gone wrong, or right.

"Helm, here," I said.

"Ready for your morning exercise, friend?" It was the Miami contact I'd chatted with before but never met. He went on: "Your long-haired acquaintance with the big, strong, strangling hands has just stolen himself a boat. He's heading due south into the Atlantic at flank speed, as we say in the Navy. Point of departure, Duck Key, just east of you. He should be passing Sombrero Light offshore just about now, judging by our last helicopter report. The boys are willing to descend and nail him for you, but they insist on the right to shoot back if shot at. This bring-'em-back-alive stuff is not in their line."

"Choosy chaps, aren't they?" I said. "Describe the boat."

"Eighteen feet. Inboard-outboard. White with red trim. One of those snubnosed, tri-hull jobs I wouldn't want to mess with in a heavy sea—any boat that blunt up front isn't an open-water craft in my book—but of course he's got no heavy seas to worry about today. Checking the manufacturer's specs, we read a top speed in the high thirties with the single outdrive he's got."

"Radio?"

"No radio."

I frowned at the wall of the booth. "What's ahead of him on his present course?"

"The Gulf Stream. Cay Sal Bank. Cuba, if his fuel holds out, but he's burning a lot of gas wide open. Chances are he hasn't got juice enough to get much past Cay Sal, even if he set out with a full tank. He'll have to start rowing after that, assuming he hasn't arranged to meet somebody with better transportation. But that's an assumption I wouldn't want to bet my life on. He most likely wouldn't be taking a little open boat straight out to sea if he hadn't arranged a rendezvous out there, somewhere."

"It looks as if a fast intercept is called for," I said. "I'll see what can be done. Tell your cautious whirlybird friends to keep an eye on him. From a safe distance, of course."

"Don't sneer. There's observation personnel and action personnel. This is a killer we're dealing with, don't forget. The boys didn't sign on to commit suicide."

"Who did?" I said, and hung up.

Haseltine looked up as I came back into the café. "Trouble?" he asked.

I reflected that it was about time for me to turn in my poker face on a new model. Everybody seemed to see through this one.

"Is that boat you've chartered ready to go?" I asked. "And how far is it from here?"

"About sixty miles; and they promised to have her fueled and ready this morning, but I'd better call if you want her right away."

I said, "Never mind, we haven't got time to drive

sixty miles, not to mention getting the boat back here." I hesitated, thinking hard. If Harriet wanted me, she'd just have to wait. I said, "That's your car outside, isn't it? Come on, let's get down to the marina. Right by the lighthouse…"

Driving down there, I worried about the possibility that Harriet might have taken the big outboard; but both her boats were still there. Well, she probably had a car, although I'd never seen it, at least to know it. I was happy to see that the dockmaster was way out on one of the piers, attending to the wants of a visiting cruiser.

I said to Haseltine: "I took a course in stealing cars once, in the line of duty. I hope boat ignition-switches work the same way. If anybody gets nosy, tell them you're Cap'n Hattie's best friend, or deck them, whichever seems more promising."

Stepping down into the boat, I got the cover off the console, revealing an impressive amount of instrumentation. As I'd feared, the keys were missing. I studied the situation briefly. A teak hatch in the console let me get my head under the dashboard. The wiring wasn't complicated. Even an incompetent thief like me could figure it out. I extricated myself briefly, lowered the big motors by means of the machinery provided, and set the manual chokes rather than try to figure out the remote-control switches on the console, thanking the luck that had let me get fairly well acquainted with a motor very similar to these not long ago.

Some tools and wire from Harriet's handy toolbox, and a little concentration, soon had the ignition switches bypassed. A length of wire from one of the batteries in the stern was put into action; and in a moment the two big motors were rumbling and spitting, shaking the fiberglass hull.

"Cast off," I said to Haseltine. "Fast. Here comes trouble."

He dropped the docklines into the boat and jumped down after them. I threw the motors in gear, as the dockmaster came running toward us, shouting something. The boat began to move. I waved at the running man in a friendly fashion, and fed more gas to the big outboards. Then we were heading out the slot between the breakwaters; and the dockmaster had stopped running and stood looking after us irresolutely. I gave him another brotherly wave.

"Get back there and set those chokes in running position before the mills flood out on us, will you?" I said to Haseltine. He disappeared behind me; and the ragged sound of the motors became smooth and even. I said, "Okay, that's fine. Now let's see what our girl friend's got here. Hang on, I'm firing stage one."

In spite of the warning, Haseltine, returning to the console, almost got left behind as I eased the throttles forward. He had to grab the back of the starboard seat to catch himself, fighting the thrust as the big boat lifted onto plane and started to go. I waited until he was safe in the chair, and shoved the levers clear to the stops. If there were any tricks to running Harriet's souped-up escape vessel at full throttle, I'd better learn them here in sheltered water, rather than waiting until we were out in the open Atlantic. The resulting noise was impressive, and the blast of air was fierce, but there seemed to be no serious control problems.

"Jesus!" Haseltine yelled over the racket. "What the hell kind of a Q-ship is this, anyway?"

"Fifty knots, the lady said. I guess she wasn't lying." I put my mouth close to his ear without taking my attention off the water ahead. "Oh, I forgot to ask. Is it against your tribal principles to be shot at, you quarter-ass Kiowa?"

He grinned, his big teeth white in his brown face. "Go to hell," he shouted, "you dumb Svenska squarehead. Watch the tide under the bridge now—"

We'd come roaring around the end of Key Vaca, named, I'd been told, after the sea cow or manatee. The long bridge of the Overseas Highway to Key West was ahead. I aimed the bow at one of the arches. Some workmen painting a railing stopped to stare at the three-thousand-pound projectile hurtling toward them. There was a clap of sound as the exhausts bounced back at us from the arch, and a funny little shimmy as the tidal currents tried to throw us off course and failed. Then we were out of the Gulf of Mexico. The broad Atlantic was ahead, and the spidery framework of Sombrero Light, with which I'd become acquainted on a previous visit to the area in more pleasant company, now dead, but that was nothing to think about now...

The big twin outboards ate up the five miles to the lighthouse in spectacular fashion. Beyond, the water

soon turned from light to dark blue. It's never really
smooth out in the Gulf Stream; and at this speed, it was
like driving a car with four flat tires down a street full of
potholes. We were both standing, to take the shocks with
our legs. Haseltine, clinging to the windshield railing
with one hand, poked me with the other and jerked his
thumb upwards.

I glanced up to see a helicopter hanging over us. When
they saw me looking, they pulled ahead, slightly off to
starboard. I swung that way, and read the course off the
compass: 193°, a little west of south. The lighthouse was
rapidly getting smaller astern. There was nothing ahead at
first, just the blue, sunlit waters of the Stream. After about
half an hour, however, I became aware of a recurrent little
flash of spray dead ahead, like a breaking wave in the
distance, only the waves weren't breaking today.

·Gradually, the fleeing boat became clearly visible.
After a while, I could even make out the wildly blowing
long dark hair of the steersman. When we were within
half a mile, I pulled back on the throttles until we were
just holding our own; this cut the decibels from behind to
where communication was possible after a fashion.

I said, "We need that man alive. Never mind the details,
but he figures in a deal I think you'll approve. You take
the wheel. Give me a little time to get ready; then pull on
past and cut across his bow. Give yourself room enough
so you can swing clear around and put her alongside just
as he hits our wake. If he's got a gun, as he probably does,
that ought to throw his aim off, we hope. Come along the

starboard side where he's sitting. When I yell, sheer off and give her the gun. Now take over…"

I slid from behind the wheel as he took it and, bracing myself in the boat, studied the tools available, but I'd already made my plan, such as it was. Boarding Morgan's boat to take him barehanded might be dramatic, but it was kind of silly. I'd already charged a gun once in the course of this operation; twice would be straining my luck. I got the big flying gaff from the rack to port.

Freshwater fishermen use a net, as a rule, to bring their fish aboard; and for some reason, salmon fishermen seem to pride themselves on also netting their trophies unmarred, even in salt water; but just about every other ocean angler after fish of any size employs a gaff: a big, sharp, metal hook with a long handle. The difference between a fixed gaff and a flying gaff is that on the latter, the gaff hook has an eye and a sturdy rope, and the handle can be removed, in the heat of action, after the hook goes home. This is for truly big fish, the kind you don't just casually lift aboard, but hoist over the side with a block and tackle.

Harriet's flying gaff was a wicked-looking implement with a handle almost eight feet long. It was equipped with a stout new line, which I coiled after making the end fast to a cleat near the boat's transom.

"Company," Haseltine's voice said, sounding quite calm about it. "Dead ahead. Coming fast. I'd judge their intentions are hostile."

I looked up. Still a couple of miles off was a big

white sportfisherman heading straight for us. Even at the distance, I could see that she was throwing a bow wave like a destroyer. I laid the gaff carefully on the floor—excuse me, cockpit sole—and steadied myself against the console.

"Okay, let's take him before they get here," I said.

The oversized outboards aft began to scream once more. Haseltine, for a man with Plains Indian blood in his veins, was a surprisingly good helmsman, better than I was in spite of my seagoing Viking ancestry. So much for heredity. I clung to the windshield handrail and watched him ease up on the smaller craft skillfully. Morgan had, of course, spotted us by now; he kept looking back, long hair blowing, and hammering at his single throttle in a futile, angry, frustrated sort of way. We passed about fifty yards to his port, and he produced the expected pistol and took a couple of wild shots at us, which we could afford to ignore at that range, the way both boats were bouncing.

Well ahead, Haseltine swung the wheel hard right, cutting across the smaller boat's bow and coming clear around to the same course once more. His timing was beautiful. Jockeying wheel and throttles nicely, he laid us right alongside just as both boats smacked hard into the big wake we'd laid across Morgan's path.

The big man was just rising to take aim when we hit; I could see his tough, craggy face intent behind the pistol, contrasting oddly with the long, girlish hair. Then his boat lurched, throwing him off balance. Well, he'd already had the two shots I'd promised Renee Schneider I'd allow him. I swung the eight-foot gaff between the boats and socked it into his shoulder. I twisted and jerked to get the handle free.

"Now!" I yelled.

Haseltine swung the wheel and hit the throttles. The boats separated. The rope came tight; the big steel meat hook took the strain; and Morgan screamed as he was yanked bodily out of his craft into the sea.

21

I was asleep, dreaming of an open boat far offshore, with no land in sight, being pursued by a much larger sportfishing vessel that was not, I knew, controlled by sportsmen or engaged in fishing. One of the three men on board the smaller boat was unconscious, soaking wet and, unlikely though it might seem, bleeding profusely from a steel hook in the shoulder. In my dream I was kneeling beside him trying to remove the gaff and plug the hole, at least temporarily. The man at the boat's helm was whistling-an off-key tune, glancing back every now and then at the vessel astern.

"Let me know when I can open her up," this one said.

"I just don't want the bastard to bleed to death," I said, in my dream.

"That's what I like about you, Helm," he said, "your tender, humanitarian impulses."

"How are they doing back there?"

"Not to worry, *amigo*. That thing's fifty feet long. Nobody's going to drive a hull that big much over twenty-five knots, not with any normal civilian powerplants, they aren't. We can play with her all day; but your chopper friends are getting nervous up ahead. I think they want to take the package off our hands, but we'll need a little time and space to make the transfer."

I said, "Okay, I've got him patched up, more or less. Cut loose your Texas wolf…"

As Haseltine shoved the throttles forward, in my dream, there was a loud hammering sound like, maybe, an overstrained powerplant tearing itself apart. Then the dream faded. I sat up groggily in my bed in my now fairly familiar resort cabin, remembering that nothing had happened to the motors. The pursuing boat had turned away when it became obvious that we could outrun it easily. There had been a tricky helicopter bit like in the movies, with a sling lowered from a winch, and Morgan, still unconscious—I'd had to rap him over the head with the billy club Harriet kept handy for subduing big fish— had disappeared skyward, to be repaired and maintained somewhere in breathing condition, we hoped, until needed. The loud knock on the cabin door came again.

"Mr. Helm?"

I found my snubnosed revolver and dropped it into my pants pocket. With my hand on it, I crossed the room and opened the door. A small, tanned boy in ragged shorts and sneakers stood there, holding out an envelope.

"Helm, Cabin Twenty-six?" he said. "For you?"

I took the envelope and gave him a quarter and closed the door. It was a cheap, small envelope, probably saturated with contact poison and crammed full of tarantulas eager to insert their lethal weapons in human flesh. I opened it anyway. Inside was a small visiting card. On the front was a name: *Paul Martin Manderfield*. On the back, neatly written in ink, were two words: *Salty Dog*.

I frowned at the card, thoughtfully. I'd expected some kind of summons or invitation, of course—that was the whole point of the exercise—but I'd kind of assumed it would be delivered by Harriet. This was better, I decided. We were getting the children and amateurs off the street. Pros were dealing with pros now; and the other party to the negotiations, whoever he might be, was making this clear to me. Good for him.

I looked at my watch. It was three o'clock in the afternoon. I was glad I'd taken the opportunity to lie down on the bed and grab a little sleep after cleaning and refueling the boat and making up some suitable lies for the dock-master. There might be a busy night ahead. Haseltine should have his chartered express cruiser here soon, if he hadn't put her on the mud or ripped her open on a coral head; and he probably hadn't. Although I still objected to the guy in principle, I had to admit that he seemed to be a pretty competent seaman, which was what counted here. I could always find some congenial landlubber to pal around with afterwards.

My pretty girl friend was at the desk in the office when I came in. "Yes, Mr. Helm?" she said.

"Is there by any chance a place around here called Salty Dog?" I asked.

"Why, yes," she said. "About five miles east, at the other end of the island. The Salty Dog Lodge, Bar, and Restaurant."

"Any good?"

"Well," she said judiciously, "they won't poison you, but you can get better food and liquor right here, or maybe I'm prejudiced."

I said, "With a name like that, I'd better go take a look at the joint, just the same. Salty Dog, for God's sake."

Back in the rental car, I examined the visiting card again. Unlike the inexpensive envelope in which it had come, it was very high class, engraved yet. The name, Manderfield, meant nothing to me. I suppose I could have used the telephone to find out if it meant something to somebody else, but I was getting a bit tired of the elaborate organizational stuff. Helicopters, for God's sake; and when the chips were really down, you still had to do the job with a simple steel hook and a length of rope while the fancy goddamn whirlybird fluttered around the sky like a helpless sparrow…

The Salty Dog Lodge had its main facilities right on the busy highway. Parking nearby, I got a glimpse of rows of cabins behind the headquarters building, running down to a small marina installation on the water. The restaurant was dark after the bright sunshine outside. The bar was in the far left corner. I could just make out a lone male customer talking to the barman. I moved that way, parked myself on a stool, and waited for somebody to notice me. After a while, the bartender moved my way.

"Yes, sir?"

"I'm looking," I said, "for a martini and a Mr. Manderfield."

"I'm Manderfield," said the other customer. "Let's be comfortable at a table, Mr. Helm. Joe will bring your drink… And another for me, Joe, please."

My eyes were getting used to the dusk; and I got a good look at him as we went through the business of offering each other a choice of chairs, as if it mattered. He was a neat, compact, medium-sized, middle-aged man in good shape, with the usual Florida businessman's tan. He was wearing light slacks and a gaudy sports shirt. His dark hair was streaked with gray, smoothly parted and combed; and he wore dark prescription glasses with strong bifocal segments that gave him an odd, four-eyed look. It was hard to feel menaced by a gent with bifocals, but I don't suppose weak eyes are necessarily an indication of good moral character.

Having got the seating problem worked out to everybody's satisfaction, we waited for the barman to produce our drinks. When they came, I tasted mine without hesitation. Manderfield had deliberately given me plenty of opportunity to have the place covered; there wouldn't be any monkey business here. In a sense, we were operating under a flag of truce—not that it couldn't be violated; but the violation, if any, wouldn't be anything as obvious and stupid as a Mickey Finn.

"You weren't very nice to our Mr. Morgan this morning," Manderfield said abruptly.

Good boy. No fancy double-talk or elaborate

introductions; and who needed introductions, anyway? He knew me and I knew him. That is, I'd never met him before, or heard his name, but I'd met a dozen like him, all professionals. I could have had the dossier read to me over the phone, but I wouldn't have learned anything I didn't already know, aside from a few meaningless details. I could spot a graduate of that particular finishing school across any street in the world.

"Mr. Morgan wasn't very nice to our Mr. Pendleton last night," I said.

"We were given to understand, by a certain lady, that you already had Morgan in custody. Imagine our surprise when he called this morning requesting a rendezvous at sea."

I shrugged. "Sometimes I bend the truth a little. It's a terrible habit I have," I said. "Anyway, we've got him now."

"He's really of very little importance, Mr. Helm. These muscle-men are all expendable, you know that."

"Thanks a lot," I said.

"Ah, but you are a little more than just a muscle-man, aren't you, sir?"

"It's kind of you to say so." After a moment, I said, "So Morgan is of no value to you. Too bad. After all the trouble we went to to catch him, too."

Manderfield laughed. "You pin me down, sir. Is one not permitted a bit of bargaining? Actually, we do have a slight interest in Mr. Morgan. Or at least in Mr. Morgan's silence."

"I thought you might," I said. "Of course, the guy

went ape about the girl who got killed, the way no good muscle-man should. He went hunting on his own to avenge her, interfering with some plans of yours; so there's also a question of making an example of him for discipline's sake. I mean, you might have condoned his going after me independently if he'd been successful; but the way he flipped, strangled the wrong man, changed his mind about killing me, and ran off with the corpse…" I shrugged. "A guy like that, you just can't afford to keep around any longer, can you?"

Manderfield smiled without humor. "How do you explain his erratic behavior, Mr. Helm?"

"It's the great weakness of your system," I said. "Your boys and girls are great, operating under detailed orders, but they don't do too well thinking for themselves. And when one of them tries to buck the machinery that made him, he's lost and he knows it. Morgan knew he was being a very naughty boy, satisfying his own human thirst for revenge. Lenin, Marx, and Stalin were all breathing down his neck as he stood there waiting to get his big hands around my neck. He knew that he was betraying socialist peoples everywhere for purely bourgeois emotional reasons. When Pendleton blundered in on him, he cracked, committed murder unnecessarily, and then, driven by guilt, decided to atone by cleaning up after himself and surrendering to the great mother machine again to take the punishment he knew he deserved."

"You seem to fancy yourself as a psychologist, Mr. Helm," Manderfield said after a moment's pause. "I think your analysis of our agents as mechanized automatons incapable of independent thought will cause you trouble one day, but that's no concern of mine. As a self-styled psychologist, can you tell me my motives in asking you to this meeting?"

"Sure," I said. "You want Morgan, mildly. You want to talk with me to see if you can figure out what I'm up to. The lady's report probably left you slightly confused. It was meant to."

Manderfield smiled. I decided that, pro or no pro, he wasn't a guy I was ever going to like very much. Some people's smiles are like that.

"Your record is impressive, sir," he said. "But you can hardly call it a record of self-sacrificing nobility. You can hardly expect us to believe that you're offering us your life in return for the lives of some people you don't even know, which is roughly what you seem to be saying."

I shook my head. "Not at all. What I'm offering you is a crack at my life. There's a difference."

"That means you expect to trick us somehow."

I said irritably, "Hell, that's what I told Hattie; didn't she pass it along? Sure I expect to trick you. It's just a question of who's got the best tricks."

"You're bluffing, Mr. Helm. You're trying to get something for nothing."

"Aren't we all?"

"You want a number of people rather badly. We want Morgan, as you say, just mildly. Since we've been assigned you, and failure is not encouraged, we'd like to get you, but it's hardly an obsession with us. There will be other times. On the whole, it doesn't put you in a very strong bargaining position, does it, sir?"

I said, "You're right up to a point. However, there's also the fact that, now that it's been called to your attention, you'd like to see this melodramatic foolishness that's being perpetrated, or at least assisted, by your allies to the south, stopped before it leads to serious trouble, trouble nobody wants around here right now."

"That's wishful thinking, Mr. Helm. We don't tell the Cubans their business, and they don't tell us ours." He grimaced. "Well, that's not entirely true. Unfortunately, like many recent converts, they take their revolutionary principles very seriously and grimly. One gets a little tired of being lectured on points of doctrine by bearded fanatics who seem to feel that Communism is their own private island invention..." Manderfield shook his head quickly, and laughed. "But that is beside the point, isn't it, sir? The point is that you're trying to claim a community of interest between us that does not, in fact, exist. Why should we care how many idiot self-styled Caribbean patriots are permitted to indulge in their gaudy antics from bases along the Cuban coast? Why?"

He was angry now, but not at me; and I realized that I'd won. He'd received orders that he didn't like. He was just taking the opportunity to gripe about them under the guise of bargaining. I didn't say anything. Manderfield gestured to the bartender, and there was silence at the table, and in the room, while the new drinks were being prepared. The only sound was the steady rumble of traffic on the Overseas Highway outside. The bartender named Joe removed our empty glasses and set full ones in their places.

"Mr. Helm," said Manderfield.

"Yes?"

"You should be at Little Grass Key, six miles due north of the Two-Mile-Channel Bridge, at exactly six o'clock. Six and six, that should be easy to remember. Make your approach from the west side of the key; there's water there. Use the open boat you used this morning. Captain Robinson says it will not be necessary to hotwire it again, whatever that may mean. Spare keys are taped under the dashboard."

"I know," I said. "I found them when I was changing the wiring back where it belonged."

"Your escort vessel, if any, must stay at least a mile away. We'll maintain the same distance. Captain Robinson, and a lady named Phipps, will be awaiting you on the island, which despite its name is little more than a sand-spit. You will take them aboard, and leave Mr. Morgan in their place." He hesitated. "I do not approve of this bargain, Mr. Helm, and see no point in it, but as you say, we are not permitted to think for ourselves. We simply follow orders…"

22

As I eased Harriet's big outboard out of the harbor again, alone in the boat this time, I made note of the fact that the light breeze was blowing from the general direction of Cuba, but at the moment I wasn't concerned with the largest island in the Greater Antilles. My immediate concern was a minor sandspit called Little Grass Key; but first, preferably without putting any dents in it, I had to get my borrowed craft a mile or so down the shore to a private dock, where my cargo awaited me.

It was all very complicated; and it had involved lengthy phone consultations to work out the intricate details. God knows how the undercover professions ever managed before the invention of the telephone—maybe that's why we don't hear much of master spies antedating Alex G. Bell. The evening's plan was a masterpiece of tricky timing, and we all had our watches and brains synchronized to the millisecond; and all it would take would be a slight change in weather, or a minor human error or mechanical malfunction, to throw the whole schedule haywire. On the other hand, maybe it would actually work out as planned, this time. I'd never seen it happen, but it might.

I switched on the depthfinder. This was a square box mounted in a bracket to starboard of the motor controls, with a big dial. Behind the dial was some kind of a spinning light that somehow, don't ask me how, made a red flash at the depth determined by the electronic gremlins inside the box. At the moment, it read five feet, not a hell of a lot of water as oceans go; but then, there generally isn't much on the Gulf of Mexico side of the Keys, where you can be fishing out of sight of land in water so shallow that you've got to push yourself along with the pole because there isn't depth enough to run the motors. Well, there's also the consideration that a silent pole doesn't spook fish the way a noisy motor does…

It was a secluded, dredged harbor protected by a stone breakwater. Coming through the narrow entrance, I recognized the white Ford station wagon from its description, and headed for the dock at which it was parked, below a luxurious residence surrounded by palm trees, with a big swimming pool nearby. I wondered why anybody with that much money would get mixed up with a bunch of disreputable characters like us. Just to see if I could do it—I'd never had a chance to play with a twin-motor rig before—I got the boat turned around by backing the port screw while running the starboard one forward. It worked, making me feel nautical as hell, a real sea dog.

By the time I'd laid the boat alongside the dock, heading out, a man had come down from the car to take my lines. Another man brought Morgan. His right arm and shoulder were pretty well immobilized. He seemed to be fairly heavily doped, which was fine with me.

"Better put this on him so he won't be so conspicuous," Morgan's baby-sitter said.

I took the jacket he handed down. Morgan allowed me to drape it over him without protest. He still was a big, formidable-looking specimen, but the switch had been turned off. I reminded myself not to take for granted that it would stay off indefinitely. I parked him in the starboard chair behind the console, and went back to retrieve my lines—well, Harriet's lines.

The man who'd brought Morgan said, "I'm Brent." He was tall and young, with crisp red hair and sideburns. His voice was familiar. He was the Miami contact with whom I'd already talked a number of times on the phone. Now, according to the evening's master plan, he was taking a more active part in the operation. Apparently he had some unique qualifications that made him a logical choice.

"Good for you," I said. "But you'd better get over there fast. Haseltine's waiting for a navigator, but he's not the patient type. You can't miss the boat. If it looks as if it's breaking the sound barrier tied to the dock, you've got the right bucket."

Brent hesitated, and said: "I'll get you within a mile of Little Grass Key. Just stick in our wake. You'll have to make the final approach yourself, of course, according to instructions. Just remember one thing: if you have to blast out of there fast for any reason, get her up on plane and keep her there. You can ride that thing on a heavy dew as long as you keep her skimming along the top; but if you get cautious and slow down, she'll settle and hit." He cleared his throat in an embarrassed way. "Sorry, Eric, I don't mean to be telling you things you already know, but this shallow-water boating's kind of a specialized deal."

I grinned. "Where boats are concerned, *amigo*, I'm a hell of a good horseman. Keep telling me. And keep your fingers crossed."

The station wagon had already disappeared inland by the time I'd eased the outboard past the breakwater. After getting well clear of shore, I swung westwards, taking it slowly. I didn't have long to wait. Just as I was coming opposite the conspicuous tower of Faro Blanco once more, a shiny red power cruiser emerged from the marina. She was a rakish job that seemed to be designed for an air speed of several hundred knots, instead of a measly forty. The cabin windshield had a slant like that of a fast sports car, and the flying bridge above continued this racy, sloping, motif. By the time all the streamlining had been taken care of, the whole superstructure had wound up so far aft that there was hardly room for a cockpit in the stern. On the mahogany transom, lettered in gold, was the name *Red Baron*.

The cruiser swung away to the west ahead of me and picked up speed. She was close enough, now, that I could hear the impressive rumble of the big twin diesels driving her. The sound was lost as I opened up my two outboards to follow, watching the figures on the flying bridge up ahead. Haseltine had the wheel, and Brent was just standing by, occasionally studying the water ahead through his binoculars, and once in a while indicating a slight change of course.

It was a beautiful evening coming up, almost flat calm now, but I couldn't really appreciate it, busy holding my station astern. I was careful to stay precisely in the flat central portion of the cruiser's wake. For one thing, it was bouncy off the sides, and for another, Brent soon began taking us through some pretty thin water. Every so often our big stern waves would break like surf on shoals no more than ankle deep, just off our course...

The island far ahead seemed to be just another strip of sand upon which a couple of hunks of driftwood had stranded during some past storm. I'll admit that I was too preoccupied with my nautical duties to realize what I was seeing until the larger boat ahead suddenly squatted, losing speed. I hauled back on my throttles and let the outboard glide alongside. Brent leaned over the flying-bridge railing.

"There's the enemy line of battle," he said, pointing ahead. Way over there, beyond the islet, lay the fifty-footer I'd seen before, its silhouette reflected in the calm water. Brent said, "Okay, it's all yours, Eric. Run straight west a quarter-mile. There's a channel leading south; take it. When you're exactly opposite them, head in slowly. Use the power tilts; raise the props to just below the surface. Don't go in too far. There's no need. It's all solid bottom, good wading. Just don't step on any stingrays."

"Thanks," I said. "I wasn't really planning to go wading, but thanks a lot."

As I've said, the Florida Keys are really a wonderful place once you get away from them in a boat. We were lying in still, clear water over a clean sandy bottom; and all around was a fairyland of islands and islets, apparently uninhabited except by birds. The sky in the west promised a glorious sunset shortly.

Morgan said, "I'll kill him. I'll kill the murdering sonofabitch. Renee…"

His voice trailed off. He wasn't looking at me. He didn't seem to be looking at anything in particular. Even my motion to grasp the throttles and ease them forward didn't cause his vacant stare to shift noticeably. We moved ahead almost without sound, the motors ticking over slowly. I stood up so I could read the water the way I'd been taught by a fishing guide. You navigate by the color down there. Dark blue is deep water, light blue-green is shallow, and white means you get out and push.

I found the darker channel leading north Brent had told me to look for, and changed course to follow it. Behind me, the rakish *Red Baron* lay motionless on the mirror-like surface. Over to the west was the big, white sportfisherman. I could see a figure up in the tall tuna-tower, and a glint of glass from binoculars watching me. I wondered if Manderfield himself was up there; or if perhaps he didn't like such high, precarious perches. I'm not very fond of them myself.

Morgan said, "A man is not a machine discipline shit. The black man was only following orders get the white goddamn bastard fuck-your lousy Russky discipline…"

Renee Schneider had described him as a thug, but Renee had been lying for effect. Paul Martin Manderfield had called him an expendable muscle-man, but Manderfield had been engaged in horsetrading of sorts. It occurred to me that I didn't know what kind of a man this vengeful Morgan was. I didn't even know if Morgan was his first name, his last, or a code name. I remembered something I'd said to Ramsay Pendleton, about leaving people behind to die. Well, Pendleton had got behind and now Morgan was going to be left.

I said, "Cut it out, friend. I'm not going to turn my back on you, and you can't take me one-handed anyway, so let's dispense with the delirious act, shall we?"

After a moment, Morgan drew a long breath and grinned briefly. "Well, it was worth a try. What happens now?"

"You get your feet wet," I said. "Satisfy my curiosity. Why the long hair?"

"Menace," he said. "It scares people to think of a professional hitman with long, girlish hair. Try it some time." After a moment, he said, "I wasn't expecting that lousy gaff. You took me by surprise. I'm not that easy. You know that."

It was a relief, in a way. Now I knew. Whatever his feeling for Renee Schneider had been, he was just another tough one, full of pride, concerned lest I downrate him because he hadn't put up a very good fight.

"Sure," I said. "Sure, I know that."

The little islet drew abeam. The chunks of stranded driftwood on the sand had become two human beings, standing, one dressed in white, the other in khaki. Even though Manderfield had said she'd be there, I was very glad to see Harriet; I was going to need her badly before this night was over. I threw the levers into neutral and, looking astern, hit the tilt switches and watched the big motors tip up until the propellers were barely submerged. I engaged the gears once more and made the turn toward the key. The steering was harder with the mills angled like that. The water got paler and shallower ahead.

"That's far enough. We can make it. Don't get my motors full of sand."

That was Harriet's voice. I cut the power and watched the two of them wade toward me. Harriet's companion seemed to be wearing rather elaborate white satin pajamas of some kind, designed more for a boudoir than a beach, let alone a wading party. Preserving the fragile, fancy garment didn't seem to concern her much, perhaps because—as I could see when she got closer—it had been wet before and was pretty well decorated with mud and sand. She was a nicely shaped lady with a face that was close to beautiful in a pert, girlish way; and short, dark hair.

As Harriet reached the boat and grasped the gunwale, I put my sneakered foot on her fingers, not hard. "What the hell are you trying to pull, sweetheart?" I asked.

She looked up at me and laughed. "You asked for a

female Phipps, didn't you? Well, you've got one. What are you complaining about? All you wanted was a token to show we knew the right place, wasn't it?"

I studied her smiling face for a moment, and grinned. She'd put one over on me, and that was fine. It got me off the hook. Now I wouldn't have to feel badly about putting one over on her.

"Sure," I said, removing my foot. "Welcome aboard, Captain Robinson. Give Mrs. Phipps a hand, will you, while I keep an eye on our male guest, here... Okay, Morgan. Over you go."

A moment later we were backing cautiously out of the shallows with Harriet at the controls, leaving Morgan standing in knee-deep water. Presently, he turned and started wading slowly toward the island. There was no place else for him to go.

23

I stood in the cockpit of the express cruiser looking through the binoculars I'd borrowed from Brent; standard, big, seagoing 7x50s. Harriet's open boat was now towing astern, squatting a little as *Red Baron* picked up speed. Beyond it, Little Grass Key was getting smaller in the distance. Back there, an outboard dinghy with one man on board was just receiving a second passenger. I watched the small boat turn and head toward the big white fishing vessel waiting in deeper water.

"What are you looking at?"

It was the voice of Mrs. Wellington Phipps, the darkhaired mother of Haseltine's beautiful blonde Loretta. I turned. She didn't look like anybody's mother. She looked like an attractive kid who'd been playing on the beach, with her grubby satin pajamas and short, tousled hair. I was quite sure, now, that I'd never seen any movie in which she'd played. I'd have remembered her.

It occurred to me that I'd arranged things very badly.

If I'd been truly smart, I'd have worked out a plan that would let me be marooned on a desert island with Mrs. Phipps, instead of giving the experience to Harriet, who probably hadn't appreciated it. Of course, I hadn't known this particular lady would be present, but never mind that.

Aside from the fact that she had a husband, assuming that he was still alive, there was only one thing about her that bothered me slightly: a funny little constraint she'd shown upon greeting Haseltine, that had been returned in kind. Well, prospective sons-in-law often had mixed feelings about prospective mothers-in-law, and vice versa.

I said, speaking loudly, as she had, to make my voice carry over the thunder of the diesels: "I wanted to see if they'd shoot him there or wait until they got him offshore where they could dispose of him directly without witnesses."

Her eyes widened. "Shoot him? Are you joking?"

I shook my head. "That's a dead man, Mrs. Phipps. He may have, a couple of hours to live if they decide to wait until dark, but no more."

"But if he was valuable enough that they agreed to this exchange to get him back—"

I said, "They wanted him back so they could shoot him, that's all. For one thing, in our hands, alive, he might eventually have been persuaded to talk about things he shouldn't. For another, there's a disciplinary problem involved. But actually, they didn't want him back very badly. He's really just a piece in a very complicated chess game, Mrs. Phipps. We all are."

"But you turned him over to them, knowing he'd be killed?"

I was disappointed in her. It was the same old illogical, automatic-humanitarian reflex. You must never allow anybody to die, even though keeping that one individual alive may cost a dozen other lives.

I said, "I had a choice. A bunch of innocent people somewhere along the coast of Cuba, or one professional killer with very recent blood on his hands. If you think I chose wrong, let me know. I can have them turn this boat around and maybe intercept that dinghy before it gets back to the mother ship. Say the word, Mrs. Phipps." There was a little silence. When she didn't speak, I said, "Excuse me, I'd better get these glasses up to our navigator before he runs us aground without them…"

When I climbed back down the mahogany ladder to the cockpit, she'd gone inside the cabin. I slid back the door to join her, and stopped inside, and whistled softly.

"Exactly," said Amanda, Phipps. "A forty-knot love-nest complete with bed and bar. Help yourself to a drink. I guess it's on the house, and I do mean house. Did you ever see such a floating bordello?"

The cabin was done in red leather and gold, with carpet to the ankles. I waded through the deep nylon to the red-leather-covered bar, wet down some ice with whiskey since that was what was handy, and joined the lady on the curving leather settee that half-surrounded a low cocktail table—black marble, no less. On the credit side, I had to admit that the sound insulation was good. In here the big motors made only a distant rumble and vibration. We could talk without raising our voices.

"I'm sorry," Amanda said. "What I said out there was stupid. Forgive me."

"It takes a little getting used to," I said. "It's a different world, with a different set of values. Pretty soon, we hope, we'll have you back in your own tidy universe where each and every human life is priceless." I drank from my glass and changed the subject: "Actually, this glamor-barge won't do forty knots with a full load of fuel. Bill is very disappointed. He's going to sue the guy from whom he chartered her. Thirty-six was the best he could get, bringing her down from Key Largo."

"I bet he will sue, too," Amanda said. "Nobody takes advantage of Big Bill Haseltine. But nobody."

I glanced at her. "What's the trouble between you two, or shouldn't I ask?"

"Does it matter? It's my daughter he's courting, not me." Her voice was stiff and formal. Then she smiled abruptly. It was a wonderful smile; and the fact that she'd undoubtedly perfected it in front of a mirror years ago, and used it professionally in front of the cameras, didn't make it a bit less breathtaking. It made you forget she was a woman with a grown daughter, not to mention, once again, the husband. I found myself wondering if it was really necessary to rescue Mr. Wellington Phipps. She said, "I'm sorry again, Mr. Helm. I didn't mean to be stuffy. I can't tell you what the trouble is. It's Bill's business. Ask him."

"Sure, and get my nose punched," I said. "I've got enough Haseltine trouble now, thanks, without asking the guy embarrassing questions about matters that are none of my business. Or are they?"

"They aren't." Amanda hesitated, and said, "You don't have to keep me company, you know. I mean, I appreciate the gesture, but shouldn't you be up there—" she gestured toward the flying bridge overhead, "—making with the sextants and parallel rulers and stuff? Hattie says you're the man in charge of everything, a very important and violent person."

I said, "The lady to whom you refer is a prejudiced source of information. As for my climbing up to that seagoing electronics lab—you never in your life saw so many screens and switches and dials on one lousy little yacht—the three of them are having the time of their lives navigating up a storm, checking all the complicated playthings before it gets dark. If I stay clear away, they may never discover that I don't know what the hell it's all about. You'll keep my secret, won't you, Mrs. Phipps?"

She laughed softly. "I know what you mean. After all the time I've spent on Buster's boats—that's my husband, you know—I still have a hard time remembering which is port. It *is* left, isn't it?"

"Uhuh, and the other side is called starboard, I think. At least that's what somebody told me once, I forget who." I noticed that she was absently pulling some damp satin away from her knee, as if she found it uncomfortable. I said, "If you're cold, maybe we can find you some dry clothes. I don't know what's on board this luxury liner, but I can take a look—"

"Oh, no, you don't!" she said quickly.

"What's the matter?"

She gave me that heart-stopping smile again. "Well, maybe you've heard I was in the movies once," she said. "Jungle epics were my forte. I was the queen of the shipwreck sagas. As soon as the wind-machines revved up and the hurricane started howling, they'd call for Amanda Mayne. I got dunked in every phony ocean in Hollywood, and some real ones—being marooned, today, was old stuff to me. And do you know, Mr. Helm, every goddamn time I crawled ashore on that same old South Seas island in my sexily tattered dress, looking, if I may say so, rather fetching, along would come the lousy hero and, quick as a wink, produce somebody's big, dirty old pants for me to climb into. I tell you, I evolved some fancy theories about the sex lives of those Hollywood producers and directors. Obviously, they were all queer for women in oversized male clothing, the grubbier the better. Don't you start doing it. I'm perfectly happy in my own beatup pajamas, thanks— although I'll admit that the next time I'm kidnaped I'll give some consideration to sleeping in my jeans."

"Do you want to tell me about it?"

"My dear man, of course I want to tell you about it. I'll be telling it at cocktail parties for the rest of my life; I'd better start getting into practice…" She stopped. When she spoke again, the lightness was gone from her voice. "Mr. Helm."

"What?"

"What are the chances?"

"Of bringing them out?" I asked. She nodded. I said, "I don't know yet. The data aren't all in, but don't get your hopes up too far. It's going to be a close one. Everybody's being clever as hell. The final result will depend on who turns out to have been cleverest."

"I want to come along. I don't want to be parked somewhere safe, waiting."

I grinned. "That's good, because as it happens I neglected to make provisions for parking you—or your daughter, whom I was really expecting—somewhere safe."

She was silent for a moment; then she said softly, "Mr. Helm, I love that curly-haired, sea-crazy sonofabitch I'm married to. Get him out for me, please. I'll spend the rest of my life on his lousy boats, bored stiff and loving it, if you'll just get Buster back to me in one piece."

"Just Buster?" I said slyly.

She made a face at me. "All right, I'm worried about Loretta, too; but just between us, the girl is kind of a pill even if she is my daughter and, well, to put it bluntly, I can live without her if I have to. That's not very motherly, but that's the way it is." She laughed shortly. "Now that I've bared my soul, just what do you want to know?"

I learned that the three-fingered Estebanian paid hand, cook, or captain—whatever Leo Gonzales' exact title had been—had produced a couple of pistols and taken over the *Ametta Too* well east of the Bahamas with the help of one of the college-boy crew members.

"Buddy Jacobsen," Amanda said tartly. "Very intense. He liked to call himself a liberal, although what's liberal about kidnaping and murder he wouldn't say."

"Murder?"

"There was another boy along, Sam Ellender, who tried to be brave and jump Leo when he wasn't looking. Buddy shot him. They buried Sam at sea, if you want to call it a burial. They stuffed him into a sailbag with an odd length of anchor chain and rolled him over the stern…"

There had been several days of sailing with the Phippses locked into the boat's big main cabin, aft. Finally, the anchor had been dropped and they'd been allowed on deck, finding themselves in a small harbor fringed with palm trees. It had been explained to them that all sails had been taken ashore, along with the dinghy and life rafts. The motor had been disabled. There was no way, they were told, that they could escape with the ketch. If they wanted to try swimming ashore, well, the island behind which they were lying was too small for anybody to hide on successfully. The other way, north, there were some not very nice shoals and swamps and channels between them and the mainland; and the mainland was Cuba, where their reception might not be very friendly.

"So we lived on board for weeks," Amanda said grimly. "In a way, I guess, it wasn't too bad, not as if they'd taken us ashore and locked us up in a shed with a lot of bugs and rats. They hadn't sabotaged the generator, so we had power and light. They'd bring us supplies when we needed them, and water when that ran short. There was always one guard on board. We might have managed to overpower him—we considered it, of course—but what would have been the point? There was really no place to go."

I said carefully, "Altogether, it was about five weeks from the time they took over the boat. Over four weeks at anchor, with absolutely nothing happening. Seems kind of pointless, if I've got it right."

She looked at me for a moment, steadily. "You haven't got it right, Mr. Helm. Quite a few things happened right at first. It was only after the first week in that place that everything settled down to a kind of dull prison-ship routing that came close to driving the three of us crazy."

"But you're not going to tell me what happened?"

"No," she said. "I'm not going to tell you. I want to see how things work out tonight. I want to think the whole thing over very carefully before I say anything about it. I want to be perfectly fair."

"Try being fair to me, Mrs. Phipps," I said. "Haseltine's involved in some way, isn't he? My life may depend on him before morning, mine and several other people's. If there's something I ought to know, you'd better tell me about it."

"If I thought it could have any effect on…" Amanda shook her head quickly. "No. I think I'm quite safe in saying that what I'm holding back can't possibly hurt."

"Sure," I said. "Okay, carry on, as we say in the Navy."

One night, after a few weeks had passed, they'd been awakened by the arrival of another boat. In the morning they'd seen a big motor yacht at anchor fifty yards away, but communication between the ships had been discouraged. Much later, only a couple of days ago, a plane landed on the air strip, which had been partially cleared by their captors.

"There were some half a dozen men there from the start," she said in answer to my question. "That's not including Leo and Buddy Jacobsen. Leo seemed to more or less take charge when he got there. It was a good thing for us, since he still felt obliged to kind of look after us, after all those years of working for us. Two more men arrived with the strange yacht. A girl, a black girl in a stewardess uniform of some kind, came with the plane. We could see her through the binoculars, with a revolver in her hand, as she helped herd the passengers out. They were rowed out to the other yacht, I suppose because it had more accommodations." She hesitated. "I don't know if it matters, but we recognized one of the plane people: a businessman friend of Bill Haseltine's named Adolfo Alire. We'd met him the year before when we sailed down to Isla Rosalia, in the Windward Islands. It made a nice cruise, and Bill had some oil business he hoped to transact, but I don't think it worked out—"

"Wait a minute!" I said. My voice sounded a little funny. "Hold everything! Isla Rosalia. That's the island where they discovered oil offshore a year ago, right after it declared its independence?"

"Why, yes, on the Caracas Shelf, whatever that may be. Way down. Nobody'd been able to explore it effectively before, let alone drill on it, because it was too deep, but with modern equipment—"

"And Haseltine was interested?"

"Of course. It was oil, wasn't it? But it turned out to be too big a deal for him, I think. He's kind of a lone-wolf operator, you know; and here there were governments and giant international corporations and cartels all competing—"

"And Isla Rosalia is the place from which your hired captain came?"

"Yes, Leo was born there. At the time, we just thought it was nice that we could help him visit his home and family for a few weeks. We never dreamed his fanatic relatives would get him mixed up in their crazy political schemes… Didn't you know?"

I said grimly, "Mrs. Phipps, you'd be surprised at what people tell us. You'd be even more surprised at what they don't tell us. Okay, give me the rest fast; we're running out of time. What happened last night? I mean, it was last night, wasn't it? You don't look like the type to spend all day in your pajamas, attractive though they are."

Manderfield must already have had her ready to use as a hostage when he set up the rendezvous with me at the Salty Dog. He must have got his instructions quickly—the instructions he didn't like—and moved fast when Harriet reported to him after our sex interlude and conversation the night before. Well, I had no reason to question the man's efficiency. I'd have been happier if I had.

"Thank you, sir," Amanda said. "It happened well

after midnight, but I'm afraid I never thought to look at my watch. There was a lot of confusion and shooting on land, awakening us. Then somebody set out flares along the airstrip, and planes came roaring in, two or three of them. We couldn't make out what was happening; but suddenly there were rubber boats all over the harbor; and men swarming aboard the *Ametta*. Our guard was disarmed. Seeing how badly he was outnumbered, I guess he decided not to resist. We were all herded into the rubber boats without being given a chance to dress, and put ashore with the people from the other yacht. Our guard was thrown in with Leo Gonzales and Buddy Jacobsen and the rest of the kidnap gang. They were also prisoners, obviously but held separately. Then a couple of men with tommy guns—well, submachine guns of some kind—came up and shone their flashlights at us, looking us over. One pointed me out, and the other grabbed me and marched me over to one of the planes, and we took off. By this time, it was close to sunrise. After a while, in daylight, we landed somewhere and I was marched to a dock and put aboard that fifty-foot yacht you saw, which promptly cast off and put to sea. Later, they seemed to be chasing somebody, but Hattie, who'd taken over as my jailer, wouldn't let me near the porthole, so I can't tell you any more about it."

"You were probably chasing Bill and me," I said. "We had a little brush with them this morning."

"You'll have to tell me all about it some time," she said dryly. "When I can stand more excitement. Anyway, eventually Hattie and I were loaded into the dinghy and ferried over to that dismal sandbar—I guess they call it Little Grass Key because there's so little grass on it. Then you came riding to the rescue, and here I am, still in my pj's."

"Back to that place you were kept prisoner first," I said. "Was the raiding party in uniform?"

"No. It didn't seem to be an official Cuban military operation, if that's what you mean. They wore all kinds of clothes and spoke several different languages among themselves, not just Spanish. And the way they were armed was out of this world. Anything that would shoot, cut, or stab, they all had it—" She stopped, as the sound of the diesels died abruptly, leaving a strange, ringing silence. "What is it?" she asked. "Is something wrong?"

"I hope not," I said. "But if there is, now's the time to find it out, rather than hours from now off the Cuban coast…"

24

"Right here," Harriet said, placing a slim brown forefinger on a small grayish strip of land in the middle of a lot of shallow blue water along the Cuban coast. On a chart, the shallow water is blue and the deep water is white, just opposite from the way you find it in nature. I suppose there's a reason.

We were gathered in the red-leather-and-gold cabin, around the cocktail table that wasn't exactly designed for navigation—that marble would play hell with a nice sharp pair of dividers. Amanda Phipps had withdrawn discreetly to lean against the bar, giving the rest of us room; I gathered she wasn't eager to rub shoulders with Haseltine. I wished I knew why, but I obviously wasn't going to learn by asking. Harriet was sitting at the table with us three males hanging over her.

"Hell, that's the old Club de Pesca," Haseltine said. "If it hasn't fallen down by now."

"That's right," Harriet said. "The old, deserted Club de

Pesca de Cayo Negro, to be exact. Black Island Fishing Club to you, Matt."

"Go to hell," I said. "I *habla Espanol* just as *bueno* as anybody, I'll have you know." I frowned at the spread-out chart. "Looks like a nice little harbor right inside the west end of it, but the water gets mighty thin once you're past that. You couldn't sneak in from the east in anything deeper than a canoe, I'd say, and you might have to carry that in places. What's that long, narrow island to the west? It doesn't seem to have a name on the chart, here."

"Locally, it's known as Cayo Perro, Dog Key," Harriet said, still translating for my benefit. "It's part of the same offshore chain."

"And the channel behind it? At least it looks as if there might be a channel."

"There is, or was. When I was there it was four or five feet deep, kind of tricky, but you could make it. We used to take the fishing boats out that way sometimes, when a norther was blowing and we wanted to get up the coast without taking a beating."

"So you've been there?"

"Yes, darling," she said. "Years ago, before Castro, when I was a mere slip of a girl, of course."

Her age, then or now, didn't concern me at the moment. I said, "So the harbor of this former fishing club can be reached from offshore either by coming in the direct channel between Cayo Negro and Cayo Perro, or by making an end run west of Cayo Perro and passing behind it. Can it be done in the dark?"

"They're all mean little channels," Harriet said. "However, with a powerboat that doesn't draw too much water, like this one, and a good depthfinder and radar, it could probably be done if the situation hasn't changed too much since I was there. But it isn't necessary, Matt."

"What do you mean?"

"It's all set up for you. It's all arranged. You don't have to pull a sneak around right end. All you have to do is sail straight in and pick up your people. You'll meet no resistance, I promise you."

I looked at her for a moment. She met my gaze steadily enough; she was telling the truth, all right. Up to a point.

"That's great," I said. "That's swell. Then you'll run no risk of getting shot as you show us the way, will you?"

There was another little silence. At last, Harriet licked her lips and said, "That wasn't the agreement, Matt."

"If there's no danger, sweetheart, why should you mind a little boat-ride?" I asked. "Anyway, the agreement was based on Loretta Phipps, not her mother, remember? If you can switch signals, so can I."

"You'd have done it anyway, you bastard."

"Sure," I said. "But now I have a good excuse, don't I? Anyway, there's no way of putting you ashore without wasting time we can't afford."

"The outboard—"

"We're taking the outboard with us. And that happens to be something I don't want you reporting to your friends right away."

She drew a long breath. "Then there's not much use

in arguing about it, is there?" she said, and I knew she'd been expecting it or she wouldn't have given in so quickly.

"But if we're going to tow my boat all that way, in open water, we'd better have a bridle on her."

I said, "Hell, use a bridle and saddle both, if it'll make you happy. Bill, go with her and see she ties the right knots and doesn't make a break for it. Remember, she's still got keys for that boat of hers somewhere; and the thing will run circles around even this souped-up sex barge, if she ever gets loose in it." I watched them disappear into the cockpit, Haseltine looking a little puzzled, as well he might. After all, he'd been more or less led to think that Captain Harriet Robinson was a trusted colleague of mine. Well, we all had our little secrets. "Where are we?" I asked Brent, standing nearby.

"Just off the Keys," he said. "We ran under the highway bridge a few minutes ago."

"What do you think of the lady's information?"

"She could be telling the truth. It's a likely hideout," Brent said. "It was one of the possibilities we considered quite seriously, as a matter of fact. It was deserted after Castro's takeover, when rich bourgeois sportsmen were no longer welcome down there. Maybe the owner's politics had been unsatisfactory, also. We have no recent reports, but at one time the harbor was considered good and the airstrip adequate, at least for small planes. There was a lodge, and there were some docks, the works. It was one of the places we wanted very much to have checked out, on speculation; but orders came through not to rock the boat in any way."

I turned to the slim figure standing silent by the bar. "What do you think, Mrs. Phipps?" I asked. "Come over here and take a look, please. Is this the place you were held prisoner?"

She moved forward, a little hesitantly. "I'm afraid I'm not much good with charts," she said. She frowned at the oversized sheet of paper on the table. After a while, she nodded slowly. "I think so," she said. "It was hard to tell anything from the *Ametta* of course; we were locked in the cabin all the time we were under way, and once the boat was anchored all you could see was the cove, just about, but later I caught a glimpse from the plane window right after takeoff. There were those two skinny islands, just like that, and the one from which we'd come had just that little hook at the west end, making the bay where the boats were lying. I could barely make them out in the weak light."

"Thanks," I said; and I looked at Brent. "Well, what do you say? I'll gamble on it if you will."

He sighed. "Well, it's the only game in town, as far as I can see. I'll stick my neck out and make the recommendations, if you feel sure enough to go in ahead and remove the noncombatants."

"It's a deal," I said. "Okay, what do I do to get there?"

Brent sat down and did some art work on the chart. "Here's our present position," he said. "Here's your course. You've got good instruments and a quiet night. No moon to amount to anything. You may even get a little high cloud after midnight, so much the better. The weather is expected to hold for the next three or four days; no major fronts in sight. Maybe a few cruising squalls here and there, particularly in the Gulf Stream, but there are always those. Otherwise just light southerly winds, not over twenty knots, probably less. Haseltine seems to know basic piloting; and of course the Robinson woman is a good navigator, if you can trust her. Between the two of them you should make it all right."

"I'm not really worried about making it," I said. "As the fellow said going over Niagara Falls with his water-wings, getting back will be the real problem."

Harriet and her husky Texas escort came back inside. "She should tow okay now," Harriet said. "I'll check her again after we get under way."

"Sure."

Brent said, "Well, I guess it's time for me to get out and walk. So long, people."

I followed him out into the cockpit, and glanced toward the distant string of lights that marked the bridge of the Overseas Highway—one of the many bridges, I had no idea which one.

"It's a long way. Sure we can't drop you closer?" I said.

"I'll be fine. I've got the tide with me," he said. He was taking off his clothes, revealing a rubber suit under them. He reached behind the flying-bridge ladder and brought out a pair of black swim-fins. "Anything else, Eric?"

"Yes. Manderfield."

"He's on a string. We know all about him. When the right time comes, we'll reel him in."

"Sure," I said. "Among the things you know, is there the fact that he's apparently got a junior-grade amphibious force, fully armed, ready to go at a moment's notice?"

I thought Brent looked slightly disconcerted, although it was hard to tell in the unlighted cockpit. "No, I don't think that's part of our information. In that case, maybe we should consider blowing the whistle on Mr. M."

"It might be a good idea," I said. "I don't like the guy. He smiles funny."

"I will so report. I'm sure it will make all the difference," Brent said. "And I'll recommend the target, giving you as much time as possible before sunrise. Let's say the bird flies at four."

"Flies, or lands?" I said. "Fast as those things go, they're not instantaneous."

Brent shrugged. "If you like, we'll say it lands at four, on the dot. That means you've not only got to be out of there by four with everybody you're planning to rescue, remember, but you've all got to be clear of the blast area. If there's any doubt of your making it by then, don't go in. There's no cop-out signal tonight." He made a wry face. "It's not nice, but it's got to be that way. Signals can be intercepted and decoded. This is a desperate, shoestring private venture on foreign soil by some desperate private citizens, one quite wealthy, with no governmental backing or elaborate communications system. It's the Bay-of-Pigs syndrome. They want no loose official ends on this one.

So there will be no abort. No matter what happens, no matter what you find or don't find, the place goes up at four. Okay?"

"Okay," I said. "Have a nice swim."

"Don't worry about me," he said. "I'm the least of your worries."

A moment later he was gone, with his unique talents. I didn't envy him the trip ashore, but then, I'm not much of a swimmer. Some people do it for fun, I'm told. I went back into the cabin, and stepped just inside the door, or whatever you're supposed to call it on a boat.

"Watch where you point that thing," I said.

Haseltine grinned, and lowered the muzzle of the ugly weapon he held: an honest-to-God old tommy gun, but with the clip, not the drum. Amanda was looking rather shocked and scared, the way many women get—and many men, too—in the presence of firearms. Harriet just looked pleasantly excited at the prospect of action.

"Christmas presents," Haseltine said. "There's one for you, too. And lots and lots of pretty loaded clips to go with it."

Well, it made sense. The old Thompson, while basically as American as chewing gum, has become an international classic these days, just the kind of weapon a few reckless characters, one rich, might be able to pick up illegally for a crazy rescue venture. It committed the U.S. government to nothing.

"Can you hit anything with it?" I asked.

He shrugged. "I know what makes it go bang," he

said. "If I don't hit the guy, I'll guarantee to make him very nervous."

That meant he was probably pretty good with a chopper. A duffer wouldn't have been so modest. I was learning more about millionaires every day, it seemed.

I said, "Well, are you two nautical experts going to run this love-tub, or do I have to? Your course is marked on the chart there. Speed twenty knots. No lights. Let's get the Cuba Express on the tracks, shall we?"

It took a little while before Harriet got the outboard to tow right at the designated speed; after that, it was just a long, dull run, with the big motors thundering and vibrating steadily as they drove us through the night. I didn't spend much time on the bridge, after settling the basic navigational strategy with Harriet. They knew what they were doing up there and I didn't. After a while, I just said to hell with it, and invaded the gorgeous love-nest forward, and went to sleep on the big soft bed—you wouldn't want to insult it by calling it a berth, even if it was on a boat. The next thing I knew, Amanda was bending over me.

"Hattie says to tell you we're getting close," she said. "How can you sleep?"

"It's easy," I said. "I'm too nervous to do anything else. What's the time?"

"A little after two. I made some coffee."

"Thanks," I said, taking the cup she offered me. "You know, you'd make some man a fine wife, Mrs. Phipps."

"Amanda," she said. "Get him back for me, Matt."

"Sure," I said. "He's as good as home right now, Amanda. Let me just go upstairs—excuse me, topside—and supervise the final details."

Outside the cabin, a cool twenty-knot breeze was blowing. That's a reasonable amount of wind even when it's you that's moving and not the air. I climbed the handsome ladder with its neat rubber treads, a little hampered by the chopper and clips I was carrying. The businesslike weapon seemed especially crude on such a refined boat. On the bridge, there was a dull red glow from the instruments. Harriet glanced at me briefly by way of greeting. Haseltine, at the wheel, gave me a little nod to let me know he knew I was there. He went on with what he'd been saying.

"...a goddamned, two-masted, rule-beater, ugly as sin," he said. "Of course they had to slap a big handicap on her. What else could they do? Just because some big intellectual brain finds a king-sized hole in the rating rules..."

"Every high-priced yacht designer in every yachting country in the world is looking for holes in the rules," Harriet retorted. "That's what they get paid for, isn't it, to build you a racing sailboat that goes just as fast as the next guy's and rates a little better? That's what wins yacht races, handicap ratings, not speed alone. When they came up with this latest lousy handicap rule that instantly made a lot of fine old racing yachts obsolete, they swore up and down it would be good for so and so many years; they promised you could build to it without losing your shirt. So what happens? The minute somebody comes through with a real breakthrough and spends thousands of dollars backing his theory, they lower the boom on him! It's a private club, that's what it is, and if you happen to be a poor damned genius from Princeton you're out."

"He isn't from Princeton, goddamn it, he's from—"

I said, "I'm sure this is fascinating, but where the hell are we now, and how's the fuel holding out?"

Harriet pointed off the starboard bow. "Cuba's over there; and the fuel is fine, thanks. Even with a ton and a half of outboard in tow, we've barely made a dent in it. Whoever built this Cleopatra's barge must have had some real long-range loving in mind."

"Any signs of naval activity?"

"Not any. Nothing on the radar. It's a deserted ocean, darling. We've got it all to ourselves."

"How good is that radar for picking up small stuff: patrol craft and MTB's, for instance?"

She shrugged. "Not too good. Wood and Fiberglas don't really register too well except at close range; not like metal. But it works both ways. We're wood and Fiberglas too. If our radar can't see them, theirs can't see us."

"It's a lovely thought," I said. "But let's bring that outboard alongside as we slow down a bit. If they do get an image, I want it to be one image, not two."

She turned to look at me directly. "I know," she said after a moment. "You're being clever."

"Brilliant," I said. "I hope."

She said, "We might as well do it now. Hold everything, Bill. Dead slow. I'll be right back."

I went with her, and we got the smaller boat lashed alongside to port, with plenty of fenders to prevent damage. Then we were back on the bridge.

"Try a thousand rpm; let's see how she rides," Harriet said, looking down at the tow. "That's fine. Course one eight oh, Bill. Due south. I hope that damned fathometer is working right. We should be picking up the outer bank... There it goes. Bottom at seventy fathoms, shoaling."

"Course one eight oh," Haseltine said.

"Steady as you go. Forty fathoms, shoaling. There's the shore, Matt; that low dark line ahead, you can just make it out. The little notch just off the bow is the pass between the islands. To port, Cayo Negro. To starboard, Cayo Perro. Right a little, Bill, we're a hair too far east. Hold one nine five until... Dead slow! Hit that switch for me, Matt, so I can read it in feet. Twenty-five feet, twenty, fifteen, fifteen... Left to one six five, Bill. Steady. Ten feet. Ten. Eight. Ten. I think we've got the channel. We'd have been aground by now if we didn't; it's shallow as hell on both sides. Just ease her on through now, holding a bit to port, we seem to have some current..."

There was a lengthy period of total silence, except for the muted rumble of the loafing diesels. The shoreline ahead grew higher and blacker.

"Seven feet," Harriet said softly. "They've let the channel fill in. I'll bet somebody played hell getting that sixty-foot ketch through here. She probably draws all of... Easy, Bill. There's a stake, leave it to port. There used to be a spoil bank just outside... Okay, I've got it on the radar. Hold your course. There it is, you can just make it out off to port. Take it close. Good boy. Now let her coast until our Admiral, here, makes up his mind where the attack should be mounted. Gentlemen, I give you the Club de Pesca de Cayo Negro."

25

Except for the murmur of the idling engines, everything was very quiet. I could make out a fringe of palms against the sky, but I could distinguish no detail below it. Haseltine had risen behind the wheel. The submachine gun in his hands gleamed faintly in the red instrument glow as he covered the starboard sector without instructions. I kept watch to port as the *Red Baron* carried her momentum into the dark lagoon. I reflected that, while we'd never be bosom buddies, probably, the big guy was useful to have around. There was a rustle of movement behind me. I looked around to see Amanda Phipps clinging to the bridge ladder, a white shape in the darkness.

I whispered, "It's safer in the cabin."

"Don't be silly," she said. "You want to head straight in, nothing to the left. There's a broken-down pier to port, and a lot of old pilings in the water that you don't want to hit. Farther along the same shore, there's another dock, kind of decrepit, but they were using it. The *Ametta* and the other boat should be dead ahead. My God, it's like a black cave, isn't it?"

Harriet said, "I've got something on the radar. Two somethings. Dead ahead. But they don't look quite right for boats."

I said, "To hell with it. You said no resistance. Here goes."

I reached for the spotlight, and switched it on, pointed forward. For a moment, there was nothing in the beam but glassy calm water. Then the finger of light touched the masts of a boat. There was something wrong with them. Not only was there a lot of disheveled-looking camouflage netting draped over them—a detail Amanda hadn't mentioned—but a sailboat's masts don't normally lie over at better than forty-five degrees on a windless night. I followed the masts downwards to the point where they emerged from the water; the boat's hull was invisible below the surface.

"Oh, no!" Amanda breathed. "Buster loved that boat!"

I wasn't concerned with anybody's yachts at the moment. "That's the *Ametta Too*? You recognize the rig?"

"Yes, of course. They must have scuttled her. The other one should be somewhere beyond her."

I raised the beam, and found it. Sir James Marcus' vessel, with no fin keel, had settled almost straight, with the upper part of its camouflaged superstructure showing.

"Cover me, Bill," I said. "Somebody may get jittery when I swing this thing toward shore. But remember, there are supposed to be friendlies around."

There seemed to be nobody around, however. I swept the light over some muddy banks, a shaky-looking dock, and the decayed pier of which Amanda had warned us, off which rotting pilings stuck out of the water like bad teeth. A second, higher sweep got me a lot of palm trees and a big, weathered building with broken windows.

"The Lodge," Amanda whispered. "Leo and the rest stayed there. But where—"

I interrupted her. "Take her in to that dock, Hattie. Starboard side to, heading out."

"Aye, aye, Admiral. I'd play hell trying to dock the other way, with that outboard alongside, wouldn't I?"

"If there's anything I hate, it's a smart-ass sailor," I said. "Okay, Chief Haseltine, look sharp. On a night like this I have to be stuck with a lousy Texas Kiowa, not even a good, fighting New Mexico Apache."

Haseltine said, "Look who's talking. Hell, your Viking ancestors couldn't hang on more than one winter in that Vinland they discovered. The local Indian tribes booted them back onto their ships and ran them to hell out of there—"

"If you comics can bear to interrupt your routine for a moment, somebody'd better help me get some lines ashore," Harriet said as we touched the dock lightly.

"I'll give you a hand," I said. Amanda dropped back down the ladder to let us through. Down in the cockpit, I stopped Harriet as she was about to climb forward along the deckhouse. "Hattie. Come over here a moment. This boat's not going anywhere."

In the aft end of the cockpit, she faced me questioningly. "What is it, Matt?"

"It occurs to me," I said softly, "that you might have some notion of ducking ashore and hiding out, leaving us to our fates. Don't do it."

She hesitated. "If I did have some such wild idea, why not?"

"Because you need us to get you out of here. If you've got some arrangements made, if you think you're going to hide in the bushes until daylight, perhaps, and wait for somebody to come for you, forget it."

She was watching me closely. "Keep talking, darling," she murmured. "Why shouldn't I wait until daylight?"

"Because this island isn't going to be here that long," I said.

There was a lengthy silence. "I don't believe you," she said at last.

"It's in the computers now, doll," I said. "Cayo Negro, Black Key. Latitude this, longitude that. Time on target, oh four hundred. Countdown will start in umpteen minutes. Of course, this is strictly top secret, and I never told you anything of the sort. It will never have happened even after it's happened, if you know what I mean. What will really have happened, officially, is that those dumb, primitive, patriot types stored a big cache of their revolutionary ammunition here, and it happened to go up, kind of accidentally."

"I still don't believe you. You're bluffing."

I shrugged. "Suit yourself, Hattie. Just remember, if

you miss this ferry out of here, you'll be in for a long ride straight up. Now let's get those damn docklines over—"

"Matt."

"Yes?"

"I wish I didn't hate you so much," she said. "You're really kind of an entertaining person, full of bright ideas."

"This wasn't my idea, and I can't stop it," I said. "So don't dream about pushing a gun in my back and making me send the abort signal. There isn't any."

"Better throw a line around that piling while you can reach it," she said. "I'll get the bow."

My job done, I watched her khaki-clad figure working confidently on the insecure, streamlined forward deck that would be a hell of a place to handle an anchor in a gale, but maybe you didn't anchor boats like this in gales. With the ship secure, I looked up at Haseltine with his squirt gun, still standing watch on the bridge.

"Anything?"

"Not a movement."

"Well, I guess I'd better go ashore and have a look around," I said. "The boat's all yours. If things go wrong, cut that outboard loose and make a run for it—"

There was a quick movement in the cockpit. Amanda Phipps was on the dock before I could grab her. I jumped ashore after her, but stopped with the Thompson ready; you can't shoot and run at the same time. At least I can't. I was aware of Haseltine on the flying bridge above me, his gun at his shoulder. We covered the white figure running toward the shore.

"Buster!" she called. "Buster, it's me, Amanda. Where are you? It's all right, dear. It's all right. They're friends."

I snapped, "Easy!" as Haseltine stiffened above me.

I'd seen it, too: a man's shape detaching itself from the shadow of the lodge building and running forward. The two shapes merged.

"Wouldn't you think grown people would have more decency than to neck in public?" I asked at last of nobody in particular.

"The trouble with you is, you're jealous," Harriet said, joining me. The trouble with me was that she was perfectly right.

Amanda was calling to us. "It's all right. Everything is all right. They were just hiding because they didn't know who we were." People seemed to be springing out of the bushes and palm trees everywhere. "Matt," Amanda called.

"I'm coming."

Haseltine said, "I'll keep an eye on the boat. You go ahead."

"Sure. Come on, Hattie. Looks like I'll have to settle for your company."

What I really meant, and she knew it, was that I didn't want her near the boats. We went up there, and were introduced to Mr. Wellington (Buster) Phipps, in dark silk pajamas, in spite of which he looked like the reasonably bright and competent gent I'd been led to expect.

"My daughter Loretta," he said. I gathered from his voice that, unlike his wife, he did not think his offspring was kind of a pill.

I could see that the girl was somewhat taller than her mother, and of course younger, and perhaps slimmer. The long blonde hair was worn far enough forward to shadow her face mysteriously, but her soft greeting and brief handshake were reassuringly straightforward. Perhaps I'd done the girl an injustice, passing judgment on the strength of a single snapshot. She had on a short, ruffly, blue nightgown-and-negligee outfit that would probably have been intriguingly transparent under normal illumination. Here, without light enough to penetrate the thin layers of nylon, she seemed to be quite properly and modestly attired—well, as properly and modestly as any young lady wandering around outdoors in her nightie and bedroom slippers.

Under other circumstances, all these people standing around under the palms dressed for bed might have seemed funny; at the moment, my sense of humor wasn't functioning very well. We got Harriet introduced; and all the time I couldn't help thinking of a big clock with a sweep second hand counting off time in a well-instrumented control room somewhere. I glanced at my watch. It read two forty-three.

Phipps was talking: "I understand Bill Haseltine's with you."

There was the same funny constraint in his voice, when the Texan was the subject, as there had been in his wife's.

"He's watching the boat," I said. "Look, I'm very eager to meet all these lovely people, but not right now. Brief me, fast. What's the situation? Where's the raiding

party your wife told me about? Where's Leo Gonzales
and his patriot crew?"

There was a brief hesitation; then Phipps said, "The
raiders are gone, all of them. Hours ago. Leo and the
others… well, they're right over there at the end of
the airstrip. Oh, don't worry. They won't cause us any
trouble. Have you got a flashlight?"

It was quite an exhibit. We could hear the flies before
we could see what they were working on. I was aware of
Harriet, not the most delicate lady in the world, gripping
my arm hard and making a funny, choked little sound as
the flashlight beam hit the row of bodies on the ground.
There was blood in great quantities. I stepped forward
and ran the light over them. They were all there, all the
ones I'd heard about but had never seen, from Leo with
his maimed hand to the pretty black girl in her splotched
and stained stewardess's uniform. They were all there;
and they were all dead.

"They were lined up, and made to kneel, and shot
while we watched," Phipps said. "A man just walked
down the row with a pistol and shot each one in the back
of the head. They called him Mr. Manderfield. Then more
pictures were taken—"

"Pictures?" I said.

"Yes," said Phipps, "there was quite a photography
session; two or three cameras with those strobe-type
flashguns, whatever you call them. Each shooting was
photographed from a couple of different angles. It looked
like multiple lightning from where we were; we couldn't

figure it out at first. Then there were all kinds of pictures taken of the bodies where they fell; and then they were all turned face-up as you see them now, and a man walked down the line and got closeup shots of each one; and finally there were some group pictures with Manderfield and his henchmen posing behind the bodies. What does it mean, Helm?"

I didn't know what it meant. All I could do was report it when I got back and hope the information would reach somebody who could interpret it. If I got back. At the present rate of progress, I'd never make it…

"Damn!" It was Haseltine's voice. "I wanted those bastards. I wanted to fry them over a slow fire! Who beat me to them?"

There was a funny little silence, as we turned to look at him. I opened my mouth to point out that he'd left his post of duty; but Harriet, the most likely source of trouble at the moment, was still beside me, and it was no time for discipline, anyway. The big man stood there grimly staring down at the dead bodies. He took a step forward and nudged one with his toe.

"Okay, Leo," he said. "That's the only way you could have got away from me. So okay." He drew a long breath, took a fresh grip on the submachine gun he still carried, and swung to face Wellington Phipps. "Hi, Buster," he said, a little defiantly.

Phipps said, "Hi, Bill."

They stood facing each other, as if neither of them knew exactly how to handle the situation, whatever it was. Obviously, they were men who'd known each other well, perhaps liked each other; and obviously there was something between them now, something big and terrible that had to be talked about, and neither knew how to approach it. Phipps cleared his throat, and Haseltine started to speak, and they were both silent once more, each waiting for the other. The impasse was broken by a fierce little rustle of movement. A fury in blue nylon hit Bill Haseltine squarely; a blonde fury with long fingernails reaching for his eyes.

"You… you callous Texas roughneck!" cried Loretta Phipps. "You incredible cheapskate! You…"

She went into some descriptive terminology that wasn't very nice; and all the time she was all over him, drawing blood. I grabbed Harriet and pulled her away, ready to throw her to the ground and flop down beside her. I mean, that kind of spectacular tantrum may look great on TV, but in real life you just don't climb the frame of a gent holding a loaded submachine gun, not with a bunch of innocent people standing around who may get their heads blown off if the safety happens to get bumped the wrong way and the guy happens to brush against the trigger accidentally while you're working him over with your nails.

"Loretta, for God's sake let me… Damn it, Lorrie, give me a chance to get rid of…"

Haseltine was doing his best to cover up, while acutely conscious every second, as a good marksman must be, of the deadly firearm in his hands. He wasn't resisting, he was simply trying to keep the action away from the chopper. As he turned from the attack, hunched over the gun, his elbow grazed the girl, knocking her off balance. She went down in a flurry of blue ruffles and white legs.

"You… you *hit* me!" she gasped, picking herself up. "You cheap, dismal brute… Oh!"

Then she whirled and ran blindly off into the darkness. Haseltine straightened up, looking after her. He checked the weapon he held, and looked at me as I came up. His face was bleeding in several places, but he seemed unaware of it.

"I'd better go find her," he said.

"I wouldn't know why," I said.

"You don't understand," he said; and that was the truth. "Here, take this. Careful, it's still loaded."

I took the Thompson and watched him disappear down the landing strip, at the end of which was a black something that seemed to be the burned-out hulk of an airplane, presumably the one belonging to the French baron I hadn't met socially yet. Manderfield had made a nice clean sweep.

I looked at Phipps and Amanda. "Any explanation will be gratefully received," I said. "No? Okay, let's get everybody aboard the cruiser. There's not one whole hell of a lot of time…"

26

There wasn't much time; but at three-twenty, Haseltine and the girl were still missing. We had the *Red Baron*'s engines turning over, ready to go. The open outboard lay along the dock just astern. For something to do, I stepped down and started both motors to make certain they'd run, and shut them off again. It wasn't time for that, yet; and the plugs might foul, idling too long. Diesels don't have plugs and can idle forever.

I pulled myself back up to the ancient dock where Harriet waited. Everyone else was on board the cabin job. I still hadn't been introduced to the aristocrats, not to mention the mere commoners, but it didn't weigh on me greatly.

"How much longer should we wait?" Harriet asked.

"Not any," I said. "You take the first section out of here now. Run east behind Cayo Perro, slow and quiet, no lights. You don't want to get to the end of the island much before four. Don't go too far. Stay hidden from seaward until you get the sign to go."

"And the sign is?"

"A lot of shooting over this way, followed by a spectacular explosion. Keep your fingers crossed. Let's hope the whiz-bang boys get the right island. Don't go on the preliminary popping. Wait for the big bang. There should be enough light with it to kill the night vision of anybody out there. That's when you go. Just turn those big diesels loose and streak for home."

"I know about the explosion," she said. "You told me. You really did mean it, didn't you?"

"Somebody's getting very tough in Washington, at the wrong time as usual," I said. "All the times they've let themselves be intimidated by some silly jerk with a gun; and now they get brave and ruthless and blow up a lot of dead bodies. And a lady named Robinson if she's dumb enough to hang around."

She said, "Assuming you're telling the truth about that, what about the shooting? Who's going to be shooting at what?"

"Sweetheart," I said, "you're just as cute as Little Red Riding Hood, but this is no time for your ducky little games. You know, because you arranged it, that the whole damned Cuban Navy is out there by now, just waiting for us to stick our noses out so they can blast them off. That's why you were going to run off and hide, and watch the lovely fireworks from the shore, clapping your little brown hands in sheer delight."

There was a little silence. "So you know," Harriet murmured at last.

I said wearily, "She'll never give me credit for one little brain cell. I don't know what I'm going to do to convince the girl I'm really a very bright fellow. She's been trying to have me killed since the first time we met; and I'm supposed to think she's given up the idea just because we made a little lovely music together? Maybe it isn't the Cubans. Maybe it's some other guys. But *somebody's* out there. You and your friend Manderfield couldn't possibly pass up an opportunity like this."

Harriet said defensively, "Well, it's what you asked me to do, isn't it? Help them set a trap for you?"

"That's right. And I'm grateful as hell. Now get up on that dreamboat's bridge and get those people out of here. It takes somebody who knows the boat, and our friend Haseltine's off chasing blondes. You know the waters better, anyway. I'll wait here as long as I can. At three-fifty I'll go, with or without passengers. The action should draw away any cats watching the other rathole west of Cayo Perro, where you'll be. After all, as far as they know out there, only one boat went in. If they see one coming out, over here, they'll all move this way to intercept. You'll have a clear run for it, off to the west."

She hesitated. "You're really serious, Matt? A goddamned sacrifice play like that?"

"Sacrifice, hell," I said. "I've never seen a Cuban marksman yet who could hit a fifty-knot target on a dark night." The fact that I'd actually seen very few Cuban marksmen was hardly worth mentioning, heroic as I was being. I went on confidently: "That little bomb of yours will take us right through them like a magic carpet; a bulletproof magic carpet."

"Who do you think you're kidding, darling? They'll have everything out there short of sixteen-inch naval guns."

I grinned. "So it is the Cuban allies. I wonder if they know they're doing Mr. Manderfield's Moscow-assigned chores for him. Well if they did, they probably wouldn't care. They've got a thing about Yankees trespassing on their shores. Considering recent history, maybe you can't blame them." I looked at Harriet for a moment in the darkness. "Get the hell out of here, Hattie," I said. "You hate my guts. You brought me here to see me die. That's why you weren't too unhappy when I made you come along; you'd even hoped for that, a little, and made arrangements in case it should work out that way. Although it involved a certain risk, being present at the kill was worth that much to you. Well, hop along and watch the show from the far end of Dog Key. I'll make it fancy enough to suit me."

She was looking at me steadily. I saw her shake her head. "No, you're not that brave," she said. "You've still got something up your sleeve."

I said, "We're wasting time. Dammit, Hattie, the whole world is crawling with people plugging to live forever. Well, it's always seemed like a hell of a futile endeavor to me. On the record, nobody's managed it yet. Methuselah racked up nine hundred years, they say, but I'll bet the last eight hundred really weren't much fun. Nobody else has even come close, that I know of. Personally, I'm off the longevity kick. I figure, if I get to operate the way I like for a reasonable length of time, I won't squawk if I don't even quite get to finish out the first century."

"And the way you like to operate is to go out of here at fifty knots right into the muzzles of those guns?"

I drew a long breath. "I was talking to a guy in Nassau just the other day," I said patiently. "As a matter of fact, it was Pendleton, the man who was later killed in my cabin, remember? We were discussing an agent I'd left behind to die, in the line of duty, some years back. Well, maybe now it's my turn to get left behind in the line of duty. Let's try it and see. Now get those people out of here—"

She said harshly: "Okay, you big, brave, phony martyr. You win! Make your turn at the stake, damn you!"

"What?"

"The stake," she said. "You remember, just before we came to the old overgrown spoil bank left when they dredged the harbor, and turned in here. There was a stake in the water, a marker, put up by the local fishermen. That's where you cut out of the channel, right to course oh five five. Have you got that?"

"Let me get this straight," I said. "I go out of here. I head out the channel. I come to the stake; and I turn right and run deliberately onto the shoals on course oh five five. Crunch. What happens then besides a lot of Cuban target practice?"

"Don't be any more stupid than you have to be!" Harriet snapped. "Do you know anything about running a fast-planing boat in shallow water?"

"Brent said put her on top and keep her there."

"That Brent had a little sense and a little seamanship, unlike some people I know! You've got about a hundred yards to get her going, once you hit the channel. When she's up and planing, back off just a little so you don't skid too wide on the turn. You haven't got much room in there. The moment you're around the stake and on course, give her everything. Ram those levers right up to the stops and forget them. Don't dodge, don't zigzag, don't slow down, don't look up from that compass, no matter what they throw at you. Oh five five and nothing either way. Keep her wide open. The depthfinder will go haywire. The steering will feel funny. Once in a while, maybe she'll touch, and the tachs will jump around like crazy. Pay no attention. What's it to you if you cream one of my props or blow one of my motors? Just keep her blasting. Do you understand?"

"It's becoming clear, gradually," I said.

"If you stop, if you even think of slowing down, if you let her settle at all, you're dead," she said. "You've got just about a seven-mile run through the shallows on that course, before you hit deep water. With a little luck you can make it. She's on the big side for it; but on this tide I think she'll clear everything if you just keep her planing right on top, really screaming. And the chances are they won't have anything out there small and shallow and fast enough to chase you across the flats. They'll have to go the long way around, following the channel and the edge of the reef, and by that time you'll have a nice big lead.

If you can't shake them after that, with the speed you've got, to hell with you."

She started to turn abruptly toward the nearby cruiser. I said, "Hattie, thanks."

She looked back. I saw her grin crookedly in the dark. "Now you can have lots of fun deciding whether I've really given you the straight dope, or whether I'm running you onto a sandbar so they can shoot you to pieces. Try flipping a coin; maybe it will help."

Then she was gone. A moment later she was up on the *Red Baron*'s flying bridge; and men fore and aft were taking in the docklines at her command. Anyway, if manpower would help, she had crew enough to run a Roman war galley. The red boat seemed to blend into the darkness a few moments after it pulled away from the dock. I couldn't help remembering that I was blessed with a light-colored craft that a blind man could spot in a Nantucket fog. I was also blessed with a couple of passengers playing some kind of childish tag out in the dark, on an island that was going to be just a big hole in the ocean in just about thirty minutes…

He came in lugging her, with a minute to spare before the deadline I'd set myself. After all, even in Hattie's nautical rocket, I had to give myself a little time to get clear. Having had to transport a few human bodies myself, from time to time, I could appreciate the strength of the big guy, marching in like that with a substantial young human female slung over his shoulder. One hand held her in place; the other carried something. As he came up, I saw that he had a pair of satin bedroom slippers there. Unique as Miss Phipps might be, and I certainly hoped she was, she apparently shared with her fellow-women the inability to stay in her shoes when the going got rough.

"Dump her in the stern and let's go," I said; but Haseltine placed her gently on the starboard seat, and put her footgear in her lap. I gave a shove, and threw the motors into gear as the boat slid away from the dock. I said, "Miss Phipps, your job is to hang on. This bucket will toss you overboard if you give it half a chance, once we're up to speed, so grab a piece of that handrail and don't let go for anything. Bill, if you don't mind, get over here to port and brace yourself against the console. The choppers and clips are on the seat up there where you can reach them. I don't suppose the lady knows how to reload a Thompson, so you'll have to keep switching between them, feeding in new clips as you get the chance."

"You sound as if you expect a real firefight," Haseltine said, taking his post and reaching for a weapon. "Who'm I going to be shooting at?"

We glided past the ancient, rotting pier and the ugly stumps in the water. I said, "Does it matter, as long as they're shooting back? When we get into the channel, I'll hit the throttles; don't get left behind. We're not going to have time for any man-overboard drills tonight. A hundred yards, and there'll be a sharp right turn; be ready for it. That should put your targets well off to port. Try for the lights; to hell with the guns and personnel. Okay?"

"If you say so, Admiral. Maybe Loretta should lie down—"

"That's up to the lady. She'll be safer down, but at the speed we'll be going she'll take an awful beating, bouncing around on that Fiberglas deck. How about it, Miss Phipps?"

"I... I'll stay here, thanks."

"Okay," I said. The spoil bank was slipping past to starboard. The jungle had taken it over, but you could still see, after all the years, that the material beneath hadn't got there naturally. It was the wrong shape. I made the turn into the channel and reached for the throttles. "Everybody ready? Here we go."

They were out there, all right. Nothing happened at first, as we picked up speed; but then we came out of the shadow of the shore, and there were suddenly more searchlights ahead than you'd see at an old-fashioned Hollywood premiere. We were barely on plane before the Thompson was hammering at my left ear. Standing at the controls for a better view, I kept my eyes from the glaring lights, watching the black water rushing toward us as she came up and out. The Plexiglas windshield twanged loudly as something went through it. Lions one; Christians nothing. The nearest searchlight flamed out. One and one. Haseltine was cursing, or praying, in a language I'd never heard as, one gun empty, he reached for the other.

The narrow channel hampered them a bit. Without shooting each other's ears off, only a few could have fun at one time. What they were, is anybody's guess. They didn't seem to be very big, but they had lots of firepower. In any case, I was trying very hard not to look at them and their damned lights and muzzle flashes. I was trying to concentrate on a stick protruding from the water ahead, nicely silhouetted by the glare. Haseltine opened up once more, in tidy little bursts.

"Hang on!" I yelled at him above the noise. "I'm coming right… *now!*"

I swung the wheel. The outboard leaned hard into the turn, shaving the stake. I said a quick little prayer of my own, and rammed the throttles forward. I'd thought we were moving pretty well already, but the burst of power was like a kick in the pants. The boat leaped ahead, just as everything landed where she'd been. Even with my eyes focused on the compass, I was aware of the ocean being turned inside-out astern.

The night was full of noise and flashing lights. The big outboards were howling out their eerie, banshee, full-throttle war song. Haseltine was reloading, cursing, and firing. Standing at the helm, I found my eyes watering in the fierce blast of air over the top of the windshield. There was no need for that now, I realized. I didn't need the extra height now. All I had to see was the compass, for seven miles; and I could watch that sitting down. I sat down, out of the direct slipstream, holding her grimly on course.

We'd taken some more hits. I couldn't tell where, but I'd felt them; but we were still afloat, still hurtling across the calm shallows with so little water under us that the depthfinder was giving no indication at all except for occasional crazy flashes all around the dial. The steering felt peculiar, as Harriet had said it would; and once in a while, as the props grazed something harder than water, the high scream of the motors would waver for an instant, only to come right back up to pitch once more. Still there were no hidden rocks to wreck us, no sandbars to bring us to a grinding halt, no coral heads to rip the bottom open.

I was aware that the black silhouette of the island was getting lower and more distant off the starboard quarter. Presently I realized that the searchlights astern were going out and the guns ceasing to fire back as we rocketed out of range. I saw that Haseltine had stopped shooting, presumably because a .45 slug won't carry more than a hundred yards with any kind of accuracy. He sat down on the seat forward of the console. Steering by compass, I didn't really need to see what was ahead, since I wasn't going to stop for it anyway; but it seemed a funny place for an experienced seaman to pick, right in the helmsman's line of vision. As the thought came to me, the big guy collapsed and slid to the floor—excuse me, Hattie, the cockpit sole.

Momentarily distracted, I remembered where I was and what I was doing, and brought the flying craft back on course once more. Loretta Phipps, her long hair and sheer garments whipping wildly in the fifty-knot gale of the boat's motion, made her way behind my chair, moving sensibly from one handhold to the next. I remembered that the girl had, after all, done a reasonable amount of yachting. She knelt, beside Haseltine, just as there was a great burst of light astern. I saw the kneeling girl look up, startled. I saw that Haseltine was unconscious, bleeding from a wound just above the belt. There wasn't a boat visible within a couple of miles of us. The light had almost faded when the concussion hit us.

Afterward, I glanced at the depthfinder. It read fifty feet, dropping fast. We were off the shallow Cuban coastal bank. We were home free. Well, almost free...

27

They never caught up with us; and if they sent planes after us, they never found us. I held on to the east and north until I found a rain squall to hide in. With the gusty accompanying wind, it got too choppy to maintain any speed, so I just shut down everything and let the boat take care of herself while I struggled to erect the canvas—well, vinyl—spray hood forward and move Haseltine into its limited shelter, working with the girl's help in the wind and pouring rain. It was daylight by this time. Loretta made her way aft through the downpour and returned clutching a first-aid kit. Apparently, she sometimes slipped and let herself betray signs of intelligence. I didn't take it too seriously. The idiot performance she'd put on earlier, as far as I was concerned, still left her far down near the bottom of the minus column.

With three of us inside, the boat's little instant tent-cabin was crowded with humanity. I wasn't sure it was good seamanship to have all that weight forward on a small vessel in the middle of a squall. However, it was just a junior-grade thunderstorm; and although we did considerable rocking and pitching as the seas built up, we didn't seem to be shipping anything except rainwater that ran right out again through the cockpit drains—all right, I'll call them scuppers if you insist. I pulled out Haseltine's wet shirt to look at the hole. It wasn't very big and it wasn't bleeding very much, at least not out where we could see it. Inside was probably a different story. I taped a large gauze pad over it for something to do, knowing it was just a formality. I might as well have used a band aid, or left the wound uncovered. The big guy opened his eyes.

"Hell of a cruise ship you run, Admiral," he whispered.

"If you'd just shot out all those searchlights like I told you, nobody'd have got hurt," I said. "I can't help it if folks can't obey simple orders."

He grinned faintly. "You bastard," he said, and licked his lips. "Loretta?"

The girl had parted the drenched, darkened blonde hair that had washed down her face; she was tucking the dripping strands behind her ears. "Yes, Bill?"

"I'm sorry—"

"It's all right," she said quickly. "Don't talk. It's all right. I… I lost my head for a few minutes, back there; but it's really all right. We'll talk about it later."

"That's a lot of bull," Haseltine breathed. "Later's a lot of bull. Now is all there is; and I want you to understand. I couldn't do it. I just couldn't do it. I wanted to, God knows I wanted to, but I couldn't. I'm not built like that. It was as simple as that."

"Of course, Bill. Just be quiet and—"

"Cut it out. Don't give me that of-course-Bill crap. And don't give me that be-quiet-Bill crap, either. I've got forever to be quiet in, don't I, Admiral? Starting pretty damn soon."

I said, "Well, I don't know—"

"The hell you don't. I know." His attention went back to the girl. "You're still mad, aren't you, Lorrie? You think I should have paid up the minute I was asked, don't you? Just like that. You think I'm just a lousy Texas cheapskate. You think I was worried about the lousy money; that's why I… I tell you, I just couldn't do it, Lorrie! Couldn't let those bastards hold me up like that. A million bucks or one buck, makes no difference. Spend every cent I've got to find you, to get the sonsofbitches who… But ransom, no. I don't pay ransom. You've got to understand. I don't operate like that. I can't."

"Of course I understand—"

He went on, as if unaware that she'd spoken: "Don't care who's snatched, even you. They can't pry it out of me like that. I don't pay off on a deal like that. You let one guy get away with it, they'll all be in there trying, every lousy get-rich-quick jerk with a gun or a knife and somebody to point it at. That bastard Leo, you'd have thought he'd have known how I felt, often as we'd sailed together. You'd have thought he'd have known I wouldn't play. Well, we never did get along. He always had the idea that, where I came from, I just had to be prejudiced against anybody who talked Spanish and, hell, maybe he was right. But I think maybe Leo just wanted to stick it into me, as much as he wanted that million-dollar ransom to finance the crummy military operation his wild-eyed Latin relatives-had suckered him into… You've got to understand, Lorrie. I couldn't do it. Couldn't…"

The squall was diminishing to a drizzle; the wind was dropping as fast as it had built up. I found a tarpaulin to spread over him, reflecting that I had, at last, an explanation for the curious, ambivalent attitude the man had shown: the trouble he'd gone to to get me on the job, for instance, and the reluctance he'd then shown to give me vital information, even going to the extent of misleading me in some instances. Believing that the girl and her family had been killed as a result of the stand he'd taken, he'd wanted to find and deal with the murderers; but he'd also been aware that many people would condemn him if the story got out. Maybe he hadn't, been quite as sure of himself and his actions as he'd wanted us to think. Maybe he'd even had a few twinges of guilt, leading him, instinctively, to try to cover up what had happened even while he was putting me to work to uncover it. Well, his secret was safe now.

After a while, the girl got up and moved away to sit miserably on the fish-box in the stern of the boat. Her thin, soaked, clinging bedroom finery, trailing soggy ruffles ripped loose by bushes and whipped loose by wind, didn't seem adequate for either warmth or modesty. I started to take off my windbreaker to put around her, but she waved it away irritably.

"I'm not cold," she said. "Why do you men always have to be wrapping us up in your damned old clothes. I'm fine. There's nothing I love like sloshing around the Gulf Stream in my wet lingerie."

I almost laughed, knowing from whom she'd inherited that attitude; but it was no time for laughter. I said, "I just wish we were in the Gulf Stream. We're way to the east of that; and we're almost out of gas. The radio's shot to hell. It looks as if we're going to have to do some drifting until somebody finds us, I hope."

It didn't seem to register. Anyway, it didn't serve as the distraction I'd intended. "I killed him, didn't I?" she said flatly. "If I hadn't acted like a crazy spoiled brat, running off to hide like that, to teach him a lesson, he'd have gone in the other boat, wouldn't he? And he'd have been alive now."

I said, "This is Big Bill Haseltine we're talking about? Do you really think he'd have let himself be shipped off to safety with the women and children—at least I hope they're safe——while somebody else played decoy for him?"

"Maybe not, but I… All those weeks that we were waiting to die just because he'd refused… When I saw him, I guess I just went mad a little, remembering all the agony we'd gone through in that place because he wouldn't… I mean, it was just money, after all; and Daddy would have paid him back, if that was what worried him."

"It wasn't," I said.

"I know that now. But at the time it just seemed so

incredible and unnecessary that we were all going to be killed because... We almost were, you know. I've never been so scared in my life. They were talking, right in front of us, about how we weren't worth anything to them any more, and how they should just shoot us and throw us in the sea. It was Leo who saved us. He sold them on the wild notion of making a much bigger deal of it since they couldn't get anything out of Bill; of keeping us alive and kidnaping those others and using us all to get real military help, not just money, for their nutty cause or movement or whatever... Do you know something? I've forgotten your name."

"Matt," I said.

"I'm Loretta Phipps," she said. "At least I used to be a lovely thing they *called* Loretta Phipps, but I was never quite sure... A lovely, sheltered, stupid thing... Do you want to know something, Matt? Being lovely isn't really difficult, if you've got a little money and the right heredity; but being stupid is very hard work."

"Why would you want to work at it?"

"Somebody's got to be stupid around the place, if everybody else is so terribly bright and beautiful, don't they?"

It seemed like an odd conversation to be holding on a shot-up, almost-out-of-gas boat drifting far out of sight of land with a dead man up forward; but at least we were off the subject of Haseltine. Loretta shivered slightly.

"I guess I will take that jacket, please," she said. "Why should I sit around practically naked just because

Mommy always made fun of… You've met my mother?"

"I've met your mother."

Putting her arms into the sleeves of the jacket I held for her, she gave me a sharp glance over her shoulders. "Oh, like that, huh? She still bowls them over, doesn't she? But I'd think she'd be a little too old for you; although I admit she doesn't look it."

"Miaow," I said.

Loretta laughed. "Well, how would you like having had to compete with that ever since you were a baby? I'm not me, not really. I've never been me. No matter how hard I try to break the goddamn mold, I'm still just movie-star Amanda Mayne's daughter… She was never *really* a star, you know. Oh, hell, I shouldn't have said that. What does it matter; and she's really very nice. I mean, if she were a horrible bitch, now, and I could feel justified in hating her lovely guts…" She stopped, shrugged, and went on: "Well, when I find out who I really am, I'll let you know."

"You do that," I said.

She gave me that sharp, searching glance once more, and grinned abruptly. "You know, I don't think you take my identity crisis very seriously, Matt."

I said, "Well, whoever you are, I think we can wait to find out until we get ashore. If we get ashore."

She looked rather surprised. "Are you really concerned about… I thought, the way you were giving orders and handling the boat, you must be a pretty good seaman."

"I try to kid people that way, but they always seem to find out the truth," I said.

"What are the weather reports, do you know?"

"Stable, except for a few squalls, for several days. No frontal activity in sight."

"Well, then there's really not much of a problem," Loretta said calmly, "as long as the boat isn't leaking seriously, which it doesn't seem to be; and as long as we're clear of the Cuban patrols. You say we're way off to the east?"

"That's right. East and north. I figured they'd probably put everything they had between us and Florida; and the only thing to do was head out this way and hope for the best."

"Well, the prevailing wind usually blows from the southeast around here. We'll have to wait a little until it picks up again after the squall; but if we put up the rest of the curtains and awnings and stuff to get more windage, and head as far to the west as we can and still keep her drifting right along, the wind and current combined should take us home sooner or later. Let's hang up all the available canvas first so we'll be ready for the wind when it comes; and then we'd better cheek to see how we're fixed for food and water…"

I sighed. I had another one, it seemed. You can't throw a rock down there without hitting a feminine Columbus or Leif Ericson. It was really a loused-up operation. I mean, I'd missed my chance to be marooned on a desert island with one beautiful, inadequately costumed lady; and now I was drifting in a small boat in tropical seas with another lovely female specimen draped in scanty lingerie—and all we talked about, for the day and a half that followed, was navigation, the weather, and how long Harriet's water and emergency supplies would hold out.

We carefully avoided talking about the object under the tarpaulin forward; although I guess it was in both our minds that something would have to be done about it if help didn't find us soon, but it did.

28

When I first saw it on the horizon, I glanced hastily at the two Thompsons still resting on the seat forward of the console, with the remaining clips. The approaching vessel looked like the white fifty-foot fishing job we'd had trouble with before, tuna tower, outriggers, flying bridge, and all. Then I realized that this was a somewhat smaller craft, but still familiar, although I'd never seen it away from the dock. Soon Harriet was looking down at us from the top of the tall structure resembling an oil derrick towering over the cabin and flying bridge of the *Queenfisher*.

"I figured, the amount of gas you had, if you made it at all you'd wind up somewhere around here," she called. "My God, some people are hard to kill."

"And some aren't quite so hard," I called back.

I saw her lean brown face change expression slightly. She glanced at the girl beside me, obviously alive, and back to me.

"Oh. Haseltine?" There was a little silence. I realized

that she'd liked the big guy. Then she shrugged up there, perhaps dismissing some half-formed hopes and plans. "Well, win some, lose some," she shouted. "Let me get down from this skyscraper before I come alongside. Meanwhile you'd better dump those armaments. We can't risk landing with them; they're illegal as hell. And I'm going to figure out how to sneak the boat into a yard where they'll keep their mouths shut about all the holes you seem to've let people shoot in it."

Women's Lib or no Women's Lib, I was getting a little tired of having my life run by the ladies. "Never mind, Hattie," I said. "We'll take care of the bodies and bullet holes and illegal weapons; that's our business. Just let me at a radiotelephone so I can check in."

Considerably later in the day, standing on the flying bridge beside Harriet after docking in the familiar marina, I watched Mr. and Mrs. Phipps, after expressing their gratitude once more, moving to a parked car with their daughter, whose costume still consisted of a borrowed windbreaker below which dangled some intriguing rags and ribbons of sheer blue nylon. Back in civilization, in the presence of her parents, Loretta hadn't had much to say by way of goodbye. Well, it wasn't as if we'd spent the past hours of peril in each other's arms.

"She's pretty," Harriet conceded reluctantly. "I didn't gather from what Bill said that she's too damn bright, however."

I said, "Cut it out, Hattie. You're not jealous, so why be snide?"

She laughed. "The old cat instinct, I guess," she said. Her smile faded. "No, I'm not jealous," she said. "Not of you and another woman. Not ever, Matt. Not after what you did to me down there."

"What did I do?" I asked innocently.

"You got yourself into that corner deliberately, counting on me—on my softheartedness—to bail you out."

"That's right," I said. "More or less."

"In other words, you played me for a sucker."

"Call it that," I said. "Actually, the original script was slightly different. I was counting on Haseltine to take the other boat out of there with the innocent bystanders. He knew enough to do it. You and I would have waited in the outboard—you tied hand and foot, if necessary. Either you'd have come through with some life-saving suggestions before the time was up, or we'd have gone to hell together. That was the way I had it figured, loosely; but Miss Phipps and Mr. Haseltine loused me up by running off to play hide-and-seek at the critical moment; so I put on my hero-martyr act for you instead, and fortunately it worked just as well, or maybe even a little better. You might have got stubborn, the other way, and decided to die just so you could take me with you."

Her eyes were hot and angry. "You admit that you faked—"

"Faked, hell!" I said sharply. "What was fake about it? The lousy run had to be made by somebody, goddamn it, and I didn't notice a long line of volunteers standing by, did you? What was so wrong about my trying to restack the deck slightly in my favor, after you'd worked hard to shuffle it the other way? Sure I did my damnedest to look brave and noble and bring tears of admiration to your eyes, not to mention words of wisdom to your lips. What the hell was I supposed to do, just drive that lousy boat out of there and get us all shot up in modest silence, when you probably had some gimmick that would give us a bit of a chance?"

She checked an angry retort, hesitated, and said, "That's another thing. How did you know I could help, at that point, even if I wanted to?"

"You said it yourself the other night," I said. "You're not a pro at killing, you said, but you are at seamanship. I have great faith in pros, Hattie. If it involved boats and water, and you wanted to badly enough, I knew you'd come up with some kind of an answer. And you did."

"Nevertheless," she said, "you counted on being able to crack me, and you did, with your phony dramatics. I meant to have you killed, and instead I got sentimental and saved your crummy life, like any mushy ingénue."

That was what she hated me for now, I realized; the fact that I'd shattered the image she'd had of herself as an efficient and ruthless avenger on the trail of the man who'd wronged her.

I grinned. "And then you came out and found me and hauled me ashore."

She said, rather sulkily, "Hell, that's a good little boat. I couldn't just leave it drifting out there, could I?" She drew a long breath. "I'm through with you, Matt. That sounds corny, but it's accurate. You'll never have to worry about any danger from me again. On the other hand, I don't ever want to see you again."

"Why?" I asked. "Because I'm the one person who knows that beneath that tough lady-skipper exterior beats a heart of pure gold?"

She said, "Get the hell off my bridge, you sonofabitch!"

I looked around as I walked away along the docks, wondering about the *Red Baron*, but the souped-up sex-barge was nowhere to be seen. I also wondered, a little, about a girl named Lacey Rockwell who, I'd been informed, had wandered into a Key West police station yesterday with an outlandish story of being kidnaped and held prisoner for weeks, for no reason she could imagine. Well, she had good news to sustain her: her brother had turned up. After spending a month out in the Atlantic bucking adverse winds and getting nowhere, young Harlan Rockwell had apparently given up his plan for a preliminary cruise through the Caribbean and headed westwards, ducking through the Windward Passage and pausing in Kingston, Jamaica to send his sister a reassuring postcard, which had just caught up with her, along with one from Panama, telling her the wide Pacific lay ahead and the great South Seas adventure was well on its way…

Mac was waiting in my cabin when I walked in. He was really giving this one the personal touch.

"What's the bad news now, sir?" I asked.

"Good news first," he said. "Various important people

are eager to thank, personally, the heroic operative whose reckless courage…" He stopped. "You know, Eric, that's not a trait we try to foster in our agents. Anyway, they want to meet you and shake your hand, sirs and barons all."

"I can hardly wait," I said. "Now that I'm properly prepared, how about the bad news?"

"Washington is perturbed, as usual," he said. "Did you have a pleasant voyage?"

"Not bad," I said. "Scratch one millionaire; no other serious casualties." I drew a long breath. "Delete that. He wasn't a bad guy, particularly in a tight spot. Where the hell would a high-priced character like that learn to work a chopper like an expert?"

"Korea," Mac said. "He was in the Marines."

"What's Washington perturbed about?"

"Some favored U.S. oil companies had the inside track as far as some Caribbean oil was concerned. The new and rather shaky island government was promised that, in return for various contracts and concessions, certain revolutionary, or counterrevolutionary, elements would be taken care of. Well, they were taken care of, all right; at least one important group of them. However, a firm with connections behind the iron curtain, as it used to be known, is claiming the credit for removing this thorn in the side of the party in power. Furthermore, it is documenting its claim with very sharp and gory color slides in great numbers. It looks as if this concern may, as a result, be given favored treatment where the offshore petroleum is concerned, an outcome very distressing to

Washington, particularly since large amounts of expensive high explosives seem to have been wasted in an attempt to achieve the same purpose—although of course nobody is saying exactly how or where they were employed."

"I was looking the other way, sir," I said. "I'm afraid I can throw no light on the subject."

"To be sure. There have also been some wild accusations in Cuban circles, concerning sinister capitalist aggressions against Communist territory."

"Jeez," I said. "I sure missed a lot, out fishing like I was, didn't I, sir?"

He looked at me for a moment. "Well, maybe some day they'll learn. Security is all very well, but if we are not told where the sensitive toes are located, we cannot very well be held responsible for stepping on them, can we, Eric?"

It was very nice of him. It meant that, although I was the big brain who'd had the genius idea of getting help from Hattie's Communist friends—thus unwittingly giving them a crack at some desirable oil properties—he was backing me all the way. Well, he usually does. Maybe that's why we stay with him, instead of moving to the glamor agencies where you're apt to find yourself hastily offered up as a sacrificial goat any time there's a breath of trouble in Washington.

Mac said, "Oh, you may be interested in hearing that a gentleman named Manderfield has been arrested for the gangland-type slaying of one Henry Morgan Valeski, usually known by his middle name, reputed to be a syndicate enforcer of some renown."

I said, "I don't know what we'd do if we didn't have the syndicate to blame things on. So they reeled in Manderfield? It couldn't have happened to a nicer guy, but do you want to know something funny, sir? He didn't know, either."

"What do you mean?"

"Their security had kept him in the dark, just as ours had kept me. He didn't know there was important oil involved, any more than I did. He was strongly opposed to making any kind of a deal with me, because he couldn't see what they had to gain by it. Nobody'd told him. Since we've got to live with it ourselves, it's nice that they're considerate enough to handicap themselves the same way, isn't it?"

"Yes. Very nice," Mac said, rising. "One more thing. The lady with former Maryland connections. Would you say a kind of amnesty was in order there? As much as can be arranged unofficially and discreetly?"

I thought of the handsome lady charterboat captain telling me to get the hell off her bridge, and grinned. "All the way, sir," I said. "All the way."

He left. An hour later, shaved and bathed and respectably attired, for a change, I started out to get something to eat and drink. Although it wasn't quite dinner time yet, I seemed to have a fairly constant craving for nourishment. There had been no real hardships; but the emergency stores on Hattie's little boat had been rather lacking in variety, and what I'd managed to grab from the galley of her big boat, after being rescued, hadn't been quite gourmet fare either. I was reaching for the doorknob when somebody knocked. I hesitated, thought of guns and knives and things, said to hell with it, and opened.

"Yes?" I said to the strange girl in the smart yellow dress who stood there. Then I recognized the windbreaker jacket she carried over her arm, and I looked again and said, "Oh, it's you. I didn't recognize you with your clothes on."

I'd got kind of fond of, or at least accustomed to, the damp, seminude, stringy-haired kid with whom I had, for a day or two, shared a platonic shipwreck, if you want to call it that. This was somebody else entirely. This was the lovely blonde creature whose self-conscious snapshot had convinced me that she'd never mean anything to me, no matter what she might mean to a guy named Haseltine. Well, I've been wrong before. I took the jacket she handed me and tossed it on a nearby chair.

"I'm hungry again," said my glamorous visitor. "I thought you might be, too. Matt."

"What?"

"I told you I'd let you know when I found out. Well, I've found out. With your help and… and Bill's, and maybe even Leo's. I'm really Loretta Phipps at last. I'm not just anti-Amanda-Mayne; I knew it the minute I saw her at the dock. She was just a nice lady who was my mother; not something I had to fight to break free from. Do you understand?"

"Not really," I said. "But we can have lots of fun while you explain it to me."

We did.

ABOUT THE AUTHOR

Donald Hamilton was the creator of secret agent Matt Helm, star of 27 novels that have sold more than 20 million copies worldwide.

Born in Sweden, he emigrated to the United States and studied at the University of Chicago. During the Second World War he served in the United States Naval Reserve, and in 1941 he married Kathleen Stick, with whom he had four children.

The first Matt Helm book, *Death of a Citizen*, was published in 1960 to great acclaim, and four of the subsequent novels were made into motion pictures. Hamilton was also the author of several outstanding stand-alone thrillers and westerns, including two novels adapted for the big screen as *The Big Country* and *The Violent Men*.

Donald Hamilton died in 2006.

ALSO AVAILABLE FROM TITAN BOOKS

PRAISE FOR DONALD HAMILTON

"Donald Hamilton has brought to the spy novel
the authentic hard realism of Dashiell Hammett;
and his stories are as compelling, and probably
as close to the sordid truth of espionage,
as any now being told."
Anthony Boucher, *The New York Times*

"This series by Donald Hamilton is the top-ranking
American secret agent fare, with its intelligent
protagonist and an author who consistently writes
in high style. Good writing, slick plotting and
stimulating characters, all tartly flavored with wit."
Book Week

"Matt Helm is as credible a man of violence as has
ever figured in the fiction of intrigue."
The New York Sunday Times

"Fast, tightly written, brutal, and very good…"
Milwaukee Journal

TITANBOOKS.COM

ALSO AVAILABLE FROM TITAN BOOKS

PRAISE FOR HELEN MACINNES

"The queen of spy writers." *Sunday Express*

"Definitely in the top class." *Daily Mail*

"The hallmarks of a MacInnes novel of suspense
are as individual and as clearly stamped as a
Hitchcock thriller." *The New York Times*

"She can hang her cloak and dagger right up there
with Eric Ambler and Graham Greene." *Newsweek*

"More class than most adventure writers
accumulate in a lifetime." *Chicago Daily News*

"A sophisticated thriller. The story builds up to an
exciting climax." *Times Literary Supplement*

"An atmosphere that is ready to explode with
tension… a wonderfully readable book."
The New Yorker

TITANBOOKS.COM